KICKED OUT WITH A COLD SHOVEL

BLOODY JOE MANNION BOOK SIX

PETER BRANDVOLD

WOLFPACK PUBLISHING
—— EST 2013 ——

Wolfpack Publishing
9850 S. Maryland Parkway, Suite A-5 #323
Las Vegas, Nevada 89183

wolfpackpublishing.com

Paperback ISBN 978-1-63977-842-3
Large Print Hardcover ISBN 978-1-63977-841-6
eBook ISBN 978-1-63977-843-0

KICKED OUT WITH A COLD SHOVEL

CHAPTER 1

"You sit tight, Flint," said "Bloody" Joe Mannion, town marshal of Del Norte in the south-central Colorado Territory. "Here's water. Take all you need. I'll be back in two tugs of a whore's bell."

"Nah, nah—I gotta help you, Joe. There's five of those scurvy devils, an' one of 'em's Bill Wade. A deputy sheriff runnin' with owlhoots." Wells Fargo Detective Flint Henry placed his right index finger on the bridge of his nose. "After what he and the others did to my express guards, he's gonna get one right here courtesy of yours truly!"

"Forget it." Mannion peeled open the right-side flap of Flint's duster and grimaced. "Christ, that's worse than I thought. If I'd known how much blood you lost, I'd have sent you packing back to Del Norte."

The Wells Fargo man grinned where he sat back against his saddle in this remote northern desert of New Mexico Territory, between the San Juan Mountains and the Black Range, with the Stalwarts rearing their foothills not far to the west. "You'd have tried, Joe."

Mannion picked up his 1866 Winchester "Yellowboy"

repeater. "I should have conked you over the head, tied you belly down across your saddle, and slapped that cayuse of yours back to town. My new son-in-law and Doc Bohannon should be tending that wound even as we palaver."

Flint Henry grinned and shook his head. It was more of a grimace than a grin. "Told you, Joe—I've cut myself worse shaving."

Mannion snorted. It was one of his own, badly worn quips.

"We got bad men to take down," Flint said, using his own Winchester to lever himself to his feet. He didn't make it. He flopped back down against his saddle with a groan and a heavy sigh. "Damn!"

"See?" Mannion said. "You need to listen to your betters!"

"Dammit, Joe." The Wells Fargo man, a little older than Bloody Joe's forty-seven years and who sported a thick, gray, dragoon-style mustache and frosty blue eyes, shook his head, removed his black Stetson, and slapped it down on the ground beside him in anger. "I do believe you're right. You're gonna have to take down those scurvy devils alone 'cause I was fool enough to get myself shot out of my saddle!"

Two days previously, the five owlhoots they'd been trailing from southern Colorado had hit a narrow-gauge train enroute to Pueblo. During the robbery, they'd killed four armed Wells Fargo messengers and a female express agent. They'd effected an ambush on the two lawmen early the previous day. Flint Henry, veteran lawman that he was, having town marshaled and worn county sheriff badges throughout the rowdy frontier west before joining the famed express agency, had insisted on pushing on. He'd claimed the bullet hadn't hit anything important, only bounced off a rib or two. Maybe it hadn't bounced off anything "important," but it had caused him to lose a lot of blood.

Mannion did not like how pale and drawn his old friend appeared.

Too late to do anything about it now.

He drew a thick handkerchief from a pocket of his black denim trousers and set it over the ragged hole the bullet had torn in Flint's shirt. "Press that to the wound. Might keep you from bleeding dry."

Henry laughed then groaned as he pressed the cloth against the wound.

He stood and looked across their camp and past their two horses tied to picket pins strung between two pines. "I've taken more than five down all by my lonesome more times than I have fingers to count."

Flint grinned. "You're not as young as you used to be, Joe."

"Don't I know," Mannion growled.

He looked at his old friend again. They'd fought in the frontier army together back before Mannion had gone to work as a town-tamer of some renown in Kansas, Oklahoma, and Texas back in the days of the great cattle drives, back before the coming of the damnable—from his point of view—iron horse.

They'd been friends for a lot of years. Mannion valued their friendship. A contrary cuss even by his own estimation, he didn't have all that many close companions. Never had. Likely never would. No, Bloody Joe was not a man to acquire many friends, but he had plenty of enemies. One of those was the deputy county sheriff running with the hooligans. Mannion had never liked Bill Wade.

Now he'd take him and the others down and throw

the cuffs on them, take them back to Del Norte to stand trial. Or kick them out with a cold shovel, so to speak. The latter would be more satisfying.

The last time he'd checked, a little over an hour ago, when it had just started to get light, the vermin had been camped on a nearby mountain slope, on a flat shelf above a wash. Mannion intended to take them down at dawn, when they were still groggy but it was light enough for him to make them out. Since the previous day's attack, Mannion had seen no sign that his quarry knew they were still being trailed.

They probably thought that when they'd shot one of their shadowers, they'd discouraged them both.

They must not know Joe Mannion's bloody reputation.

Mannion squeezed the Yellowboy in his gloved hands and gritted his teeth. They'd get to know his reputation soon enough.

He squatted down beside his friend. "I'll be back soon. Uh...if it just so happens I'm not..."

Flint grunted a laugh. "You'll be back, Joe."

"Yeah, well, just keep that firestick close...just in case. They might backtrack me and I don't have time to cover my trail."

"Give 'em hell, Joe!"

Flint extended his hand. Mannion shook it then turned away and strode across their camp. They'd built no fire, worried their quarry or their horses would see it or smell it. All Mannion had in his belly was jerky. Once he'd taken down the five scurvy devils, he'd build up the fire and fix him and Flint a rudimentary meal before getting his friend to the nearest town and sawbones.

They both—but Flint especially—needed sustenance.

He jacked a cartridge into the Yellowboy's action

then off cocked the hammer. He made his way to a break between two ridges sloping down at the end of the camp, dropped to his haunches, and stared down through the dry wash below and up and across it to the forested slope on the other side of it. The five killers were camped on the other side of that ridge's near shoulder, just above the wash that curved around the base of it.

Mannion, a veteran hunter of men, catfooted down a crease in the ridge to the wash and climbed the bank and into the woods on the other side. He climbed to what he figured was about sixty yards above the wash, descended half that distance, then dropped to a knee behind a pine. From here, he could see the killers' camp as well as the outlines in the murky light of their horses picketed on the far side of the wash, to the right of a large, stone escarpment.

One man was building up their cookfire. Clad in long-handles, flannel shirt, and boots, he leaned down low over the fire ring, tossed his long hair back behind a shoulder, and blew on the coals while gingerly adding tinder.

Another man had just sat up and was stretching.

Slowly, quietly, holding the Yellowboy down low by his side, Mannion stepped out around the pine and moved slowly down the declivity. There was just enough milky light that he could see and avoid the obstacles.

Most of them, anyway.

He was roughly thirty feet from the outlaws' camp when his right foot came down on a twig, snapping it.

He stopped, grimaced, and inwardly cursed.

None of the men below appeared to have heard it.

But on the other side of the wash, a horse lifted a shrill whinny.

A man yelled on Mannion's right, *"Law, boys!"*

Joe threw himself forward, landing belly down on the ground as a rifle screeched roughly fifteen yards away. He could see the orange stab of flames in the corner of his right eye. The bullet slammed into a tree bole with a dull *thunk*!

While the others shouted the alarm below, Mannion rolled onto his left side, raising the Winchester, aiming quickly, and squeezing the trigger. Bill Wade himself—stocky and bearded—must have been on guard duty. Mannion hadn't seen his empty bedroll because of the pines obscuring the camp. Now Wade yelped and flew straight backward, firing skyward the fresh cartridge he'd just racked into his Winchester's action.

Pistols and rifles started barking on the bench below Mannion, several thudding into the ground and into the trunks of the trees around him, spraying bark and pluming dirt and pine needles. Joe twisted around to see one man on a knee wielding a revolver while the other three had grabbed rifles or carbines and were jacking and firing, jacking and firing, shouting curses as their empty cartridge casings arced back over their shoulders to clink onto the ground behind them.

Mannion had the advantage of the high ground.

He managed to dispatch first the kneeling man—slender and with short, blond hair spiked from sleep and clad only in wash-worn balbriggans. Next, Joe dispatched the man nearest him. That man cursed and flew back to roll up into the fire he'd just coaxed back to life, screaming as flames clung to his shirt and longhandles. He scrambled wildly back to his feet and went leaping off the shelf and into the wash.

Joe let him go since the other two were hurling lead dangerously close to him.

He shot the shaggy-bearded man first and then the

older man whom Mannion recognized as Carl "Dad" Carlson, whom Mannion had sent to the state pen several years back for cattle rustling in the San Juan Mountains north of Del Norte. Dad fell straight back against a birch tree, his eyes snapping wide in shock at his imminent demise. His old Spencer repeater sagged in his hands to rest across his denim-clad thighs.

His washed-out blue eyes found Mannion.

"Damn, Bloody Joe," he croaked out, "I figured you had to be o' them on our trail. Just had to be. Damn, you're a determined cuss!"

With that, he spasmed, dropped his chin to his chest, and slid sideways to lay on his left shoulder, jerking as he died.

Remembering Bill Wade, Mannion jerked a look to his right. The man was just then running, then crouching, up into the pines. The rogue lawman's rifle had slid toward Joe when he'd dropped it. Longish, dark-brown hair hung down over Wade's shoulders from beneath the cream, funnel-brimmed hat he wore. Cradling his right arm in front of his chest, he reached across his body to shuck his bone-handled Colt from the holster tied low on his right thigh.

Mannion levered a fresh round into his Yellowboy's breech and aimed. He held fire as Wade slipped between two boulders, taking a hard left behind one and disappearing.

"*Dammit!*" Mannion bit out.

Disgusted with himself for not having scouted the camp better and seeing that Wade's bedroll was empty, he heaved himself to his feet. He paused to cast a quick glance to the shelf below him. Three of the shooters down there lay unmoving. The fourth one had fallen in the wash beyond and below the shelf, his flannel shirt and longhandles sending up thick tendrils of white smoke and short, orange flames. His feet were bare, the soles coated with sand.

Satisfied he'd taken care of business on the shelf, Mannion began striding up across the belly of the incline, toward where Bill Wade had disappeared behind the boulder. Walking with the Yellowboy aimed straight out from his right hip, Mannion saw large drops of blood on fallen leaves and pine needles, beginning to glisten now as the dawn light grew.

When he was within ten feet of the two boulders, he broke into a run. As he did, Bill Wade stepped out from behind the boulder on Mannion's left, extended the Colt in his left hand, and sent two rounds toward Joe, both bullets screeching through the air inches to Mannion's left. The lawman pressed his back against the right boulder then stepped into the mouth of the natural corridor between the two rocks.

He eased the pressure on his trigger finger.

Wade was gone.

Mannion hurried forward, stopped at the end of the eight-foot corridor and tracked the Yellowboy first to his left and then to his right. He heard shambling footsteps and turned to look up the slope on his left in time to see Wade just then disappearing around the far side of a large, gray stone escarpment sheathed in pines.

Mannion hurried around the scarp.

He stopped when Wade stepped out from behind a large pine fifteen feet away and up a steep rise. The man had lost his hat and his hair hung in his eyes. He raised the Colt in his left hand, turned sideways, and bellowed, "*Why won't you die, you son of a bitch?*"

Mannion threw himself to the ground as Wade's Colt barked twice loudly, then a third time, the third round grazing Joe's right elbow through his dark-brown corduroy shirt.

Mannion pulled up the Yellowboy, aimed quickly, and fired once...twice...three times.

The three slugs punched holes across the center of Wade's chest. Wade staggered backward, blinking rapidly, head lolling on his shoulders. He got his feet set beneath him and, blood pumping from his chest through his pin-striped shirt between the flaps of his brown leather vest, glared at Mannion and shouted, "Oh, go to hell!"

He dropped to his knees, then to his face and chest, and rolled wildly down the rise, piling up in front of the lawman. The crooked deputy stared at Mannion through eyes glazed in death.

"Not yet, Bill. Soon, likely. But not yet."

CHAPTER 2

MANNION LEFT BILL WADE WHERE HE'D FALLEN.

The crooked lawman didn't deserve a proper burial or to be hauled back to town. Nor did the other four. Let the carrion eaters do their work.

Mannion went down to the outlaws' camp. He found two sets of saddlebags stuffed with scrip and specie— paper money and gold coins. It was a ranch payroll that had been headed for Pueblo from a bank in Gunnison when the outlaws had taken it off the train. Sixty thousand dollars' worth. It must be a large ranch. The bags were piled up between two mussed bedrolls. Mannion shouldered the loot and glanced around at the surrounding ridges, wondering what was giving him such an uneasy feeling.

He saw no sign of anyone on the lurk, but he sensed he was being watched.

Damn peculiar.

He took the saddlebags over to where the horses were picketed on the other side of the wash. He freed all five then shouldered the loot again and followed the wash around the base of the ridge. He climbed the hill on the opposite side of the wash from the outlaws' encampment, strode through the break in the ridge, and stopped.

Flint lay just ahead, head tipped back against his saddle. The man lay slack-jawed, his body still. He didn't appear to be breathing and his face was even more ashen than before.

Joe stared at him, dread oozing up along his spine. By not riding back to Del Norte after they were bushwhacked, had he killed his old friend? Mannion opened his mouth to speak but suddenly Flint's eyes fluttered open. He looked at Joe and held up a hand. He gave a feeble smile.

"Haven't given up the ghost yet, Joe. I see you haven't either. I heard. They didn't give up without a fight."

"Nope, they did not." Mannion walked into the camp and set the saddlebags down. "Sit tight. I'll build us a fire, cook some coffee and a can of beans."

Flint held up his hand, palm out. He'd closed his eyes again. "Just for you, Joe. I'm not hungry."

"Never mind. I'll saddle the horses. Going to get you to Santee Springs, get that wound tended."

He walked over and opened the Wells Fargo's man's duster and winced. More blood had seeped through the handkerchief the man held against the wound. Mannion cursed then propped the man's head up while he switched out the saddle for a feed sack and eased the man's had back down. He walked over to where he'd picketed the horses, saddled both mounts, and led them into the camp. He dropped the reins of his big bay, Red, and led Flint's gray gelding over to where its rider lay. He prodded Flint's left foot.

"Enough beauty sleep, old-timer. You know it's not gonna do any good, anyway." Mannion chuckled.

Flint's eyes did not open.

His chin was dipped low and his lips were partly open beneath the gray mustache. Concern rose in Mannion. He dropped to a knee, touched the man's shoulder.

"Flint?" Nothing.

Louder: "Flint?"

Still nothing.

He placed his gloved hand on his old friend's chest. It wasn't moving. He couldn't feel a heartbeat.

"Flint?" he prodded again, his concern rising.

He placed his hand on Flint's shoulder again and gave him a none-too-gentle shake.

"Flint, goddammit. Open your eyes!"

The man's eyes were open just a slit. Mannion could see just a little frosty blue. Neither lid moved. Mannion placed his hand on Flint's chest again.

No movement.

"Ah, hell!"

Mannion removed his hat, slammed it down on the ground beside him. "Damn you anyway, you stubborn old rattlesnake!"

The gray gelding lowered his head, gave his rider's right ear a sniff, turned to Mannion, dubiously, and twitched his ears.

Joe sucked down the start of a lump in his throat. "He's gone, boy." The horse eyed him with what Mannion saw as bald accusing. "I killed him. Should have taken him to Santee when we were close. I just wasn't sure there was a sawbones there. Dammit!"

He placed his hand on his old friend's shoulder again, gave it an affectionate squeeze. "So long, Flint. I'll be along soon, I expect."

He set his hat on his head. He rose and tried to suck down that growing lump in his throat once more. He was a hard man, was Bloody Joe Mannion. He wasn't used to getting lumps in his throat. He didn't like it. He walked over to the bay and unstrapped his folding shovel from the saddle.

Flint Henry was one man he would not leave to the carrion eaters.

———

MANNION DUG THE HOLE GOOD AND DEEP.

When he finished, he eased the body, wrapped in Flint's bedroll, into the hole then filled in the hole and piled rocks over it to keep the wildcats and coyotes out. He fashioned a cross from two stout branches and rope. He'd have preferred to give his friend a proper burial, but it was a three-day ride back to Del Norte, and the body would not keep in the southern Colorado heat.

He stood over the grave, his hat in his hands while the hot desert sun hammered down, reflecting off the rocks so brightly that it stung his eyes. No words came to him except, "I'm sorry, pal. Rest well."

He heaved a weary sigh, placed his hat on his head, and walked over to his horse. By now it was late morning. He'd unsaddled both mounts rather than let them stand saddled in the sun. Now he resaddled them both. He'd take the gray back to Del Norte; find it a proper home.

It was the least he could do for Flint.

He slung the loot carrying the saddlebags over his own saddlebags on Red's back, then swung up into the leather. Again, he looked around.

All morning he'd had the sensation of being watched. Now, without the distraction of digging the grave, the sensation was stronger than ever. He'd looked around several times, but he hadn't seen anyone. It was still the case. Only the cactus-stippled desert with its mounds of sand and rock, the large bulk of the Black Range rising in the southeast, the San Juans hulking up in the northwest, the Sangre de Cristos looming in the north and east. The Stalwarts were a smaller range to the west.

No movement around him except birds. Once, maybe an hour ago, he'd spied a lone coyote slinking through the ravine before it had seen him and disappeared into a trough between escarpments.

Mannion sipped brackish water from his canteen. He had his own canteen and Flint's canteen. He'd fill them both at a runout spring he remembered maybe an hour's ride north, on the way back to Del Norte. He capped the canteen and hooked the lanyard around his saddle horn; it hung down on the opposite side of the saddle from Flint's. He cast one more cautious glance around, glanced at the lonely grave mounded with rocks between two gnarled cedars then swung Red north and clucked him into a trot.

He trailed Flint's gray by its bridle reins. He glanced back to see the horse also give his rider's resting place a parting look, and that damned knot Joe hadn't been able to get rid of since it had started growing nearly three hours ago swelled just a little more.

Remonstrating himself for his carelessness, he put Red onto the old Indian hunting trail he and Flint had taken, trailing the killers, and eased him into a fast walk. He had a wife now to go home to. He'd married the beautiful Jane Ford for a second time over the winter, in a double wedding with his beloved daughter, Evangeline Mannion, and the town's young doctor, Ben Ellison.

Thoughts of Jane and Vangie and even his new son-in-law soothed him. He'd be glad to get home, to get out of this damnable hot country, to rid himself of the inexplicable sensation he still had of being watched.

He rode another twenty minutes. Between two haystack buttes peppered with sage, cactus, and greasewood, to the left of an ancient, rocky riverbed, he reined Red to a sudden halt. Flint's gray, whom Flint had always just called Hoss, gave a blow as it stopped just off Red's left hip.

Mannion frowned down at the trail that had turned to sand a few minutes previously. The prints of several shod horses scored the trace. The riders had ridden in from the north, just as Mannion and Flint had done. But here, they'd veered off to both sides of the trail, three riders angling off into the wash, three angling off to the west and around a butte.

The prints were not easy to make out, mixed in with both the killers' and Mannion's and Flint's trail. But Bloody Joe had been lawdogging long enough to have become a practiced tracker.

Yep, there were prints down there, overlying the others.

Seven.

Mannion looked around, squinting against the bright sunlight. The sensation he'd had of being watched was validated by that spoor. The feeling grew into a cold hand of apprehension--chill witch's fingers splayed against his back, between his shoulder blades.

He and Flint had been followed. They'd been so intent on the killers' trail that they hadn't paid close enough attention to their own back trail. Now those seven riders were following Mannion. He whipped around to look behind him. He couldn't see them, but they were behind him, all right. His sixth, cautionary sense had not been fooling with him. It had been alerting him to danger.

As he continued to study his back trail, he slid the

Yellowboy from its scabbard. He levered a live round into the action, off cocked the hammer.

He turned back forward and clucked Red ahead once more. Needing both hands free, he dropped the gray's reins. Not wanting to be left alone out here, Hoss would likely follow of his own accord, which he did as Mannion booted Red into a fast trot, wanting to reach a high shelf roughly a mile ahead. From there, he'd take a closer look at the terrain around him with his field glasses.

As he rode, black Stetson pulled low to shade his eyes from the sun's glare, he pondered who those seven shadowers might be. He remembered riding through a road ranch two days before. He and Flint had stopped to water their horses at the proprietor's well. Several other horses had been tied to two hitchracks fronting the lowslung, tin-roofed place.

Two had been tied to one rack. Seven had been tied to the other rack. Two men in rough range gear had been standing in the saloon's open doorway, partly obscured by shadows within, the sun glinting off the dimpled beer schooners in their gloved hands. Both wore battered Stetsons. They were unshaven. Nothing distinguishing about them.

They were gazing out with mute interest at the two newcomers at the well, lips moving as they'd spoken furtively, quietly between themselves.

Were those two men part of the seven who'd followed Mannion and Flint out from the road ranch? And were likely behind him now?

Mannion remembered there'd been Winchesters sheathed on the seven horses. Nothing strange about that in this hard country, but he also remembered the dark interest in the eyes of the two men studying him and Flint from between the two open batwings. He'd passed them off as men he might have run into before and not on a friendly basis. In fact, they might have spent some time in Hotel de Mannion, which was what the locals in and around Del Norte jokingly called Mannion's office and jailhouse.

Bloody Joe Mannion had a lot of enemies.

But if the two he'd seen at the road ranch were part of the seven who'd been shadowing his and Flint's trail, they probably had more than revenge in mind for what they saw as past injustices. They'd likely seen the five owlhoots with the bulging saddlebags and figured Mannion and Henry were after them. So they, in turn, were after Mannion now that he'd acquired the loot. They knew that, because they'd been watching him. His sixth sense convinced him of that. Which meant they also knew he was alone—and very flush...

He glanced behind him again, looked forward, then snapped his head back around. A mare's tail of clay-colored dust was curling up behind a distant rise.

Mannion touched steel to Red's flanks. The stallion lunged into a full gallop, laying his ears back. He sensed trouble was afoot. He likely hadn't scented the trackers earlier because they'd probably lain up a good way's away from Mannion's and Flint Henry's camp to keep the two horses from scenting them and giving the warning.

They hadn't lain so far back, however, that Mannion's sixth sense hadn't known they were there. Now he'd have to scour them from his trail. Seven against one were tall odds, but he'd thrown that dice before and come out of it with his guns smoking.

The trail led him and both horses to the top of a rocky dike. He continued down the other side for a good thirty feet, stopped Red, swung down from the saddle, and dropped the reins. The gray rode a little farther down the slope then stopped and curveting, gazing dubiously back. Mannion fished his field glasses out of his saddlebags and, binoculars in one hand, Yellowboy in the other, climbed back up to the top of the rise and hunkered down in some rocks off the trail's right side.

He leaned the rifle against a rock, doffed his hat, got down flat on his belly and, holding his hands over the ends of the glasses so the sun wouldn't reflect off the lenses, peered through a gap between the rocks. The mare's tail of dust had grown a little larger. The riders were closer.

Judging by the size of the cloud, it was likely made by three, maybe four riders. Too small for seven. Apprehension returned to Mannion.

Where were the others?

He turned his head to peer over the rocky wash on his left.

Nothing but a lone hawk lazily circling the wash's far embankment, on the scout for mice and rabbits.

Mannion peered to his right and lurched with a start as the crack of a rifle sliced through the otherwise silent air. The report echoed eerily. He saw where it had come from. Two riders sat their horses on a rise maybe a quarter mile away, almost directly west of the trail he'd been following.

They both sat on the shoulder of the slope. One held a rifle straight up in the air above his head and squeezed off another shot. Then, still one-handed, he aimed the rifle down at Mannion. Not to shoot—they were too far away for accurate shooting—but to indicate Joe's position to the other four he could now see galloping down a rise roughly two hundred yards to the south.

When they gained the bottom of that rise, they swung off the side of the trail, to Mannion's left. They were galloping hard, crouched low over their horses' polls, the flaps of their dusters whipping out behind them, six-shooters and rifles glinting in the brassy desert light.

"Ah, I see," the lawman said, the short hairs standing on the back of his neck as he studied the four riders through his field glasses. "You're gonna try to swing around behind me, catch me in a whipsaw."

He lowered the glasses and turned to his right.

The other two were galloping toward him down the cactus- and rock-littered slope, both men now holding their rifles straight up from their right thighs.

"Not hardly," Joe snarled. "Not my first rodeo!"

He gained his feet and jogged back down to where Red stood, glancing edgily toward the two sets of riders, whickering softly, reins dangling. Flint's gray was a good distance down the rise, also glancing at the two sets of riders, twitching his ears and switching his tail.

"Easy, boy," Joe said softly as he approached the bay. "This is not the time to bolt and leave me alone out here!"

He knew the horse wouldn't bolt, though. He'd trained him too well.

He gained the stallion, grabbed the reins, dropped the field glasses back into his saddlebags, and fairly leaped into the saddle. Rather than turn Red north, because he figured that's what the ringtails after him expected him to do, he turned him south, galloped up and over the rise and headed straight back in the direction from which he'd come, head down low, hat brim pulled lower.

He held the Yellowboy by the neck across his saddlebow.

"*Hy-yahhh*, boy!" he bellowed into the horse's ear as

he galloped hell-for-leather down the rise's south side. "Split the wind, boy! If I ever needed you to, it's *now*!"

Red did just that.

This wasn't the bay's first rodeo any more than it was its rider's.

CHAPTER 3

AS MANNION AND RED GAINED THE BOTTOM OF THE slope, Joe heard shouts coming from both flanks.

And then the screeching reports of rifles.

He glanced behind to see both sets of riders—two to the west, four to the east—just then galloping around the shoulders of the rise he'd just been on, determinedly spurring their horses toward him. He and Red galloped up and over the top of the next slope. Flint's gray had gotten discouraged by the gunfire, veered from the trail, and disappeared. Mannion didn't blame him. As he was galloping across a broad flat, Joe glanced behind once more.

The two sets of riders were one set now, barreling toward him along the trail, roughly a hundred yards behind. They were triggering their rifles, smoke and flames lapping from the barrels aimed straight out from their shoulders. Joe kept Red at a lung-grinding pace for another hundred yards then, knowing that even the big, stalwart bay could not hold the pace much longer, he swung him off the west side of the trail and headed for the high, apron slope of a rocky-topped bluff.

There, he'd give the horse a breather and try to hold his pursuers off, try to take down as many as he could with the Yellowboy. He gained the base of the bluff and spurred Red up the slope at an angle, heading for the rocks above. As he did, some of his pursuers' bullets landed perilously close, pluming dust, tearing up sage and cactus, and ricocheting off rocks with angry spangs.

One such ricochet hammered off a rock to Mannion's right and sliced a long burn across the nub of his left cheek, evoking an angry curse. As he and the horse fairly leaped onto the crest of the bluff, two more slugs slammed off the rocks around them.

Mannion crossed the crest of the bluff, put Red down the other side for ten yards, then leaped out of the saddle, dropped the reins, and brushed his fist across his cheek with another curse, seeing the blood on his glove. Then he ran back to the top of the bluff ringed with large rocks and stippled with sagebrush and greasewood.

The riders were fifty yards away, galloping up the bluff, leaning low in the saddle, still triggering lead at their quarry.

Mannion dropped to a knee, levered a round into the Yellowboy's action, raised the Winchester to his right cheek, aimed quickly, and fired. The man he'd targeted screamed and flew straight back over his horse's arched tail, rolling wildly, arms and legs windmilling, back down the steep slope while the man's horse turned sharply left, directly into the path of another horse and rider.

The horses screamed as they collided, both falling violently in a welter of flying dust, the rider on the second horse screaming as he flew forward over both mounts, losing his hat and his rifle.

The others reined their own mounts to skidding halts, one man shouting, "Take cover! Take cover!"

Mannion took a shot at the second fallen rider, his bullet blowing off the ear of a prickly pear to the left of the man's scissoring right boot as he ran wildly to Mannion's right, diving behind two gravestone-sized rocks roughly forty yards below.

"Dammit!" Joe groused, ejecting the smoking cartridge from the Yellowboy's breach and seating fresh.

He took aim again but held fire. The other riders were scrambling into the rocks at the base of the slope and up the slope several yards from the bottom, to Mannion's left. Mannion swung the Winchester to his left, lining up the sights on another target.

Again, he held fire. When he'd swiveled at the waist, he'd felt a nasty pinch in his left side. He looked down to see blood staining his shirt, oozing through a round, ragged-edged hole.

"What in hell?" he grumbled, shocked. "I took a blue whistler!"

He hadn't felt it till now. Too much adrenaline coursing through his veins; he'd been so intent on gaining the crest of the ridge, his only chance of holding his would-be killers at bay.

Rifles crackled below.

Mannion lay flat, poked the Yellowboy between rocks, and returned fire. He emptied the Yellowboy once, reloaded, and continued firing. By the time he'd emptied the Winchester once again, he'd blown a hat off one attacker and evoked a yelp from another as his bullet carved a notch along the man's right arm, causing the son of a bitch to pull his head and rifle down.

The lawman held fire, keeping his head down.

Not finding a target, his attackers did the same.

He cursed as he unknotted his neckerchief and wadded it up. He pulled his shirttails out of his pants, lifted the left one far enough that he could see the wound. A flesh wound, only. It had gone right through the side of his belly. Burned like the blazes, though, now. He cursed again with more venom when he stuffed the neckerchief into the ragged hole to try to staunch the blood.

It was only a flesh wound but it was bleeding bad.

That nasty task completed, he picked up the Yellowboy again and loaded it quickly while gazing down the slope at where his assailants were holed up behind rocks from anywhere between fifty and eighty yards away. He could hear them talking among themselves but the wind had come out, obscuring their words.

A rifle cracked below.

The bullet slammed into the face of the rock to Mannion's right, spraying rock dust and shards. Joe aimed the Yellowboy toward where the slug had been hurled, but the hatted head of the man who'd fired it was just then jerking back behind cover, a low hummock of ground from which a stunt cedar bristled.

"Mannion!" one his assailants yelled from below and slightly left of the man who'd just fired the bullet. "Blue Bowdrie here!"

The man's voice was pitched with a vague amusement.

Mannion frowned, pondering. Then he yelled through the narrow gap in the rocks before him. "Do I know you, Bowdrie?"

"Probably not, but I know you!"

"You were at the road ranch!"

"Yes, that's right."

"Well, it's not nice to meet you, Blue Bowdrie. I take it you're after the loot...?"

Mannion heard several men chuckle beneath the

rustling wind that was kicking up small dust devils here and there across the belly of the slope below him.

"How did you figure that one out, Bloody Joe?"

More laughter. Mannion ground his back teeth.

"The joke's on you, Bowdrie," he shouted, cupping his gloved hands around his mouth to be heard above the wind. "They didn't get more than a few hundred dollars, turns out!"

"Like hell!" was the outlaw leader's shrill response, followed by the man's own delighted laughter. "Bill Wade knew exactly what was in that express car. He wouldn't have called in his boys for a few hundred dollars. I'm thinkin' over fifty grand!"

Yeah, Joe thought, stretching lips back from his teeth in frustration. At least.

Wade had been suspected of straddling both sides of the law for a long time, but nothing had ever been proven against him. He likely would have been fired by the sheriff who'd hired him, but the cowardly old rascal, Titus T. Willoughby, was afraid of the man.

Mannion had to admit that Wade had been an effective law bringer, if a crooked one. He'd made the mistake of leaving one of the express guards alive to identify him just before the poor man had given up the ghost. That's how Mannion and Flint Henry had known whom they were chasing when they'd picked up the thieving killers' trail near the sight of the holdup. Henry had just happened to be in Del Norte when the cable announcing the holdup had arrived at the Western Union office.

"Leave the loot there, Joe!" shouted Bowdrie from below. "You can just walk away!"

Mannion croaked out a dry laugh at that and shouted, "If you know my reputation, you know that's not gonna happen. I tell you what—you boys pull out and I'll let *you* live!"

That evoked more laughter, which swirled around on the wind.

So it went for several long hours—heated exchanges, occasional gunfire. Mannion held his ground. He held the high ground, so all he had to do was hurl a bullet down to the wolves at the base of the bluff, keeping them pinned down behind their rocks.

At night, however, that would be another matter.

Once it was dark, they'd steal around him. Then he'd have complications.

He had to do something to lighten the odds against him lest he should make his beloved Jane a widow, his beloved daughter, Vangie, a fatherless daughter. At least, she had a man now to take care of her. And a good one, even if Ellison was a city slicker who'd gone to medical school at Harvard.

Ah, hell—Joe didn't hold his soft hands against him overmuch. He made a good living and would take care of Vangie once he'd taken over Doc Bohannon's practice, once the older medico retired, which he would do in a few years.

Shadows grew long.

When the sun angled down behind the western ridges, silhouetting the dramatic peaks of the Stalwarts against it, and the first stars started twinkling to life in the east, Mannion had figured out what he'd do.

There had been only sporadic shooting in the past half hour, to which Mannion had replied with even more sporadic fire of his own, just to let them know he was still up here. He knew the outlaws were trying to get him to go through as much ammo as they could, so when the buzzards snuck around him, he wouldn't have much lead left to defend himself with.

There likely wouldn't be much shooting again until good dark. Then a few would remain below to distract him while the others worked around him.

That's why he had to make his move now and hope the owlhoots hadn't foreseen his ploy.

He had to get off this butte and into the rocky, dike-stippled country to the southeast. In the dark they couldn't track him.

He'd left Red ground reined down the opposite side of the bluff. Fortunately, despite the gunfire, the bay had stayed with his reins, idly cropping grass. Joe had taught him well. A damn good horse. Sometimes Mannion didn't think he deserved him, with all the shooting the poor animal had had to endure in the company of his hard-luck and badge-toting owner.

Joe rose to a crouch and catfooted across the crest of the bluff and down the other side. Red had moved only a few feet away from where Mannion had ground tied him. Now the hard-luck and badge-toting lawman slid the Yellowboy into its boot, grabbed the reins, and heaved himself heavily into the saddle, suppressing a groan as his bullet-torn side cried out in pain.

He reined Red around and booted him down the long, easy slope toward the flat desert below, toward a broad, deep wash that was a butterscotch snake tracing its serpentine curve ahead and right. He'd ridden only a hundred feet or so when a rifle spoke from the other side of the ridge behind him.

Then, faint with distance, came Blue Bowdrie's call: "Hey, Joe—you still up there?"

Mannion grimaced, cursed.

They wouldn't wait till dark, he knew. Bowdrie had suspected his ploy. He'd send men to scout the crest soon, and when they saw he was gone, they'd come for him.

He had to make it to that wash and not move again until after dark.

If he made it that far. As he spurred Red into a gallop, he gritted his teeth against the pain in his side. He looked down to see a damned bloody mess.

He groaned, clutched the horn with both hands, trying like hell to stay in the saddle.

"Hold on," he urged himself. "Hold on. You drop now, you're a dead man." He glanced behind him toward the top of the ridge he'd just left, and which was barely visible now in the murky blue twilight. "Hold on till you make the ravine..."

A man shouted behind him, his voice coming from the crest of the ridge: "Just like you thought, boss—he's makin' a getaway! Headed south!"

The shrill cry echoed, chilling Mannion's bones.

"Come on, Red," Joe urged, touching the bay's flanks again with his spurs. "Just a little faster...if it kills me..."

CHAPTER 4

IT WAS PLENTY DARK WHEN MANNION REALIZED THAT Red had carried him into a rough country of shelving dikes and deep washes. He must have fallen asleep for a bit. Now the bay had stopped and stood tensely expanding and contracting his muscles beneath the saddle.

Red's head was up, partly turned to see behind him, audibly sniffing the breeze that seemed to have died now that night had descended. The sky was bright with pointed stars.

The bay was listening. He was hearing something.

Now Mannion's heart quickened when he heard it, too—the hoof thuds of approaching horseback riders. Men's voices carried in the near complete silence relieved by the mournful howls of a lone wolf perched on a distant ridge.

The thuds grew quickly louder until Mannion could hear the squawk of saddle leather and the jangle of bridle chains. He looked behind him to see shadows jostling, starlight reflecting off a gun or a bridle bit.

"Damn dark," one man said in a hushed voice. "But I think his tracks lead this way."

Heart thudding, Joe neck reined Red sharply to his left, putting the stallion up close to the concealing shadow of a steeply slanting ridge wall, so close that his left leg was taut against the formation's crenelated face; he could feel the stones and gravel through his black denim trouser leg. Cool and quiet here against the stone.

As the riders approached behind him and on his right now, just then coming around from behind the dike, Joe felt the cold sweat of fear pasting his shirt against his back. Fear or maybe pain and blood loss—a combination of the three.

He slid his right hand across his belly, which was cold and oily wet with the blood that had poured out of the wound. He wrapped that gloved hand around the walnut grips of the big Russian .44 holstered for the cross-draw on his left hip. He unsnapped the keeper thong from over the hammer then gritted his teeth against the soft *snicking* sound as he slid the silver-chased revolver with a seven-and-a-half-inch barrel from the hard, oiled leather.

The horse-and-rider-shaped shadows of the two riders —yes, just two; they must have split up to look for him in the darkness—appeared over his right shoulder, moving up even with him, fifteen feet away, between him and the murky drop-off of what Joe assumed was an arroyo.

Keep moving, he silently willed the two riders. *Just... keep...moving.*

As though they'd heard his silent plea, they stopped their horses suddenly just ahead of him and on his right, fifteen to seventeen feet away. One of the horses had lifted its head sharply, jostled the bit in its mouth.

It had scented Mannion.

"What is it, hoss?" asked its rider.

Holding their reins taut in their hands, both men looked around. They curveted their horses and turned their heads to stare straight at where Mannion and Red were concealed by the formation's dark shadow.

Truly concealed?

Or...as their eyes adjusted...did they see him?

Both men froze in their saddles, heads turned to face Mannion. Their faces were black ovals beneath their hat brims—one short-crowned cream hat, one high-crowned dark hat. Both horses snorted and sidestepped.

Keep riding, Mannion silently urged his stalkers. *Nothing to see here, boys...except death*, he added just as the man on the left cursed suddenly. His right hand moved, and Joe saw the glint of starlight off rifle bluing as the man whipped his carbine around, aimed toward the formation.

The big Russian in Joe's right fist leaped and roared, orange flames stabbing from the barrel. Each blast sounded enormous in the silent, starry night. Each man grunted in turn and their horses pitched, throwing each man from his saddle.

Then both horses bolted, galloping back in the direction from which they'd come, reins bouncing along the ground beside them. The blasts of the Russian echoed, dwindling as they vaulted toward the stars.

One man lay on the ground before Joe—a still shadow. The other man groaned and thrashed as he tried to rise. Mannion booted Red ahead and saw the white line of teeth between the man's spread lips.

"Three down," Joe growled.

The man looked up at him. Mannion could see the whites of his eyes as they snapped wide. "N-no!" he pleaded.

The Russian barked again, flashing, revealing the

hatless man on the ground before him. He slumped over onto his back with a groan and lay still.

"Four to go," Mannion said.

Men shouted in the darkness around him. Mannion holstered the Russian, secured it with the keeper thong, then booted Red on ahead. He'd let the bay pick its own way in the darkness.

"Don't know how much hay you got left in the burner, old pal," Joe growled groggily into the bay's right ear. "Hope...just...a little...more..."

It was him who'd run out of fuel. The stars swirled above and around him. His head was light. He looked at Red, saw two manes, two heads.

He stopped the horse, pricked his ears to listen.

Galloping hooves thudded distantly.

"This way!" a man shouted. "The shots came from this way! I seen the flashes!"

"Louis!" another man shouted above the loudening thud of hooves. "Willie!"

They were heading toward Mannion.

"Well, ol' pard," Joe said, lifting his right leg, which seemed to weigh as much as an anvil. He skidded it across Red's back and half fell to the ground, his sudden meeting with it jarred the wound painfully. He felt as though a rabid dog's teeth were chewing into his side. "Time to fork trails...for now..."

He tied the reins around the horn. Then he removed the saddlebags bulging with loot, draped them over his left shoulder. He walked around to the bay's right side, slid the Winchester from the scabbard.

"Go, boy." Mannion slapped his hand sharply against the bay's right hip. "With everything you got left—*go!*"

The horse whickered and lurched into a run.

Red's shadow dwindled in the night until it was only

Mannion and the stars here. And the growing thuds of approaching riders.

The wolf had stopped howling.

Mannion peered toward the arroyo curving darkly on the other side of the dark shapes of the two men he'd killed. He stumbled around the bodies, peered into the ravine. He couldn't see much. Too dark out here.

He began walking along the edge, to the southwest.

"Gotta...find a way...down."

He set his right foot down...too close to the edge.

The brushy ground gave way beneath him.

Suddenly he was lying supine. The stars were above him, winking indifferently at his plight. He fell straight down, his right hand opening, releasing the Yellowboy. The saddlebags slid off his shoulder. His hat flew off his head; he could feel the coolness of the desert night air against his scalp. He struck the side of the ravine with a grunt, heard the crunch of brush beneath him, then rolled, his right boot striking a rock with a dull thud.

He fell through open air again, down the curving belly of the ridge wall, he suspected in a vague way, time having slowed down almost amusingly.

The hard ground of the arroyo came down to slam him about the head and shoulders. He heard the metallic thud of his rifle landing on the ground beside him. It was followed by the double thumps of the saddlebags landing on the other side of him from the rifle.

His head pounded. His shoulders ached. Every joint in his battered body cried out for mercy. That rabid dog was having none of it. It continued to chew into his left side, ripping and tearing, growling like it had found its last meal and it was going to enjoy it, by God!

He heard the thuds of horses passing along the ravine straight above him. Sand and gravel rippled down the

side of the ridge wall to his right. It ticked against his
right pant leg.

Quickly, the hoof thuds dwindled to silence.

Then there was only Mannion and the stars and the
rabid dog here on the bottom of the ravine.

Joe felt himself smile. "Well," he heard himself growl,
groggily. "That's one way to skin a cat!"

Merciful dark enveloped him. Whether it be death or
slumber, he didn't know.

At the moment, he didn't care.

———

BLUE BOWDRIE WAS NOT AN UNHANDSOME MAN.

His deeply tanned face was even-featured. Long, dark-
brown hair hung to his shoulders and, for a sometime
cowhand/sometime border tough, he was not poorly
dressed. At least, his trail clothes—Spanish-style red shirt
with puffy sleeves and green piping in the shapes of
cactus on its breasts as well as blue denims over which he
wore hand-tooled brown leggins, and brown leather
stockmen's boots—were not old and ragged.

He was roughly five foot ten and well filled out
without either being fat or overly muscular. When
women first saw him in one of the brothels he and his
partners frequented between the Mexican border and
Dakota Territory, where Bowdrie and "his boys," as he
called them, worked on ranches between stage or ranch
holdups, they saw a fine cut of a man. One that they
would not mind lying with as much as they minded most
of the jakes who came inquiring about their talents.

It was when they got a close look into the man's eyes
that something withered inside them, and a chill of
apprehension rose in their backs. There was a dark seedi-

ness in those light-tan orbs. Some might even say the dark, flat light of unbridled lunacy. Yes, when women got a good, close look into those eyes they saw the eyes of a man they'd just as soon not spend another hour with, let alone another night.

Most of them sported bruises in the wake of such a coupling. Simply because Bowdrie just seemed to enjoy inflicting pain for pain's sake. Usually, he smiled when he did the inflicting, usually suddenly, out of the blue, and that's where the evil really shone in his eyes. Sometimes it was only a slap or, a little worse and if he'd been drinking too much Who-Hit-John, a punch across the jaw. Sometimes, however, when he was really in a dark mood, he'd take the belt, buckle first, to a girl's backside.

They were lucky, however, if he only took it to their backside.

He'd cut girls before with the Arkansas toothpick whose handle jutted up from behind his right shoulder, from a long, slender, hard leather sheath strapped around his chest beneath his arms. Usually that happened only in the border country, where a man—especially one with Blue Bowdrie's well-known reputation in the American Southwest and northern Mexico—could get away with such a deed. North of the border, he'd found it often brought more trouble than it was worth. So he usually inflicted his pain where it would show and warn the girl or girls that if they reported him to their madam or to anyone else, he'd come back for them and hack certain parts from their bodies.

He had that seedy, lunatic light in his eyes now as, sitting astride his dun gelding, he peered through his brass-framed spyglass out across a bristling bowl of desert roughly two hundred yards from the base of the cactus-stippled bluff he and his two remaining "boys" sat their mounts on.

The other three survivors of their so far misbegotten attack on Bloody Joe Mannion were the Mexican half-breed, Enrique Martinez; the big, blond, droopy mustached Swede, Anders Anderson; and the Alabaman, Reb Winslow. The two men they'd found around midnight had been the Texan, Willie Green; and the Cajun, Louis Palovar.

Willie had been Blue Bowdrie's first cousin. They'd grown up together and had had some fine times in Old Mexico. They'd been blood.

And Mannion had killed him. And Blue Bowdrie had spent a good part of the rest of the night after he'd found him and Palovar digging a grave. Outlaw or not, that's what you did for your blood. The others had buried Louis, as well, because he'd been a close partner of theirs, and you had to show the other men you respected them well enough to give them proper burials.

That bonded a gang together. Looking out for each other.

And exacting revenge for each other, if it came to that.

Well, it had come to that for Willie Green and Louis Palovar, as well as for Dick MacGregor, whom Mannion had killed previously. They hadn't taken the time to bury Dick, because they'd had to get after Mannion who had left the rest of them feeling like fools.

Very angry fools.

Bowdrie had vowed that once he and the others had killed Mannion, he'd backtrack and give Dick—or what was left of him by then, after the scavengers had had their fill—a proper burial.

Those deaths including the death of his blood kin

were why Blue Bowdrie had such a wild mad on this morning, just after sunrise, the shadows shortening and the coppery desert sunlight growing broader and longer across the desert.

Blue Bowdrie lowered his spy glass and turned to the three others lined out to his right, atop their mounts. He jutted an arm and an angry, gloved index finger out across the flat below and beyond.

"That's the son of a bitch's horse!" he bit out, showing his teeth beneath his thick, dark-brown mustache, squinting his seedy, light-tan eyes malevolently.

"Ah," said the Alabaman, Reb Winslow, leaning forward against his saddle horn as he studied the big bay calmly cropping bromegrass around the base of a rock casting an oblong of shade off its western side. "If Mannion ain't lyin' dead or wounded over there—maybe Willie or Louis put a bullet in him?—then all we gotta do is backtrack his hoss, an' we'll have our man...an' Bill Wade's loot."

He smiled easily, as was his way, belying the cold-blooded killer inside him. He turned to Winslow. "Eh, partner?"

Blue Bowdrie cursed and gigged his dun savagely forward. "Come on!"

CHAPTER 5

SAM MCDOWELL TOSSED A SUN-BLEACHED DRIFTWOOD branch into the box of his buckboard wagon and cursed.

He'd just caught sight of men riding toward him, trotting their horses around a long bend in the broad arroyo. Four, in fact. Three white men, as far as he could tell from fifty yards away. One, riding far out on the right side of the group, appeared to have some Mexican blood.

The calico mare hitched to Sam's old wagon whickered edgily and shook her head.

"Easy, Honey...easy," Sam said, moving up to place a placating hand on the mare's rump as he watched the four riders straighten out and ride directly toward him now as they came around the bend.

Sam didn't recognize any of the four. He knew most of the cowpunchers in this neck of the New Mexico desert in the foothills of the Stalwart Range, where his home was. None of these was any of them. That meant they were likely rustlers or outlaws on the run, because that was the only other kind of man you saw out here, this far off the beaten path. Why Pa had ventured out to this canker on the devil's behind—when Sam had been only eight years old and his sister, Ilsa, had been Sam's age now, thirteen—baffled the boy.

He'd said he'd liked the peace and quiet. Well, he got it, too, lying dead as he was six feet under, several hundred feet up a gentle rise behind their cabin.

Sam glanced up into the buckboard, at Pa's old Spencer repeating rifle snugged into a sheepskin-lined leather sheath beneath the driver's seat. He glanced toward the riders closing on him now from twenty-five, thirty yards away and narrowing the gap quickly on their trotting mounts. He glanced at the Spencer again, back at the riders.

The lead rider was smiling. The man riding beside him, tall and lean and wearing an old Confederate campaign hat, was smiling, too. Those smiles did little to ease Sam's tension, but they did make him rethink going for the long gun. Besides, he wouldn't be able to make it to the Spencer, anyway. No time to shuck it from its sheath, pump a round into the action, and get it leveled on the four strangers before they were on top of him.

His heart was beating fast. He wished so badly it wouldn't do that. A man needed to be brave. That's what his father had told him on his deathbed, dying in his room in the cabin under Squaw Ridge, a rustler's bullet in his belly.

"You have to be brave, Sam. Be brave for your sister. You're the man of the place, now."

Dammit all, anyway, his hands were sweating inside his gloves.

"Good morning to you, young man," said the lead rider, a darkly handsome man somewhere in his late twenties, early thirties, Sam guessed. All four riders reined up in front of Sam. "How are you this fine, New Mexico mornin'?"

He cast his tan gaze around as if in appreciation of the rough desert landscape around him, the junipers and cedars climbing the ridges of the arroyo, the distant tabletop mesas, the golden sun vaulting into the sky. Maybe even the dark-eyed juncos and American goldfinches piping in the brush.

Pa hadn't known much about ranching, him having been a city doctor before Ma died. But he'd known his birds and had passed on that knowledge to Sam and his sister, Ilsa.

Sam absently patted the nervous mare's rump again and ran his tongue across his dry upper lip. He swept his too-long, blond hair back from his face with his other hand and said, "I'm all right."

"Workin' hard or hardly workin'?" asked the man in the gray campaign hat. He had a long, narrow face and pale blue eyes, a deep scar running in a crescent shape under the left one, just above the colorless patch beard carpeting his narrow jaws. He leaned casually forward against his saddle horn, quirking his mouth corners affably.

The other two men—one big, blond, shaggy, and droopy-eyed, the other definitely having some Mex or Injun blood, maybe both—glanced at each other and chuckled. The big, blond man had double bandoliers crisscrossed on his broad, lumpy chest. He was like a big, blond bear. Sam would not want to tangle with that one.

Sam gave a nervous chuckle and said, "I reckon...I don't know..." He wasn't sure how to answer the question. He'd been working hard since before sunup. He always did.

"What you doin' out here, kid?" asked the darkly handsome man, also leaning casually forward against his saddle horn. The handle of a big knife jutted up from

inside the collar of his shirt. Likely an Arkansas toothpick, Sam thought. He was a bit of a student of knives.

Sam glanced at the deadfall branches and driftwood
mounded in the buckboard's box. "Gatherin' wood," Sam
said, feeling stupid about having to explain the obvious.

"How old are you?" the darkly handsome man asked.

"Thirteen."

"Where's your Pa?"

"Back at the cabin," Sam said, suppressing the auto-
matic urge to jerk his head in the direction of the log
shack he shared with his sister roughly an hour's ride
higher in the mountains, to the west. He did not want
these men to know where he lived. And that he and his
sister lived alone there.

"I see, I see," said the darkly handsome man,
exchanging a quick glance with the man in the gray
Confederate hat and with the petal-soft Southerner's
drawl. Turning his gaze back to Sam, the handsome man
said, "You see a man out here? A man alone? On foot?"

Just then, Sam spied movement behind the four
strangers, to his right. He slid his glance in that direction
to see another man...yet another stranger...lying at the
base of the arroyo's wall, partly obscured by brush and
rocks. The man lay flat on his back. He gave his left arm
a feeble wave to get Sam's attention. Now that he had it,
he raised one, gloved finger to his lips.

Sam wasn't sure, but he thought he saw a five-pointed
star pinned to the breast of the man's shirt.

Sam's heartbeat quickened even more.

He slid his gaze back to the darkly handsome man
clad in a red, Spanish-style shirt and wearing a tan
Stetson with a band studded with hammered silver disks,
and said, "Uh...no...no, I haven't. I haven't"—a quick
glance back at the man lying at the base of the arroyo

wall then quickly back to the darkly handsome man again —"no...no, sir, I haven't."

His heart was beating so hard he feared it would burst out of his chest.

"Well," he added quickly. I best get back to work. This wood ain't gonna load itsel—"

He'd just started to turn away from the men and the wagon when the big, blond bear of a man gigged his horse over, blocking Sam's route toward the side of the arroyo and a good pile of driftwood washed down from the higher reaches during the last heavy rain.

The blond-bearded, heavy-lidded man glared down at him from beneath the floppy brim of his black, bullet-crowned hat. "You sure, kid? If I find out you're lyin', I'll cut your tongue out, dry it, and hang it around my neck!"

The men behind him chuckled.

Feeling the blood rush out of his cheeks, it took Sam several seconds to find his voice. His ears rang with terror. Part of him—the cowardly part—wanted to go ahead and point out the man lying on the opposite side of the arroyo.

Why couldn't they see him? All they had to do was turn that way.

The brave part of Sam—the part of him he'd promised his pa he'd cultivate—told him not to do it. There was a struggle deep inside him, however, and for a good three or four seconds he wasn't sure which side was going to win.

Then he brushed the sleeve of his blue wool work shirt across the sweat popping out on his forehead and he said with feigned indignance, "I ain't lyin'! I ain't seen no one, an' my word is bond!"

Inwardly, beneath his knee-quaking trepidation, he smiled. That last part was not half bad. He hadn't realized he was going to say it before he'd said it. It was one of Pa's old phrases; it had just come spurting its way out of his mouth.

At the same time, he felt a little sheepish. Obviously, his word was far from "bond." But unless he wanted to get that lawman over there killed for sure, for these men were obviously bad men that the lawman had likely been hunting, he had no choice but to lie. If they killed the lawman, they'd likely kill him, too, because he'd see them do it.

He stared up at the big bear of a man, trying to look tough. He just wished his knees would stop quaking. He wondered if these men could see it.

"All right, all right," said the darkly handsome, tan-eyed man, moving his horse up beside that of the big blond bear of a man. He smiled down at Sam and said, "We believe you, boy. You're not stupid. I can see that. You wouldn't lie to us. You just give a yell if you see him. Big man with a badge on his shirt. Might be wounded. We found his hoss, but not him—no, sir."

He glanced at the big blond man. "Yep...must be wounded. Maybe dead."

He turned back to Sam.

"What's your name, kid?"

Sam hesitated, not wanting to tell them his name. But he couldn't come up with an alias on the fly, so he went ahead and told them.

"Well, then, Sam—where do you live?"

Sam hesitated. Inwardly, he cursed. If his sister would have heard the curse—the really bad one—she'd have made him chomp down on a bar of soap for a good twenty minutes in the kitchen. Ilsa was like that.

Time for another lie.

He canted his head in the opposite direction of his

and Ilsa's cabin at the foot of Squaw Ridge. "Up that way."

"Mine diggin's?"

"Yes, sir," Sam lied again, inwardly wincing. Ilsa, who'd become his mother of sorts—or, rather, *mother hen* —had lectured him time and time again to never lie or curse, so whenever he did either one—even when it was perfectly reasonable to do so—he felt guilty.

The darkly handsome man put his horse up closer to Sam, until Sam could see his face more clearly, and see deeper into the man's eyes. Part of him recoiled at the sight. Suddenly, he found himself looking into a pair of devil's eyes. They were light brown and at first they looked warm and sympathetic. But now, looking deeper into them, Sam could see an amber spec in each, as though a demon inside him, with its own pair of amber, devil's eyes, was peering out.

The man smiled, but that only made it worse.

"Your word is bond—eh, Sam?"

"Th-that's right, sir."

"'Sir'—I like that." The devil-eyed man glanced at the big man beside him, who gave a low growl that was sort of a dry chuckle.

"All right, then." The man with the devil's eyes glanced at the men behind him, glanced at Sam once more, with those amber devil's eyes peering out from deep inside his own. He winked and said, "Take care, Sam. Maybe run into you again out here."

"All...all right," Sam said, fashioning a smile he knew was composed of as much wood as that he was gathering for his and his sister's potbelly stove.

The men clucked their horses into trots, heading up the arroyo, leaning out from their saddles, looking for sign of the man they were hunting, not knowing he wasn't fifty feet away.

When they were gone, Sam gave a deep sigh of relief.

But his trouble was not over.

He patted the calico again, said, "Stay, Honey,"—his sister had named the horse—then pulled his felt hat down tighter on his head and, glancing cautiously back toward where the bad men were disappearing around another bend in the arroyo, he walked toward the man on the arroyo's other side. He stepped through brush and over rocks.

Right away, he could see that the man had fallen into the arroyo from above. There was a good bit of dirt, sand, and gravel mixed with the blood on his shirt and on the bulging saddlebags and rifle that lay on either side of him, on the rocks and small shrubs.

The man was big with long, salt-and-pepper hair hanging to his shoulders. A shaggy matching mustache mantled his mouth. A high-crowned, broad-brimmed black Stetson lay nearby, as well.

The man had seemed to be dozing, his belly rising and falling sharply as he breathed. Now he opened his eyes suddenly and stared up at Sam. Again, the boy was taken aback by a man's eyes. This man's eyes were gray, like a wolf's eyes. There was a fierceness in them, but not an evil fierceness like those of the man with the devil's eyes. The badge on the man's shirt further put Sam at ease.

At least, at relative ease. He was still nervous as hell— er, *heck*...

The man stared up at him. It seemed to take him a few seconds for his eyes to focus. Then he lifted his right hand slightly and growled out, "Beat it, kid."

Sam was taken aback. "Huh?"

"You heard me." The man's head jerked as he coughed. "Beat it!"

Sam drew a deep breath, shook his head. "You're in a bad way, Mister."

"No shi—er, I mean...no *kiddin'*."

Despite the direness of the situation, Sam had to smile inwardly a little at the correction. Was he looking down at an adult version of himself? He wouldn't mind. The man was big, broad-shouldered, flat-bellied, and with a wolfishly handsome face. He was old, definitely, but strength still radiated from him. It did despite all the blood on his shirt and running down the left leg of his trousers.

"Just the same," the man croaked out. "Leave me. I'm trouble for you. Leave me...forget you ever saw me."

"I can't just leave you here."

The man had let his eyes flutter shut. Now he opened them, and they fairly glowed with that wolf-like fierce-ness. He gritted his teeth and said, "Leave me here. I won't...won't...get you killed."

Pain must have racked him. He shook then lifted his head again and coughed. When he rested his head back down on the ground again, he said, "I only waved 'cause I knew you'd spot me if you hadn't already. If they'd killed me, they'd have killed you, too."

Sam had to admit, with another pang of his customary guilt, that that had been one of the reasons he hadn't pointed the man out to the bad men. The other had been the courage he'd promised his father.

He could not let this lawman die out here alone. He had to show courage. He had to do what he could for him. That meant that he had to get him in the wagon and haul him home to where he and Ilsa could tend him. There might be no saving him. His shirt was a bloody mess, and his face, arms, and legs were all scratched and bruised.

But Sam had to try.

If he didn't, his pa and his own guilt would haunt him forever.

He dropped down to his haunches. "Mister, I'll tell you what I'm gonna do."

Again, the man opened those gray wolf's eyes.

Sam steeled himself against them. "Whether you like it or not, I'm going to get you into that wagon and I'm gonna haul you back to me and my sister's cabin. I can't do it alone. You're gonna have to help if you can. If not, I'm gonna unhitch Honey and gallop home and fetch my sister out here to help."

Sam glanced toward where the four obvious killers had disappeared up the arroyo. Then he looked at the big, wolf-eyed man again staring up at him out of the severe planes and deep lines of his face tanned to the texture of saddle leather. "Just hope them four don't come back and find us."

The wolf-like man grimaced and snorted, making his broad chest jerk. "You're a piece of work, kid."

"My sister often says the same thing, sir. Be right back."

Sam fetched the wagon, leaped down, and grabbed the man's right hand and arm. "You ready?"

The man groaned. He didn't curse this time.

CHAPTER 6

SOMEHOW, SAM MCDOWELL MANAGED TO GET THE BIG man into the back of the wagon, stretched out against the right-side panel. To make room for the man, Sam had tossed out some of the wood he'd gathered and shoved the rest aside. He had no blanket with which to pad the bed and apologized to the big man who was so fatigued and otherwise defeated that he merely gave his right hand a dismissive wave.

The man said something in a garbled voice. Sam could make out only the word: "Bags." Sam picked up the saddlebags that had fallen into the ravine along with the big lawman. He was surprised at how heavy they were. He could hear coins jiggling inside.

Judging by the weight, there was a good bit of loot in those bags. What else could it be but loot—given the wounded lawman and the obvious border toughs who were gunning for him? Sam set the bulging bags in the wagon beside the lawman then retrieved the Winchester Yellowboy, as well, taking a minute to brush the sand and dirt off the pretty gun and to admire its solid, well-balanced litheness and beauty. He traced his fingers over the intricate scrolling on the brass receiver, knowing it was the brass of the receiver that had given the rifle its famous nickname, *Yellowboy*.

Sam had seen such rifles in wish books he and his sister kept in the privy with a box of straw, and often wondered if he'd ever own one someday. He figured not. He figured that he'd likely be trapped out here on the ranch with his sister for the rest of their lives, never being able to afford anything more than Pa's old Spencer, which Pa had purchased for a few dollars from the old mountaineer Pa had bought the cabin from.

Sam set the rifle under the driver's seat, sort of wedged between the box's front panel and the leather-sheathed Spencer for some protection. If those hardtails returned, it would be the Yellowboy Sam would use to hold them off. Both fear and delight rippled through the boy as he climbed up into the driver's boot. He'd love to shoot such a fine weapon as the Winchester but knew that if it came to that, he and the big, wolf-like man breathing heavily in the wagon behind him would likely be filled so full of lead they'd rattle when they walked, as the old saying went.

They'd die hard.

Sam gritted his teeth as he took up the reins and released the brake handle and clucked the mare ahead then turned her back around to head northeast along the arroyo floor. If it came to shooting, he'd get one of them, by God!

Courage, he told himself. *Courage...*

As he put the wagon up the arroyo a hundred yards and then followed an eastern side canyon, he had to admit he wasn't feeling very courageous right now. Dread lay heavy in him. It draped his shoulders like a cold, wet blanket, making him shiver at times. As the wagon bounced along, climbing into the mountains, evoking more than a few grunts and groans from the man in the back, Sam cast several cautious looks over his shoulder, scrutinizing the trail behind him, his entrails tied in knots with the dread that he might see those two smiling killers on his back trail...and the big blond bear of a man and the little half-breed Mexican who sported two big pistols and two big, silver-capped bowie knives on his hips.

He and the lead rider—the man with the amber demon's eyes peering out from inside his own, and who had the handle of a big knife jutting up from behind his right shoulder—likely knew how to wield those knives to great effect. The darkly handsome devil with his Arkansas toothpick and the little, round-faced, long-mustached Mexican with his two fancy bowie knives in hand-tooled buckskin sheaths. They'd likely see a boy who'd lied to them and then helped the man they were after as a great opportunity to cause some pain that they would likely take great delight in.

That's who those men were, Sam knew. He lived remotely and rarely mixed with others, but he had a good imagination and a level-headed sense about the world. Besides, when Miss Cobb had closed her school to marry a rancher and have a baby, she'd given Sam several old dime novels to help keep him in trim with his reading, knowing the boy was not prone to crack more highbrow fare such as *Ivanhoe* or *David Copperfield*. Thus, Sam McDowell was rather well-read on the subject of frontier evil.

Even more so after this morning...

His and his sister's cabin was in a broad valley at the base of a forested mountain an hour's ride from where he'd run into the outlaws and their quarry, so Sam had to listen to the big man's agonized grunts and groans for longer than he wanted to. He supposed it probably felt a lot longer to the lawman, however, and for that he was genuinely sorry. He honestly thought that the man would expire before Sam ever reached the cabin. He was still grunting and groaning, however, when Sam pulled the buckboard off the main trail and through a fringe of ponderosa pines and over the wooden bridge spanning Bayonet Creek—so named for the old mountain man who'd originally settled here and had been found in his cabin after a long winter by his friends with an Apache bayonet sticking out of his frozen and thus well-preserved carcass.

Sam gave another little shiver at the thought. He wasn't sure why Pa had wanted to settle with two young kids here in such a remote place. He had to admit, however, that the place had grown on him. Over the past four years, and even after Pa's violent death, it had become home. He and his sister lived a relatively simple, uncomplicated albeit hardworking life here.

At least they had until about an hour ago...

Ilsa was out hanging fresh wash on the rope line strung between two ponderosas fronting the cabin, the fire over which she'd boiled the clothes still sending up wisps of pale gray smoke and short, yellow flames dancing in the pine-scented breeze. A hide-bottom chair was positioned close to the fire, on its right side. On the chair was a nest made from a stout quilt from which Sam could see Ilsa's pet, a half-grown raccoon named Pearl, peering out. Their half-collie, half-shepherd dog, King, came running out from where he'd been curled up on the humble log cabin's front porch, near the two chairs on which Sam and Ilsa sat out in the early evening, watching the sunset and the first stars twinkle to life, happy to take a break together between the day's seemingly endless chores and sleep.

Ilsa had heard the mare and the wagon clattering over the bridge and had been edging over toward where she had a double-barrel shotgun leaning against one of the pines to which an end of the wash line was tied. Now she stopped and shaded her eyes from the sun with one hand as she scowled curiously toward Sam.

"Ilsa," Sam said, drawing the wagon up in front of the cabin, King barking wildly, tail wagging, causing the mare to arch her neck and playfully chop at the dog with her front feet. "We got trouble! I got a wounded man in the back! He's been shot!"

"What?" Ilsa said sharply, incredulously, standing frozen in place near the pine against which the shotgun leaned, her long, black, wool skirt dancing in the breeze. She wore her customary elk hide vest over a white blouse, the sleeves rolled to her elbows. Her long, coal-black hair blew around her smooth, lightly tanned, dark-eyed face. Ilsa took after their mother, of black Irish heritage, while Sam, blond and blue-eyed, took after Pa, a blond-headed Scot with a good bit of Nordic blood.

Sam set the brake and, ignoring the dog barking and leaping around him, always happy to see him even when he left the yard for just a few minutes, clambered down from the wagon and hurried around to the back. He released the tailgate and glanced back to see Ilsa standing in the same place, both fists on her hips now, angrily, head canted to one side.

"Ilsa," Sam called. "He's a *lawman*!"

Ilsa began striding toward him, her expression no happier than it had been a minute ago. Sam looked down at the man in the wagon. He appeared to be asleep now, chest rising and falling slowly, heavily, eyelids fluttering as his eyeballs rolled around behind them. The muscles in his face leaped around and he moved his lips, softly groaning, in deep agony.

Sam glanced at his sister just now approaching the wagon, holding the hem of her skirt above her brown ankle boots. "He's in a bad way, Ilsa. A real bad way."

Ilsa stopped beside Sam and gazed down at the stranger. She crossed her arms on her chest and said with sharp accusing, "He's been shot!"

Sam looked at her. "I know. There's four hardtails after him!"

"Hardtails?"

"Ilsa, we have to get him inside and haul out Pa's old medical kit."

"And just what are we gonna do with it?"

"I don't know. I reckon we'd best boil water or somethin'. Isn't that what Pa always did?"

"Pa did a lot of things. He was a doctor, Sam! But he's dead—don't you remember?"

"What was I supposed to do, Ilsa?" Sam said, indignantly. "Just leave him out there?"

"Yes!"

Both Sam and his sister jumped at the same time. The stranger had fairly bellowed the reply.

Sam looked at the stranger. His gray wolf's eyes were wide open now, and he was staring up at Ilsa. The man's jaws were set hard as stone and those gray orbs fairly throbbed with emotion.

He rasped out, "Now that you got me this far, you'd better get me into the cabin or shoot and bury me. Those jackals find me out here, we're all dead!"

Ilsa looked at Sam, her dark eyes wide with shock. Sam looked back at her, his damnable heart drumming against his breastbone again. Brother and sister shuttled their fearful gazes back along the trail through the pines up which Sam and the wounded stranger had come.

King was mewling and standing on his hind legs, front paws on the tailgate, sniffing the newcomer.

Ilsa turned back to the stranger and released the tail-gate latch. "Let's get him out of there," she said.

The tailgate dropped down beneath the bed of the wagon.

"Out of the way, King," Ilsa said, hazing the dog aside. "Get out of the way. Go to the cabin!"

She pointed and the dog slinked off, whining.

"How are we going to get him out of there, Sam?" Ilsa said, raking her enervated gaze up and down the broad length of the man before her.

Suddenly, with a fierce growl, the man shoved up on his elbows and looked at Sam. "My rifle!"

Sam quickly fetched the Yellowboy and handed it to the man who took it in both his big hands, turned side-ways, and slammed the rifle's brass butt plate against the wagon's wooden floor. With another fierce growl, casting a quick glance toward the trail leading into the yard, he used the rifle to slide his big bulk down the length of the wagon until his legs were hanging over the end of it. He thrust the rifle at Sam.

"Take that!"

The stranger heaved himself forward until both feet were on the ground.

"Give me that!"

He took the rifle back from Sam, slammed the butt against the edge of the wagon, and groaned as he levered himself to his feet. Sam looked at the man's face. It was red and swollen—several large, purple veins in his fore-head and around his eyes throbbing till Sam thought they would burst. His long, sweat-damp hair danced across his collar and craggy cheeks.

He took the end of the rifle's barrel in his right hand, leaned against it, and flung out his right arm in an arc. Sam and Ilsa leaped against him. He hooked his arm over them, and they each wrapped one of their own arms around the stranger's waist, helping balance him as he began limping and shuffling toward the cabin—so quickly that Sam and Ilsa, stumbling over each other's feet, had trouble keeping up with him.

As they passed the fire, Sam heard the chittering of Ilsa's raccoon, which she'd found orphaned along the creek earlier that spring. King stood at the edge of the porch, regarding the big stranger warily. As Sam, Ilsa, and the stranger began climbing the porch steps, King backed away along the porch to one side, head and tail up, whining, his dark eyes cast with incredulity and fear.

The threesome shuffled across the porch. The stranger ducked his head to pass through the low doorway and rasped, "Direct me!"

Sam could feel his big, quivering body weakening.

Ilsa looked at Sam. "Pa's old room!"

They guided the stranger through the kitchen then the living room part of the cabin. There were three tattered-quilt curtained doorways in the cabin's rear wall. Sam and Ilsa guided the stranger toward the far left one. Ilsa reached forward to slide the quilt to one side and then she, Sam, and the stranger, ducking his head again, pushed through the doorway and into the room.

It was larger than the other two, which belonged to Sam and Ilsa. Sam and Ilsa rarely came in here to be reminded of their father by the heavy furniture, which included a heavy armoire, small but stout liquor cabinet, chest of drawers, a zinc-topped washstand, and a large bed neatly, tightly made with a faded purple star quilt.

The smell of their father, including his nightly cigar and glass of good bourbon, lingered here two years after his death.

The stranger stopped at the side of the bed.

"Put an old towel on it," he wheezed, his knees beginning to buckle. "For the blood!"

Ilsa lurched forward, drew the covers back, then opened the armoire and plucked two heavy towels from an upper shelf. She hurriedly spread them on the bed. She'd just pulled away when the big stranger collapsed face forward. He could only half help them roll him onto his side, lift his legs, and lay him out the length of the bed.

Sam could hear King whining in the cabin's open doorway.

The stranger reached out with a quivering hand, wrapped his fingers around Sam's left wrist, squeezed. "Saddlebags...*inside*! Whiskey!" he said through gritted teeth, his gray eyes burning through Sam's. "Then heat two knives. Get them glowing hot. Bring them here!"

His head fell back against the pillow, his eyes closed, he gave a heavy, ragged sigh, and he was out.

CHAPTER 7

A WHISTLE SOUNDED UP THE FORESTED SLOPE ON BLUE Bowdrie' left. He glanced at Anders Anderson riding beside him, and both men checked their horses down, closing hands over hogleg handles.

They removed their hands from their pistols' grips as they watched the gray-hatted Reb Winslow and the Mexican half-breed, Enrique Martinez, ride down out of the trees. Martinez had let his low-crowned, straw sombrero hang down his back by its braided rawhide thong. His sweat-damp, dark-brown hair showed the lines of the hat. As he and Winslow checked their blowing mounts down before Bowdrie and Anderson, Martinez brushed his gloved fist across his bushy mustache and muttered a Spanish oath.

"No sign of him?" Bowdrie said.

"Not a thing, jefe," said Martinez, lifting his chin and scraping the four-days' growth of beard stubble on his naturally ten neck. "Lady Luck has not smiled down on you, either, uh?"

"Maybe," Bowdrie said.

"We been followin' the tracks of a lone horse—Mannion's horse," said Anderson in his deep, guttural voice. He glanced at Bowdrie. "At least, we *think* it's his horse."

"Likely only one lone horse out here. We're only about a half a mile from where we last seen that bay. Trouble is," Bowdrie added, scowling angrily at the flinty ground around him and his three remaining "boys," "this ground is too hard to hold a print for far. We lost his trail a couple hundred yards back."

"You think he's heading back to his rider?" asked Winslow.

"It's the only lead we got," Bowdrie said. "We sure as hell haven't been able to find any sign of the man himself. All we know is he's on foot. Why, is anyone's guess."

"Took a bullet, maybe, eh?" said Martinez with a coyote grin, showing his small, crooked, tobacco-stained teeth. "Maybe one of Willie's or Louis's..."

"Maybe," Bowdrie said. "Or maybe one of us winged him before. Trouble is we haven't even found any blood... much less those damn saddlebags."

"Probably holed up somewhere," Anderson said. "Bleedin' out. If he ain't dead already."

Just then a rifle report sliced through the afternoon air, causing birds to wing up out of the pines on the north-facing slope, to Bowdrie's left. All four men automatically reached for their rifles jutting up from their saddle scabbards. Then, his eyes finding five riders galloping down from a forested ridge a hundred yards ahead and on his right, Bowdrie turned his hand palm out, and said, "Hold on."

The other three turned to follow their leader's gaze toward the five riders angling down the slope in their direction, the hoof thuds rising quickly as the newcomers closed the gap between them and Bowdrie's bunch. The five all wore the attire of your average range rider—chaps, dusters, work shirts, vests, and billowy neckerchiefs.

"Sit tight, fellas," Bowdrie ordered. "We'll hear what they have to say..."

"Easy pickin's," said Martinez with a shrewd grin. "And nice horses."

Bowdrie shot him a hard look. "You listen to me, bean-eater. Those horses are nothin' compared to the loot Mannion has!"

The leader's outburst, common as it was, successfully cowed the Mexican, whose naturally tan cheeks turned a darker shade of brown as he lowered his sheepish, brown-eyed gaze to his saddle horn. "Si, si, jefe. Pardon!"

Bowdrie gave a caustic snort. The Mex's suddenly deferential demeanor didn't fool him. He knew he'd have to sleep lightly for the next several nights lest Martinez should slide one of his pigstickers between Bowdrie's ribs one night while the outlaw leader slept. That they were down to only four men might spare him, however...until they found the loot. That much loot was dangerous, and he knew as well as the others did that if they did find it, they'd all have to sleep lightly until they'd divvied it up and gone their separate ways.

Bowdrie regarded the five men before him, blinking against their own dust catching up to them. The lead man appeared thirty or so, tall, lean, grim-faced, with sandy hair and long, sandy, mare's tail mustaches.

"Who're you and what're you doin' out here?" he asked curtly, keeping his right hand splayed across his right thigh, near the Schofield .44 holstered there. "This is open range but my cattle...Bar Z cattle...graze on it."

His gaze was direct. Not belligerent but close.

Bowdrie gave his easy smile and held his right hand up, palm out. "Easy, now. Easy. Pull your horns in, um... Mister, um..."

"Trainor," the tall man said. "Zeke Trainor." He narrowed one eye that had just turned belligerent; he pointed his left index finger at Bowdrie, commandingly. "And you don't give the orders out here. I do."

Bowdrie shared an easy smile with the easy-smiling Reb Winslow then turned back to Trainor. "Look, Trainor, we ain't long-loopin', if that's what you're thinkin'."

"That's what I'm *always* thinkin'. We live a piece off the beaten path out here"—Trainor glanced at the hard-eyed men flanking him—"and me and my hands are the only law."

"Well, now you got help," Bowdrie said.

Trainor scowled, incredulous.

"We're part of a deputized posse out of Del Norte in the Colorado Territory," Bowdrie lied. "We were led out here by the town marshal up thataway—Bloody Joe Mannion."

Trainor cast his skeptical glance to one of the men flanking him then turned back to Bowdrie.

"It appears you recognize the name," Bowdrie observed.

"Yeah, I know the name. You're part of Mannion's posse, you're sayin'?"

"That's right," Bowdrie said. "We were runnin' down five train robbers led by a crooked deputy sheriff from up north—Bill Wade."

Trainor blinked. He'd heard of Wade, too.

"We caught up to him. Cut him an' the others down... but not without a fight. Bloody Joe took a bullet. His horse ran off with him on it. Now, we found the horse, but not Bloody Joe. We think he might be lyin' wounded out here somewhere. Kinda like to find him before we head on home."

"Si, si," said Enrique Martinez quickly, so delighted by Bowdrie's tall tale that he was eager to take part in it himself. "Wounded or dead—who knows, *ya sabes a lo que me refiero?*" You know what I mean? "Pitiful end for such a famous hombre!"

Bowdrie shot the Mexican a quick, cutting glance then returned his gaze to the tall, lean rancher before him, whose interest in the story seemed to have grown.

"I take it you haven't seen him," Bowdrie said to Trainor.

"No, I haven't seen him." The rancher frowned, canted his head to one side. "You're sure it's Mannion out here?"

"Unfortunately," Bowdrie said. "Uh...he has the loot the robbers stole off the train. Not quite sure how he got it, but he has it, all right. Not sure what he may or may not have intended to do with it, but he has it, all right. If you happen to find the marshal and the loot, let us know, will you? We'll make sure they're both safely returned to Del Norte." He glanced at his men. "Me and my fellow citizens will get it safely home and into the hands of those it belongs to."

He grinned his affable grin. Winslow grinned his, as well.

One of the men flanking Trainor lifted an arm and pointed a finger at Bowdrie. "He's full o' crap, boss. That there is Blue Bowdrie—border tough!" He locked gazes with Bowdrie himself and flared his nostrils as he said, "He shot my brother, Ned, in Las Cruces a few years back. They got crossways over a faro game! I seen it all!"

Bowdrie stared mildly back at his accuser—a lean,

blond, blue-eyed man with thick lips and buck teeth. He wore dusty blue denims and a faded canvas duster. "You were there an' didn't lend a hand?"

He smiled.

The blond man glared back at him, his cheeks dimpling over his jaw hinges. He slid a flap of the duster back behind the worn grips of the .44 holstered for the cross-draw on his left hip.

Bowdrie chuckled and leaned forward against his saddle horn. "Mister, do you really want to die here today?"

Trainor glanced from him to the blond man. "Keep it holstered, Canton! You're not getting into a shooting match!"

"Tell him that, Mister Trainor," said Canton, tonelessly. He kept his challenging gaze on Bowdrie but his long face was mottled red and white with apprehension.

Trainor turned to Bowdrie. "Keep it holstered, Bowdrie. And get off my land!"

Bowdrie cut his own hard gaze at the rancher, his eyes appearing even harder in contrast to the easy smile lingering on his lips. "And if I don't?"

Trainor blanched a little, as though he'd seen the demonic light in the gunman's eyes. He spat to one side and reined his Appaloosa around. "I have more men than these on my roll. And some are fast. As fast as you. So get the hell off my land!" He glanced at the others, all showing an apprehension similar to Canton's. "Come on, you men. We have work to do!"

Casting Bowdrie and his brethren one more cautious, apprehensive look, the others reined their mounts around and galloped off after their boss. Canton was the last to leave. He let his own glare stay on Bowdrie until

Bowdrie laughed, mockingly. His face turning a darker shade of red, the blond drover reined his own mount around, put the steel to it, and galloped after the others, the flaps of his faded duster whipping out around him in the wind.

"If I may say so, jefe," Martinez said, tentatively, "we should have cut them all down. Buried them in shallow graves." He shrugged exaggeratedly. "I am just saying."

"Yeah...maybe," Bowdrie said, staring after the cowboys. "On the other hand, killin' 'em might be more trouble than it's worth."

"Likely have to do it sometime, boss," Anderson said.

"Oh, yeah. I don't doubt these hills are gonna run red with blood before we're through." Bowdrie smiled. The idea didn't bother him all that much. He clucked his mount forward and cast his scrutinizing gaze at the ground. "Come on—let's try to run down that damn bay!"

———

MANNION TOOK A DEEP PULL FROM THE BOTTLE SAM had brought him.

"Damn...er, I mean, *dang*," Joe said, when he'd pulled the bottle back down. He looked at the labeled bottle. "That's good Who-Hit-John!"

He winced as Ilsa gently sponged the blood from around the wound as Mannion lay with his head and shoulders propped up against the headboard on pillows. Ilsa and Sam had managed to wrestle the shirt off the lawman's shoulders and tossed the bloody rag in a corner. Then they'd cut off his equally bloody, wash-worn long-handle top and discarded that, as well. Joe kept passing out, but he was trying to remain conscious now so he could drink the whiskey. He needed the whiskey to help quell the almost unendurable pain that awaited him when Ilsa and Sam pressed the two knives, which were heating in the potbelly stove in the main part of the cabin, against both wounds in his left side—the entrance and exit wound.

He could smell the odor of hot steel emanating through the open bedroom door.

He'd had wounds cauterized before, sometimes without whiskey. That had been no fun at all. In fact, he almost felt like sobbing, just remembering it.

Ilsa plucked the bottle out of Mannion's hand. "Pa liked the good stuff."

"I'm a rotgut man myself," Mannion said. "But it'll do in a pinch, I reckon."

Ilsa looked at him. She was a pretty, dark-haired, dark-eyed girl. Not hard to look at, at all. In fact, Mannion thought the boys—if there were any boys around here except her brother—probably fought like cats and dogs over such a treasure. Her eyes were deep and soulful. Eminently expressive. Commanding.

"A rotgut man, eh?" Those eyes shot him a glance of reproof. "We've brought a rotgut man into our house, Sam." She looked at Mannion again. "This is going to burn."

"I know."

She tipped the bottle over the wound and worked some of the whiskey deep into it and out the other side with a sponge. Joe stiffened, extending his legs straight out before him and sucking air sharply through gritted teeth.

"Yi, yi, yi," Mannion said. "That's the way to do it, girl!"

"Pa showed me."

"Pa?"

"Dead now," Sam said, standing beside the chair Ilsa sat in, close against Mannion's left side. "He was a doctor in Pueblo before we moved out here. He tended a lot of the local ranch hands. Broken bones, snake bites... gunshot wounds."

"I take it he's dead," Mannion said, the whiskey's burn coursing through every fiber of his being. He knew it was nothing compared to what would come next, so he plucked the bottle out of the girl's hand and tipped it back until the bubble had rolled up and down three times.

"Two years," Ilsa said. "Rustler shot him. Or so we figure. We heard the shot. It was at night and Pa had heard the cattle stirring. He rode out to investigate. We hauled him back to the headquarters belly down across his saddle, Sam an' me."

Mannion frowned at the pair. "So...you're all alone out here?"

They both nodded.

Ilsa took one more swipe at the ragged wounds in Mannion's side, dropped the sponge in the bloody bowl of water on the bed beside Joe's left knee, and glanced at her brother. "Bring the knives, Sam."

Sam glanced at the lawman, nodded, and left the room.

Ilsa gave Mannion a dark look.

"Don't worry, darlin'," Joe said, smiling at her. "This ain't my first rodeo."

He winked.

Her perfectly molded, impossibly smooth cheeks colored a little.

Oh, sure, Joe, Mannion castigated himself. *Flirt with a girl even younger than your daughter, you old goat!*

He chalked it up to the drink.

He'd chalked a lot of things up to drink over the years.

He winced when he saw Sam reenter the bedroom, two wide-bladed knives glowing like molten iron lying across a blue-speckled, tin plate. The boy walked over and set the plate on the bed, beside the basin of bloody water.

Ilsa looked down at the glowing knives, then at Mannion. She shook her long hair back from her face and said, "Marshal, what's your name. In case..."

"In case I kick off?" Joe said, staring down in horror at the two glowing blades. "Joe Mannion. I'm from up Del Norte way."

"*Bloody Joe?*" said Sam, eyes snapping wide in shock.

"One an' the same," Joe said.

"You recognize the name?" Ilsa asked her brother.

"Who hasn't heard of Bloody Joe?"

Mannion laughed. "I see my reputation precedes me even here." He looked at Ilsa. "If I don't make it, I'd appreciate your getting word to my wife, Jane. She runs the San Juan Saloon in Del Norte."

Jane will tell Vangie.

Ilsa nodded. "Of course, Marshal Mannion."

She picked up one of the knives, handed it to Sam. She picked up the other one.

Mannion sat up a little straighter and leaned forward, giving access to both the exit and entrance wounds in his side.

"All right, children," he said, stealing himself against the misery that would soon be his. "Give me hell. Er, I mean *heck!*"

He chuckled.

———

SAM HELD HIS GLOWING KNIFE AGAINST BLOODY JOE'S Mannion's exit wound.

Ilsa held hers against the lawman's entrance wound.

Brother and sister scrunched up their faces against the stench of scorched blood and skin.

"One more second, Sam!" Ilsa yelled above the sizzling sound.

Yep, that's just how it sounded, Sam thought. *Like meat sizzling in a cast-iron pan.*

"All right," Ilsa said.

They pulled their knives away.

Mannion, however, had passed out as soon as they'd each pressed their blades to the wounds. He lay back against the bed, partly turned to his right. His eyelids fluttered; his breath rattled in his throat.

Sam remembered that rattling sound in Pa's throat just before he'd passed.

"I hope we didn't kill Bloody Joe Mannion," Sam said.

Ilsa dropped her knife on the plate and pressed her hand against the lawman's broad, bare chest. She shook her head. "He's still alive. Now, only time will tell."

"Right."

Sam felt his gaze drift to the saddlebags hanging over the back of a chair in a corner near the end of the bed. He looked at Ilsa, surprised to find that hers had gone there, too.

They looked at each other, and each jerked with a self-conscious start.

"Well, Sam," Ilsa said quickly. "I'll start cleaning up and start supper. You better get to the afternoon chores."

"Right, right," Sam said, glancing at the saddlebags once more. "How much you think is there, though?"

"Best not think about it, little brother." Ilsa flicked his chin with her thumb then picked up the bloody washbasin.

Suddenly, King started barking out in the yard.

The barking grew louder and louder and more incredulous.

"Oh, God!" Ilsa said, setting the washbasin on a table. "Who do you suppose that is?"

Dread touched Sam.

Had the brigands who'd shot Mannion followed him and the lawman here?

Sam and Ilsa shared an anxious look. Then Sam strode quickly through the doorway and across the cabin to the closed front door. King was barking near the cabin now—growling and barking fiercely.

A wooden thudding sounded on the cabin's front stoop.

Thud! Thud! Thud! Thud-Thud-Thud!

"Oh, God!" Ilsa said. She'd followed Sam out of the bedroom and now stood behind him, raising a hand to her open mouth.

"Stay back, sis."

Courage, boy. You're the man of the place now.

Sam grabbed the Spencer off the table, pumped a cartridge into the action, then shouldered his sister aside as he moved to the door. He closed his hand around the handle and tripped the metal and leather latch. He gritted his teeth as he began inching open the door.

From the other side of the door:

Thud! Thud! Thud! Thud! Thud!

Sam drew the door wide and peered out. His lower

jaw sagged in shock when he saw the horse hammering its right, shod front hoof against the stoop's bottom step.

"What is it?" Ilsa asked behind him.

Sam turned his wide-eyed gaze to her. "It's a big, bay stallion!"

CHAPTER 8

AGAIN, ILSA CLOSED HER HAND OVER HER MOUTH AS she stepped up into the open doorway beside her brother.

Sure enough, the horse facing her and Sam was a big, sleek bay. He looked extremely nervous, agitated. Again, he slammed his right front hoof onto the stoop's bottom step, ignoring the angry barking and raised hackles of King. He looked at Sam and Ilsa in turn and gave his head such a violent shake he nearly threw off his bridle.

"Easy, boy," Sam said, stepping slowly onto the stoop, holding both hands up, palms out. "It's all right. It's all right." He glanced over his shoulder at Ilsa and said, "You suppose it's..."

"His horse," the girl said. "Your Bloody Joe Mannion friend. Has to be. He came looking for him."

"Easy, boy. Easy," Sam said walking slowly down the steps. "King, go lay down!"

The shepherd-collie wasn't having it. He continued rushing the horse and barking. None of it seemed to phase the stallion who continued looking at Sam and Ilsa but mostly it was trying to get a look through the cabin's open door behind them. It had been looking long and hard for its rider and must have winded him somewhere around where Sam had picked him up. The horse must have followed Mannion up here by scent.

The stallion backed up a couple of steps. Again, he shook his head and stomped his foot.

"Easy, boy," Sam said. He cooed to the horse as he slowly approached, reaching for the bridle.

Sam closed his hand around the cheek strap and cooed again at the big mount, trying to sooth it.

"Jeepers, he's agitated," Sam said.

"Take him around back," Ilsa said. "I'll open the curtains on Mannion's window, let him look in. Maybe that'll settle him down and then you can stable him. We have to get him out of sight pronto!"

"Right, right."

Sam bent slowly over and picked up the horse's bridle reins. He slowly straightened, wanting to make no sudden movements. Ilsa was right. He had to get the stallion out of the yard and into the stable as soon as possible. The owlhoots after the loot were likely scouring the country. They might follow the tracks of Sam's wagon. If they saw the bay in the yard...

Sam shuddered at the thought.

He and Ilsa were right independent. But they could not hold off four hardened killers. Especially not with as much loot as appeared to be in those saddlebags on the line. Sam already knew from earlier how determined they were.

Ilsa swung around and hurried off toward the lawman's room.

As she did, Sam got the bay settled down somewhat. After a little gentle coaxing, he was able to lead the mount around behind the cabin. He walked up to the window as Ilsa stared out through Mannion's window. Sam could see the big lawman lying on the bed to the window's right, the head of the bed abutting the cabin's rear wall, the man's feet extended, under the quilts, toward the opposite side of the room.

Sam led the horse up to the left side of the window, so it could see into the room, toward the right side and its rider.

"See, boy?" Sam said as Ilsa turned away and walked out of the room. "He's right there. He's beat up a bit, that's for sure. But Sis an' me—we're takin' good care of him. You see him, boy?"

It took the horse a minute to understand what it was being told. Then it peered into the room and blew, switched its tail. Its gaze held on the big man lying beneath the quilts. The horse stepped up a little closer to the window, turned its head more to the right. It stared at the big man on the bed with mute, growing interest.

It blew. It whickered deep in its chest, gave its tail another switch. A satisfied one.

Ilsa had come up to stand beside Sam. Seeing the satisfied expression on the horse's face, the way the sight of its rider seemed to instantly calm it, brought tears to her eyes.

"Oh, gosh—look at that, Sam. That horse does purely love that man!"

"I know," Sam said softly, smiling up at the big mount, its gaze held fast on the big man in the bed.

"Best see if you can stable him now." Ilsa brushed a tear from her cheek with the back of her hand. "You know, Sam—I'm sure that horse left a mighty clear trail. Right up here to Mannion's window."

"I know," Sam said, nodding. "Just as soon as I get him stabled, I'll see if I can wipe some of it out."

Ilsa looked at him darkly and nodded. She turned around and walked slowly back around the corner of the cabin.

Sam knew how she felt.

They had a famous lawman in the cabin. One with a target on his back. One with a whole lot of loot.

That meant Sam and Ilsa were caught in one mighty big whipsaw.

"Come on, boy," Sam said, gently patting the bay's snout. "Let's get you into the stable and whip you up some water and a bait of oats. What do you say to that, eh?"

Contented now, the bay answered the tug on the lead line.

Sam led the bay back to the corral and stable flanking the cabin. In the corral, the calico, Honey, and Pa's thoroughbred, Lightning, stood watching the bay and the boy dubiously from over the closed gate. Sam led the bay into the stable, dropping the reins once he was inside then quickly closing the doors behind him.

The faster he could get the lawman's horse out of sight the better.

But he still had to deal with the bay's tracks. Those four toughnuts were likely scouring the craggy country below the ranch for the lawman. If they came upon the bay's tracks, they'd follow them for sure. They'd see the wagon tracks, too.

Once the stable doors were closed, Sam led the bay into one of the four stalls. He brought water in a bucket from the rain barrel outside then forked hay into the stall and set a bucket of oats down in front of the horse, who still seemed agitated but not as badly as before. He knew his rider was near. He was a smart horse, though, Sam could tell. He'd seen Mannion in the bed and knew he was injured and was likely worried about him.

"You're a fine horse," Sam said, giving the bay's long neck an affectionate caress. "I'll give you a good rubdown later. I have to go wipe out your tracks, so we don't have any unwanted guests here this afternoon."

He left the stall and saw by the golden light filled with dust motes slanting through the stable's two front windows, one on either side of the door, that it was, indeed, afternoon. Time had flown since he'd been accosted by the four hardtails and then found the wounded lawman.

Odd how quickly life could change. It had been that way when he and Ilsa had heard the shot echoing off Squaw Ridge behind the cabin and they'd ridden Honey up to find their father slumped over on the ground, not far from where he'd been shot off his horse.

Sam drew a deep breath, hitched his denims up higher on his skinny hips, then left the stable through the side door, entering the corral. He led Pa's black thoroughbred, Lightning, into the stable to saddle and bridle him. The thoroughbred was one of his and Ilsa's rare valuable possessions. A wealthy former patient of Pa's had gifted the family with the horse when George McDowell had left his practice in Pueblo the year after Ma had died to take up the life of a gentlemen rancher out in the rugged mountains of northwestern New Mexico.

Pa had never said as much, but Sam suspected the reason he'd wanted to leave his practice was his heart had been broken after he hadn't been able to save Ma from the cancer that had taken her. He hadn't had the heart for it anymore. He'd just wanted to head up into the high, craggy ridges of these Stalwart Mountains and lick his wounds in private—with his only son and daughter by his side.

When Sam had Lightning saddled, he led the big black out of the stable and around to the front of the cabin. Ilsa was out there on the stoop, staring worriedly toward the southeast, back along the trail that climbed up from the lower country to the ranch in the high, piney country. She'd placed the raccoon on a blanket on a chair beside the cabin's front door. The little tyke, whom Ilsa had named Pearl, was sitting up and washing herself like a cat.

Ilsa's long, coal-black hair jostled in the breeze.

"Any sign of 'em?" Sam asked.

Ilsa shook her head. She had her arms crossed, and her face was pale and drawn with concern. "Not yet." She glanced at the thoroughbred, then at Sam. "You be careful out there, little brother. Don't go far and hurry back."

"I'm gonna ride out a mile or two, wipe out the bay's trail before it reaches the canyon." He meant the canyon that trailed up from the low country, giving access to the higher valley in which their ranch sat.

Ilsa glanced to the west; dark clouds were piling up over pine-studded ridges. "Looks like rain. If we get enough, it'll wipe out the trail."

Sam stepped up onto the stoop and reached through the cabin's open door for the Spencer. "Can't chance it," he said as he walked down the porch steps and slid the rifle into the leather sheath he'd strapped to the thoroughbred's saddle. "I'll ride down a ways and make sure it's blotted out."

As he untied Lightning's reins from the hitchrack, Ilsa stepped up to him and wrapped her left hand around his right wrist. "Sam, aren't you scared?"

"Heck, yeah!" he said with a dry laugh.

"I don't think I've been so scared since Pa died."

"Me, neither." Sam looked up at her—she was three or four inches taller than her brother, him four years her junior—putting on the toughest face he could manage. "We have to be brave, Sis. We stood against rustlers since Pa died. We can stand against this."

Ilsa placed her hand on his shoulder and narrowed her eyes at him as she said, tears glazing her eyes and emotion making her voice sound tight, "You do Pa proud, little brother."

Sam turned away, flushing, and led Lightning over to the steps. He climbed to the highest step then leaped into the saddle. Distant thunder rumbled. He looked up at the slate-gray clouds piling up over the ranch. "I best get moving."

"If it starts to rain hard, come on back home, Sam."

"I will, Sis. You got your shotgun?"

"It's inside. You got your rainslicker?"

Sam jerked his thumb over his shoulder to indicate the yellow canvas slicker wrapped around his bedroll lashed behind the cantle of his saddle.

He turned back to his sister gazing up at him worriedly. "Keep an eye out, Sis. I'll be back for supper...I hope."

"I'll be waiting."

Sam pulled his floppy-brimmed felt hat down lower on his head, reined Lightning around, and clucked the mount toward the trail leading out of the yard. He didn't have to cluck twice. The thoroughbred hadn't been ridden in a while and he was chomping at the bit to hightail it into the tall and uncut country beyond the ranch yard.

When horse and rider had left the yard, clomped

across the bridge spanning the creek, and rode out through the pines and into the open valley, Sam reined up to study the trail meandering ahead of him between the high, pine- and fir-studded peaks. No sign of anyone on the trail so far. Good.

He clucked Lightning into a trot and relaxed his body, riding easily in the saddle, just like Pa had taught him to do. More thunder rumbled. Again, he glanced up at the clouds, a little disappointed to see them sliding across the sky behind him and off to the southwest. There's a chance the storm might skirt him and the trail. It might discourage the outlaws, though. Maybe keep them in camp, giving him a chance to wipe out the bay's trail before they found it.

When he was a couple of hundred yards from the ranch yard, he booted Lightning into a lope, keeping a keen eye on the trail ahead and the broad valley around him, glad to see no sign of the men stalking Bloody Joe Mannion. Gradually, the floor of the valley dropped and pinched off between two close ridges. Between those ridges was where the canyon dropped down toward the low country, one of the only two or three trails offering access to this high valley.

Pa sure did find himself a remote enough place—Sam would give him that.

Mostly, Sam liked it up here, though. He supposed he sort of took after Pa in his feeling at home with the peace and quiet, being sort of off by himself. Ilsa seemed to be that way now, too, though she'd really chafed when Pa had first told her and Sam where the little ranch he'd bought was located.

Back then, she'd been Sam's age now—thirteen. Being a pretty and social girl as well as naturally likable, she'd had quite a few friends and some young male admirers back in Pueblo. She'd also enjoyed school. Sam had been a shy, awkward loner from a young age; he'd had only one close friend, a fishing buddy named Lyle Kendrick, and he'd been too restless to enjoy being cooped up in the classroom.

So the lack of schooling and the remoteness of their new home had never really bothered him. Leastways, it hadn't till Pa died. Now, with just him and Ilsa living up here together and having to work so hard to keep food on the table and the rustlers off their range, he had to admit he sometimes found himself wondering what living down in the low country again would be like.

Maybe someday he'd find out. He and Ilsa had never really talked about moving. Pa was buried up here, behind the cabin, and where would they go where they'd be as free as they were up here?

As Sam rode down into the narrow canyon between those two craggy ridges, he kept an eye on the storm as well as on the trail ahead. Sure enough, those storm clouds appeared to be passing him by. The ranch might have gotten a few sprinkles but down here, Sam could see blue sky between the high, thin clouds that were the tattered edges of the squall.

Damn the luck.

As he rode, he could see the bay's hoofprints clearly marking the sandy, gravelly trail of the canyon floor. Soon, down where several trails branched off toward other ranches and a remote mine, he'd wipe out the prints, making it harder for anyone tracking the bay to track it up into the valley.

He followed the steeping canyon floor around a bend then reined in sharply.

He pricked his ears, listening. He'd heard something. Lightning had heard it, too. The horse stood staring straight ahead, twitching its ears. A slight breeze gust carried men's voices up the canyon.

Familiar voices.

"Ah, no," Sam said, his heart picking up its fearful beat.

He'd just started to rein Lightning around to head back up the canyon when he spied movement on the trail ahead—a horse's head just then appearing as it rode out from around a bend roughly sixty yards down canyon. The horse's head was followed by the rider sitting astride the animal—a lean, dark-haired man with a concho-studded hat!

Bowdrie saw Sam a second after Sam had seen Bowdrie.

The robber drew his horse up sharply, eyes widening. He jerked his right arm and index finger up and forward, pointing. "Hey, there's that kid!"

"Damn!" Sam said as he sucked a sharp breath through gritted teeth.

He put his head down and batted his heels against Lightning's flanks, galloping back up the canyon.

"Wait, kid!" Bowdrie shouted. "We wanna *talk* to you!"

A revolver cracked behind Sam, the bullet screeching off a rock just inches to the right of Lightning's scissoring hooves.

CHAPTER 9

ANOTHER BULLET SPANGED OFF A ROCK JUST AHEAD OF Sam and on his left.

At the same time, the thunder of the revolver that had fired the shot echoed around inside the canyon, making both Sam and the thoroughbred flinch. Sam glanced behind. All four cutthroats were galloping toward him, strung out single file fifty yards behind.

Sam turned his head back forward. A trail branched off the canyon's left side, climbing through pine and boulders toward a ridge crest. Sam hadn't taken that trail before, so he didn't know where it led. That didn't much matter at the moment. If he kept running Lightning straight up the canyon, he or the horse or both of them were going to get a bad case of lead poisoning.

Without a second thought, he swung the stallion onto the trail. Lightning put his head down and shot up the steep slope, the trail tracing a serpentine course through pines, rocks, and boulders. It must be an old Indian hunting trail because no prospector or rancher would want to negotiate such a steep route to his diggings or ranch headquarters. An old hunting trail now probably used by rustlers.

"Heading up that ridge!" Sam heard Bowdrie shout behind him.

Again, a revolver cracked. The bullet screeched off a rock somewhere behind Sam, as now they were working up into plenty of cover. Riding low in the saddle, giving the thoroughbred its head, he looked up to see a cloudy sky through the pine crowns ahead another fifty yards.

"Come on, boy—keep goin'!" Sam desperately urged the stalwart mount. "We gotta get shed of them polecats!" He only vaguely remembered reading that line in a dime novel.

More angry shouts behind Sam. More gun cracks.

The stallion followed another bend through the rocks and then the trees fell back behind him and Sam, and the thoroughbred gave one more lunging leap, and they were on the crest of the ridge. Sam steered the mount behind some boulders, leaped to the ground, and hastily tied the reins to a gnarled pine growing up through a crack in one of the rocks.

He shucked the Spencer from the saddle sheath and ran back toward the lip of the ridge, dropping to a knee between boulders, gazing down the trail up which he'd come. He could see the four riders climbing the serpentine trail, heading toward him.

"Courage, Sam," he told himself, working the Spencer's cocking handle, levering a round into the action. "Courage!"

Quickly, he lined up the sights on one of the riders. There were too many rocks and trees for him to tell which one. He didn't much care. He was just trying to discourage them, slow them down so he could hop back up on Lightning's back and light a shuck away from those four devils.

He let out a breath and squeezed the trigger.

The .56-caliber rifle leaped in his gloved hands, belching smoke and flames from the maw. The man he'd aimed at gave a shrill howl followed by the even shriller whinny of his mount. The horse pitched, throwing the rider off his back and into the rocks along the trail.

Sam's eyes snapped wide in shock. "*Holy Moses—I hit one!*" he yelled with unabashed, astonished glee, pumping his left fist in the air.

He'd really only meant to fire close, to slow the riders' pace.

But now it occurred to him, as they all shouted curses and leaped from their saddles, shucking their own rifles from scabbards, that while he'd slowed their pace, all right, he'd also made them angrier than snake-teased rattlesnakes!

Rifles flashed and roared in the rocks down the slope below Sam, the bullets slamming into the rocks around him and blowing a pine twig from a near bole. He hunkered low in the rocks to avoid the bullets as well as the dust and gravel and rock shards the bullets were throwing at him.

When the shooting dwindled, Bowdrie shouted, "Work around him, boys! I want to cut off that little cata-mount's ears before the storm hits!"

Sam looked around.

Storm?

He looked up, shocked to see that the wind must have changed direction. Dark purple storm clouds had piled above him. Just as he noticed them, a sharp witch's finger of lightning ripped through the sky above and to his right. It was followed a second later by an earth-shuddering clap of thunder. There was a sizzling sound and a sharp whiff of brimstone. Sam turned to see a pine not far down the slope on his right fold up like a Barlow knife, its upper half burning brightly. There rose a loud crunching and crashing sound as the top half of the tree slammed into the bottom half, broke off at the ragged, burning hinge, and tumbled straight down through its own lower branches to the ground.

The earth shuddered beneath Sam with the impact.

"Holy *Christ*!" bellowed one of the men on the slope below Sam.

Behind Sam, Lightning whinnied shrilly once...twice...three times...

No! Sam thought.

He's gonna bolt for sure. He's gonna bolt!

Panic overwhelming Sam, he leaped to his feet and ran with the heavy Spencer held high across his chest. Just as he rounded the boulders behind which he'd tied the thoroughbred, he saw the stallion gallop off across the top of the ridge, its black coat glistening with the rain that had begun slashing down from that angry sky so suddenly that in the chaos, Sam hadn't noticed.

He did now.

Suddenly, he was as soaked as though he'd dove into a river for a summer swim. Only, the rain was cold. So was the wind, slashing right through him, getting at the very marrow in his bones.

Shouting rose behind and around Sam. The four brigands were making good on their intention to work around him. He took off running in the same direction as his horse, the wind blowing his soaked felt hat off his head. He spied a glimpse of movement to his right, between rocks. Before he could change his course, a brown-skinned man with long, dark hair, mud-brown eyes in a hawk-like face with a thick, brushy mustache stepped up in front of him. He grinned and spread his arms wide, his right hand wrapped around the neck of a Winchester.

He tipped his head back and yelled something in Spanish, mustached upper lip stretched back to show long, tobacco-stained teeth. He meant to encompass Sam in his arms. Panic was a wild stallion inside Sam; he didn't stop. He swung the butt of the Winchester forward and with a fierce grunt, slammed it into the dead center of the Mexican's belly. The man gave a deep, guttural cry of his own as he doubled over like the lightning-struck pine had just done, the smoke from the burning of which liberally peppered the rain-laced wind.

The Mexican dropped to his knees, groaning and lowering his rifle.

Sam leaped around him and ran for all he was worth across the rocky flat before him until the ground dropped away and he was sprinting down a gentle slope through pines. As he leaped deadfalls and raced around rocks and thickets, the entire sky flashed around him. Thunder crashed, sounding like what he'd imagined a fierce battlefield in the War Between the States might have sounded like, howitzers and Napoleon cannons blasting.

Distantly behind him, his pursuers were shouting but the shouts were nearly drowned by the wind, rain, and the thunder that made the ground pitch beneath Sam's running feet.

Ahead of the boy, the ground slanted down on his right. He thought he'd heard only a few seconds ago Lightning give another shrill whinny from that direction. Sam switched course to race down the slope but stopped suddenly when, through the billowing sheets of rain, he saw the jaws of the earth suddenly open before him, showing a dark, craggy mouth of crooked teeth that were the rocks poking up from the far side of a deep, narrow canyon.

Sam ground his boots into the spongy ground, dropped the Spencer, and flung his arms straight out in the air to each side of him, trying mightily to not only halt his momentum but to thrust himself back from the edge of the canyon he suddenly found himself teetering over, the stubborn hands of gravity shoving him forward. But as he did, a cold rock dropped in his belly. He felt the soft ground slowly give way beneath his boots.

Then suddenly the ground was gone.

"Ah, *shiiiit!*" he cried as he heard the clacking of rocks and the crunching of grassy ground give way beneath him.

And then he was falling straight down the side of the canyon.

For one long second or two—a second or two that seemed a day or two—the world was a blur of upward sliding rock as he faced the opposite side of the canyon, dropping feet first through thin air. He struck ground on the heels of his boots and fell back hard against the canyon's near wall.

Eyes rolling back in his head, the world a blur before him, he slid down the wall to the ground.

Deeply disoriented, his ears ringing and his vision blurry, he spent a minute trying to figure out what had just happened. He seemed to be caught between two worlds—consciousness and unconsciousness, dreaming and reality. Slowly, his vision as well as his head clarified. He looked around, scowling incredulously, the rain still pounding down on him, streaming down his face and

forming a wavering pale curtain in front of him—
between him and...what?

More thin air.

He must not have landed on the canyon bottom.
Because there was another drop-off before him, not three
feet straight out from where his feet and legs extended
straight out in front of him. He leaned forward. Another
cold stone—this one even larger than the first one—
dropped in his belly.

He was staring straight down at the canyon floor that
was a river of fast-rushing, dark-brown water speckled
with chunks of mud, sod, and driftwood. He was still a
good hundred feet up from the bottom of the canyon. He
glanced up. As far as he could tell in the slashing rain, the
top of the chasm was about fifty feet away.

He'd dropped fifty feet...onto what?

He lowered his gaze once more to what he was
sitting on.

It was a four-and-a-half-foot wide ledge of sand and
gravel, with a lone cedar and tufts of sage. He turned to
his right and heard a scream hammer out of his lungs and
throat. At least, he thought he'd screamed. No one else
out here to hurl out an embarrassingly girlish yell like
that. At least, no one else alive, that was.

As for the fellow sitting beside him, only three or
four feet away and slumped sideways against the canyon
wall, he'd been dead a long, long time.

Sam heard himself give another yell. He slid a few
inches farther away from the man slumped beside him.

No, not a man. A skeleton with just a bit of mummified skin clinging to his bones. Mummified skin and what
appeared the remains of a dark-blue uniform tunic and
the tattered remnants of army-blue slacks with a few
inches of remaining yellow stripe running down the

outside of the legs. Long, tangled, grisly patches of color-less hair clung to the scalp to hang down over the poor fellow's shoulders that were nearly all bone.

Pale, bleached bone.

The skeleton's main, most startling feature was the fletched arrow sticking out of his ribcage, the feathered end resting on the ground.

"Soldier," Sam said, his innards churning with revulsion. "Galldang...soldier." He glanced toward the top of the ridge above him. "Musta fell down here, too. Or... came down to avoid the Injuns that prob'ly stuck that arrow in his guts."

Sam stretched his lips back from his teeth as he stared at the dead man.

Dead a long time. Hard to tell how long. Ten years, at least.

An image of another skeleton flashed in Sam's mind. A smaller skeleton.

His own skeleton ten years in the future. For that's what he would sure as hell be if he couldn't figure a way off this ledge.

Panic shot through Sam as he jerked his gaze to the top of the canyon once more.

Just as suddenly, he pulled his head back against the canyon wall and tucked his legs beneath him, trying to make himself as small as possible. Several small rocks and pebbles had just tumbled down the wall, bouncing. They'd been loosed from above.

Sam waited nearly a minute then slid his head out from the canyon wall again. Just a few inches. Far enough that he could see more clearly up the wall to the crest. His heart leaped. A man stood on the ledge above him, staring down toward him. Sam wanted to pull his head back again, but what was the point?

Bowdrie had already seen him. The outlaw stared straight down the wall at him, unmoving. He was merely a silhouette against the dark forest above and behind him and through the wavering curtains of rain. But Sam knew it was Bowdrie, all right. The figure was Bowdrie's medium size and the silver conchos trimming his hat flashed in the lightning.

Also, there was something about the man's dark stare down the canyon wall that told Sam it was the evil-eyed Bowdrie. Maybe it was just the boy's imagination, but he thought he could see those small, red, amber eyes fairly glowing within the man's deep, dark eye sockets. They burned like the small embers of a still hot but dying fire.

The man's lips pulled back from his mouth. Sam could see the white line of his teeth against the darkness of his silhouetted face. Bowdrie's right leg moved. A stone came bouncing down the cliff wall. Sam pulled his head back and watched the stone flying past him and into the murk below.

When he slid his head back out from the wall and stared toward the top, the man had disappeared.

Sam shuddered.

He hadn't even been worth a shot.

Because he was a goner.

The outlaw had left him here to die alone.

Well, not alone. But the fellow beside him wasn't really much company. But then, he hadn't been anyone's company for a good, long time.

Ten years or more.

Sam pulled his head down, placed his hands on his temples, and sobbed.

Courage?

To hell with it.

CHAPTER 10

ILSA HUGGED THE HALF-GROWN RACCOON IN HER ARMS and shuddered at the chill pushing against her.

She stared out bleakly at the falling rain. It was letting up a little, but lightning still lit up the sky to the southeast and thunder rumbled like boulders rolling down a steep ridge. It was still storming off in the direction in which Sam had gone to wipe out the prints of Mannion's horse. The storm had switched direction just after it had struck the ranch, an end of it sliding off toward Sam.

The boy should have been back by now. He should have returned when the rain struck. There was no reason not to. The rain would have wiped out the prints of the lawman's horse. Sam would have known that.

The reason he hadn't returned was because he hadn't been able to.

Had he run into the outlaws after the loot?

Holding Pearl taut against her, Ilsa gave another shudder. Not from cold this time. From fear. From terror of what might be keeping her brother away from her.

The raccoon looked at her and gave a chittering cry,

narrowing its little, dark-brown eyes. Pearl knew Ilsa was worried. They'd been together several months and, aside for Sam, they were each other's sole companions. They sensed each other's moods.

Now Ilsa was deeply worried about her brother and Pearl sensed it.

Ilsa drew the blanket she'd draped around her shoulders and Pearl closer against them both and turned to the cabin's open door.

"Let's go inside, Pearl. Let's sit by the fire."

She noted the brittle fear in her voice as she stepped into the cabin and closed the door behind her. She made Pearl a little nest on a hide-bottom chair near the potbelly stove and the table, and then Ilsa went out to the porch to fill a coffeepot with rainwater. She set the pot to boil on the stove, glanced out through the window left of the door, hoping again to see her brother riding into the yard atop Lightning.

Nothing out there but the storm, however.

Ilsa rubbed her hands on her skirt over her thighs, nervously, then went to her father's old room. She cracked the door and peered inside. The lawman lay as before under the covers on the bed, breathing loudly as he slept. A lamp burned on the table beside him, the wick turned low. The wan light shone in the sweat glistening on the lawman's face.

Fever sweat.

She'd given him some bone broth earlier. He'd gotten as much down as he could, seeming to realize he needed it to heal. He wanted to heal as quickly as Ilsa wanted him to, and to leave.

"Why did you have to come here?" Ilsa whispered through the crack between the door and the frame. "We were doing just fine before you showed up."

Instantly, she felt chagrined by the animosity she heard in her voice. But the lawman and the men after him—all five from the vile outside world that Ilsa's father had brought her and Sam up here to escape—might have cost her brother's life. Without Sam, she'd be alone.

Just her, King, the horses, and Pearl.

She drew the door closed with a click and brushed a tear from her cheek. She glanced toward the chair in which she'd built the nest with the blanket for Pearl. The raccoon stared at her, eyes worried inside the dark fur ringing them.

"I'll be all right, girl," Ilsa said. She drew a deep breath and walked to the front door once more. "As soon as Sam gets back. He just holed up out of the storm, that's all. As soon as it lets up over there, he'll be back." She smiled suddenly. "He'd never miss supper."

That made her choke back a sob. She sobered suddenly when King started barking outside. Heart thudding, Ilsa drew the door open and peered out toward the bridge spanning the creek. As she did, she gasped suddenly and closed the door again, almost slamming it and making the window rattle and the frame shake.

Sally chortled anxiously from her chair near the stove.

A horseback rider was just then crossing the bridge. All Ilsa could tell through the gray curtain of rain was that he was a full-grown man out there clad in a high-crowned Stetson and yellow rain slicker. Too big to be Sam. Besides, the horse was a lighter color than Lightning.

One of the outlaws!

King barked with more and more vigor, territorial anger.

Heart pounding, Ilsa picked up the double-barrel Parker shotgun leaning by the door. She broke it open out of habit to make sure both tubes were filled then snapped it closed. She sidled to the window by the door and cast her gaze out between the open, gingham curtains. She gasped again and pulled her head back from the window, squeezing the shotgun in her hands. The man had just pulled his horse up to the hitchrack fronting the cabin. He wore a high-crowned Stetson and chaps over denim jeans.

He looked vaguely familiar and there appeared no one else with him.

Of course, the others could be keeping out of sight.

"Ilsa...er, Miss McDowell?" came the man's familiar voice above King's incessant barking and the rain that had lightened to a near drizzle, though the sky was still the color of oily rags hanging down close over the pines surrounding the cabin. "It's Zeke Trainor!"

Relief touched Ilsa. But just for a second. A fresh wave of anxiety came to replace that which she'd felt before.

What was Zeke Trainor doing here? In weather like this?

"Miss...?" came Trainor's voice again. "Would you call this consarned cur off?"

Ilsa squeezed her eyes shut. Holding the Parker straight up and down before her she wondered what she should do. For a moment, she considered remaining silent, figuring maybe he'd suspect no one was here. But that was ridiculous. He could see the lamplight burning in the windows to either side of the halved-log door. He'd probably even seen her furtive peek out the window.

She drew a deep breath as an idea came to her. She turned to the door, drew it open quickly and stepped out, drawing it closed behind her. She took one step forward and raised the shotgun in her hands, angled at a slant toward the awning over the porch. King stood beside Trainor's dun, hackles raised, tail arched, barking furiously at the neighboring rancher.

"I'm sorry, Mister Trainor—I'm alone and not taking visitors."

"Ah," he said, giving his head a single nod. "I see. Could you call the damn dog off, anyway? He's spookin' my hoss!"

Ilsa stomped her foot once and told King to lay down.

The dog gave a few more anxious barks then swung around, mounted the porch, and lay down against the cabin's front wall, flanking Ilsa. He continued to mewl deep in his throat.

Still, Ilsa could hear the rain ticking off the hat of her visitor. It dripped off the ends of his long, sandy mustache that was the centerpiece of his long, narrow-jawed, deep-eyed face. Inwardly, she shuddered, remembering the feel of that mustache brushing against her neck.

"Where's Sam?" the man asked.

Was that a suspicious look on his face or was it only her imagination, kicked up by the threat of the men searching for the lawman in her father's bed?

"He rode out to check on the north herd."

"In this weather?"

"He left before the storm rolled in."

"Ah."

"What can I help you with?"

"I'd like to talk to you. A pressing matter." Trainor lifted his chin and sniffed the smoke from the chimney pipe flatting out over the yard. "Is that coffee I smell?"

"Is it...is it about Sam?" she said suddenly, hearing the anxious tremor in her voice.

Maybe Trainor had come upon her brother out on the range. Her heart fluttered at the thought.

Trainor frowned beneath the dripping brim of his Stetson. "I thought he was with the north herd."

"He is."

"I came from the Bar Z...to the south."

"Oh." She glanced down, feeling blood rise in her cheeks. She swallowed. He knew she was lying.

"Say, now." Trainor swung down from his saddle. He stepped toward the hitchrack with the reins in his hand. His boots squawked in the damp sand and grass. "You look a might off your feed, Miss McDowell. Ilsa." He crooked the corners of his mustached mouth in a smile as he gave the reins a cursory wrap around the hitchrack's worn, gray crossbar.

Again, inwardly, she shuddered at the memory of that day at the creek.

"I didn't invite you to step down from your saddle," she said as King leaped to his feet and began barking defensively again, standing close by Ilsa's right side.

"Long ride over here," Trainor said loudly enough to be heard above King's barking. "You could at least give me a cup of coffee while I let my horse blow a bit...before the long ride back." He closed his gloved, right hand over the worn walnut grips of his holstered .44. "And would you please tell that cur to pipe down!"

"King!" Ilsa said. She knew the rancher wasn't above shooting the dog.

King gave a shrill yip then slinked off to the far end of the porch and lay down again.

Ilsa just stared at her visitor, tempted to level the shotgun at him. She couldn't shoot him, though. Even after he'd accosted her when she'd been wading in the creek. Not that she didn't want to. But it would only bring more trouble.

Slowly, cat-like, he mounted the porch steps, keeping one eye on King who kept both eyes on the intruder. When he'd gained the top of the porch, Trainor stopped and held up his hands, palms out. "I'm not here for any kind of repeat of...you know—at the creek. We both have bigger fish to fry."

Ilsa frowned a little, curious.

"We do?"

He lifted his chin to indicate the closed door behind her. "Let's go inside, sit down and talk like reasonable people."

"I don't think you're reasonable, Mister Trainor."

"Today, I'm reasonable." His gaze was direct, his brown eyes grave.

She couldn't let him in the cabin. The lawman was in there. No one must know he was here. That the loot from the train was here. She didn't trust Trainor, a neighboring rancher with seven or eight men on his roll, farther than she could throw him.

"Tell me out here."

Keeping his hands raised, palms out, Trainor stepped forward.

She leveled the Parker on him. "Stop!"

He kept coming. Damn him, he kept coming, keeping his eyes on hers. He held out his hands, wrapped his hands around the shotgun, and gave it a quick jerk, pulling it out of her hands.

"Damn you!"

"You know you're not gonna shoot me. I'm here to discuss a problem. One that we share."

"I told you—"

"Inside," he added.

He stepped around her, tripped the latch, and nudged open the door. He looked around as though suspecting someone else might be inside. Seeing no one, he stepped into the cabin. Pearl gave a frightened trill, leaped down from the chair, and slinked under the hutch abutting the right wall, in the parlor side of the cabin. The raccoon lowered her head to peer out from behind her natural mask.

Ilsa's heart pounded. She held her breath, hoping that the lawman didn't snore loudly enough for her uninvited guest to hear. If Trainor had been a good neighbor, she'd have gladly told him about the lawman and the men hunting him. Even about the loot. But she knew from experience the man, who ranched with a wife and two kids at the foot of Thunder Ridge, on the farther southern edge of the valley, in a shallow canyon, couldn't be trusted.

That day at the creek hadn't been the only time she'd realized that. They'd met up on the range before, and she hadn't liked the way he'd looked at her. Those looks had started, as they had from other men, ever since she'd begun filling out her skirts and blouses. The day at the creek she'd managed to fight him off, but the encounter had terrified her. Repelled her.

No, Zeke Trainor was not to be trusted.

Casually, as though he were just any neighbor, he sauntered into the kitchen part of the cabin. He lay the shotgun across a corner of the table, drew a chair out with his boot, removed his hat, set it crown down on the table, then slacked into the chair, making the old hide-bottom creak beneath his weight. His short, sandy hair showed the indentations of his hat just above his ears. He drew up the Colt's revolver holstered on his right hip, making the sitting more comfortable, and sighed.

Ilsa stood in the open doorway, staring coldly, anxiously in at him.

She couldn't help glancing at the lawman's closed door. Trainor's suspicious eyes followed her own to the door before returning to her.

"Now, then, Miss Ilsa," he said. "How 'bout that coffee?"

She drew a breath, smoothed her skirt down against her thighs, stepped inside, and closed the door. She went over to the stove and tossed a handful of Arbuckles from a burlap pouch into the pot. When the coffee returned to a boil, she set it on the warming rack, added water to the pot to settle the grounds, and filled two stone mugs with coffee. She brought the mugs over to the table, set one down before Trainor and one before the chair she always sat in, opposite the one Trainor was in.

She did not sit down, however. She didn't want him to think she was feeling one bit hospitable.

She glanced at the shotgun then, standing at the corner of the table, a good eight from her uninvited guest and crossed her arms on her chest. "All right." She shook her hair back from her face. "What brings you here, Mister Trainor?"

Trainor lifted his coffee, blew ripples on the smoking surface, and sipped. "Good." He set the cup back down on the table and turned to her, his expression again grave. "Ran into four men down by Taylor Wash."

"Four men?"

"Four hardtails. They were looking for another man. A lawman. Mannion from Del Norte. Said he was wounded, and he had saddlebags full of loot."

"So? What does that have to do with me?"

"Just wondered if you'd seen him's all."

"No," Ilsa said, shaking her head. "I haven't seen him."

"Wasn't long after we left the hardtails one of my men brushpopping strays found a good bit of blood on the side of that dry wash near the canyon. Wagon tracks, too. The wagon was headed up this way." Trainor paused and took another careful sip of the hot coffee. When he'd swallowed and set the mug back down on the table, he brushed a fist across those ugly, drooping mustaches, and looked at Ilsa.

He canted his head to one side, skeptically. "Yours an' the boy's is the only ranch up here."

Ilsa's throat was dry. Her tongue felt overly large for her mouth. "I don't know what you're talking about. I've seen no lawman...no loot."

"You're sayin' he's not layin' back there, in your old man's bedroom?"

Ilsa tried to quell the quivering in her right knee. She also tried to keep the tremor from her voice. She felt the blood wash out of her face as she said, "No."

Trainor stared at her. He glanced at the door behind her, returned his gaze to her face, and quirked the corners of his seedy, mustached mouth. He looked her slowly up and down and said, "Why are you so cold to me, Miss Ilsa? You need a man in your life."

"You're married, Mister Trainor."

"She's a cold woman, old before her time."

"You have two kids."

"They could do without May as easy as I could. May herself? Hell, all she talks about is goin' back to Nebraska." Again, he ran his goatish, brown eyes up and down Ilsa's body. "They'd prefer you."

"Well, they're not going to get me. And neither are you."

"You could give me a chance, at least."

"How old are you, Mister Trainor?"

"Thirty-six."

Ilsa narrowed her eyes at him in disbelief. "I'm seventeen!"

She jerked with a slight start when a raking snore rose from behind the door where Mannion lay in Pa's old bed. She jerked her enervated gaze to Trainor. He didn't react to the sound.

Had he not heard it?

Keeping his lusty gaze on her, the rancher said, "We could make a good life with that loot, Miss Ilsa. You could move over to my place. Bring the boy—I don't care. Add another few rooms to my house, even a front porch. My kids ain't half bad. A little rambunctious, but what kids ain't?"

"Please leave now, Mister Trainor." Again, Ilsa glanced at the shotgun resting over a near corner of the table, nearest the door.

"I know he's in there."

"What?"

Trainor gave a heavy-lidded smile as he glanced at the lawman's door. "I know he's in your Pa's old room. The loot's in there, too?"

Ilsa was so anxious she worried she might pass out. Her vision was a little blurry and the cabin seemed to be rising and falling slowly around her, as though it were a boat rising and falling with the swells of a large body of water. "I asked you to leave."

Smiling that lusty, heavy-lidded smile, Trainor kept his goatish gaze on her, letting it roam down to where it should not go, to her sharply rising and falling chest clad in her white blouse and elk hide vest. "Not just yet." He placed his hands on the table and rose from his chair. "We got a future to discuss."

He started to move around the table.

He stopped suddenly when a click rose behind Ilsa, making her start again with a sharp intake of air.

Trainor's gaze drifted behind her.

She heard the squawk of hinges. She turned to see the lawman's door open, and the lawman's bare-chested figure step out of the doorway, extending two silver-plaited revolvers straight out in front of him.

CHAPTER 11

SAM STARED STRAIGHT OUT OVER THE CANYON. THE rain was lightening. He hardly noticed. The rain was the least of his problems.

He looked down at the ledge he was on, suspending him precariously over the flooded gorge below. He looked at what remained of the dead soldier to his right, the fletched end of the arrow resting on the ground, the stone tip embedded in a rib. A fresh wave of panic overwhelmed him.

He heaved himself to his feet and fairly leaped at the stone wall, shoving the tips of his glove fingers into cracks or over stone dimples, scraping at the wall with his feet, desperately climbing. Trying to climb, rather. He made it only a foot up the wall when both hands, not finding anything to grab on to, slid down the wall. Sam's face slid down the wall as well, his feet struck the ground and he stood there, breathing hard and scowling up the wall at the ridge.

Air rushed in and out of his lungs as that wild stallion of panic inside him lost its head and made for the proverbial hills.

He squeezed his eyes closed and pressed his left cheek against the cliff face.

He said aloud, tightly: "No! I have to slow down. I have to *calm* down. I have to breathe evenly and *think*... take it one move at a time. Or sure as there's a devil in hell I ain't gonna make it out of here!"

He stepped back from the wall and stared up at it, scrutinizing it closely, blinking against the rain that had waned nearly to a mist. His eyes searched for cracks, fissures, small thumbs, bulges, and dimples in the rock that might provide hand and footholds. The panic in him waned. His heart slowed.

Hope grew.

He glanced down at the dead soldier. "The reason you didn't make it out of here, poor fella, is because with that arrow in you, you couldn't climb. Well"—Sam rubbed his hands together, trying to dry them—"I can. And I'll be jiggered if I ain't gonna do it, too."

He gave a resolute nod, stepped up to the wall once more, looked again at the possible route he'd just traced with his eyes, and reached up for the first two handholds —a small ledge of rock three feet above him and to the right and a crack between two striations roughly the same distance up and to his left. He glanced down and found the first two footholds. Thrusting his hands up, he lifted his feet, finding all four hand- and footholds with a feeling of satisfaction. Grunting, he pulled himself up with his hands and pushed himself up with his feet, gritting his teeth against the strain.

It would have been a whole lot easier had it not been raining. The face of the cliff was slick. But Sam kept his head about him, consciously kept himself calm, and looked above for the route he'd mapped out in his head from below.

Fifteen tough minutes after he'd started, he found himself halfway up the cliff.

A wave of dizziness swept over him. He could see the shelf he'd been on nearly straight below and it looked so small from this height. The canyon beyond and below it looked like the mouth of some giant, angry god opening wide for him. It grew wider with each inch he slowly, painstakingly, grunting with every thrust and pull, clambered up the face of the cliff.

"Don't look down," he told himself, staring at the wet, gray rock before him. "Keep your mind on each move of your hands and feet. Each one. One at a time."

He drew a breath, looked up for the next handhold, and continued climbing.

He was only half-consciously aware that the dizziness nearly left him. He didn't want to think about it. All he could think about was where he was going to place each hand and each foot.

A couple of times, while pulling with his hands and thrusting with his feet, he lost hold. Panic seeped back into him as he fought to regain his purchase, hanging on the wall either one-handed or with only one hand and one boot planted in a crack or grinding into a slight bulge or ledge. Each time that happened, his stomach rose nearly to his throat. But he fought down the fear and the disorientation that came with it.

"Nope," he told himself quietly but determinedly. "You're fine. Just find another grip. There's plenty here. Didn't look like it from below, but there's plenty. Just... keep...climbin'..."

The crest of the ridge crept down toward him. It seemed to come down awfully slowly...more slowly than he was climbing, though he knew that wasn't possible. But it kept coming down until his head was maybe five feet from the crest. So close that he could see the forest that flanked it. Another foot and he could see more of the trees, hear the rain, which had finally stopped altogether, dripping from the branches.

Another foot...another...another...

He placed his left hand on a stout root curling out of the cliff face just inches below the crest. He gave it a gentle tug to test it. It held. He pulled on it harder and removed his right hand from its current hold and thrust his elbow up toward the flat crest of the ridge.

The root wasn't as stout as it had looked.

One end of it pulled free of the cliff face. Chunks of wet sand spilled down the wall. Sam's left hand flew down against his side and both feet slipped off what he'd rested them on.

"No!" he cried, slamming his right elbow over the lip of the ridge.

He grunted as he ground that elbow into the ground, rocks and pebbles gouging into it through the soaked sleeve of his shirt. He looked down to see his feet dangling down against the wet stone wall.

"No!" he cried again as he thrust his left hand up and entwined those fingers with the fingers of his right hand.

He poured all his strength into his arms now, from his fingers to up high in his shoulders, levering himself up higher then shoving himself forward. He kept levering and grunting, eyes squeezed shut, until he rolled slowly over on his right shoulder and his legs snaked up out of the canyon to extend straight out before him now as he lay flat on his back—at the top of the ridge.

He opened his eyes. He smiled. Late, coppery sunlight peered out between the ragged edges of clouds that were turning whiter than gray.

He was breathing hard. His right shoulder was sore.

Slowly, his heart stopped racing and his breathing slowed. He spread his arms and legs, opening his hands to feel the hard, stable ground beneath him. He glanced to his right. The canyon lay only three feet away. Too close. He rolled twice to his left and stared up at the widening gaps between the clouds once more.

What sounded like a hoof thud rose behind him.

A horse snorted.

The smile vanished from his face.

"Oh, God, no!" he said aloud.

The outlaws had been waiting for him!

He sat up suddenly and turned to see Pa's rangy thoroughbred walking slowly toward him, head down, reins trailing along the ground to either side.

"Lightning!" Sam raked out with uncommon relief.

The horse stopped six feet away. It shook its head, regarded the boy dubiously with its chocolate-brown eyes.

"Oh, God," Sam said. "Oh, God. Oh, God. Oh, God." He heaved himself to his feet with a grunt. He was dizzy; the fear of falling remained in his bones. Heavy-footed, he walked forward, took the horse's long, sleek black snout in the crook of his arm and caressed the left wither. "I thought for sure I was a goner, boy." He shook his head, the entire harrowing experience weighing heavy in him, hard and solid beneath the lightness of his relief. He'd never felt so close to death.

He glanced at the canyon. The dizziness returning, he turned to the horse, grabbed the reins, climbed a log, toed a stirrup, and swung up into the wet leather saddle. "Let's get the hell out of here, boy. I wanna get a long... long...long way from here!"

It was as though the mouth of that giant, malevolent god kept trying to suck him back down its throat.

He reined the horse away from the canyon, took a minute to get his bearings, then batted his heels against the thoroughbred's flanks, heading roughly northeast, hoping he'd make it back to the cabin before nightfall.

He was suddenly powerful hungry and Ilsa would be worried sick.

———

MANNION HELD HIS TWIN RUSSIANS STRAIGHT OUT IN both hands.

He felt his hands quivering a little. He was weak from blood loss and that rabid dog was still chomping down in earnest on his left side. He suppressed the pain, willed his hands and guns still as rage burned inside him.

As he'd known it would but hoped it wouldn't, trouble had followed him here.

He gritted his teeth, clicked the Russians' hammers back and narrowed his eyes at the tall, thin, horse-faced, sandy-mustached man standing off the corner of the eating table, near the door.

The man regarded Mannion with wide, grave eyes.

Slowly, he raised his hands, turned them palms out toward the big, bare-chested man filling the doorway. "Easy," he said. "Easy, now...Mannion."

Ilsa turned to face the lawman. She looked at the big pistols in his hands. She turned to Trainor then back to Mannion. She looked into his eyes, and her own eyes gained a cast of incredulity, trepidation. She stepped into the line of fire between Mannion and Trainor and raised her own hands slowly.

"Get out of the way," Mannion said, nudging the Russians to the left.

He kept his own gaze on the fearful eyes of the horse-faced man standing by the door.

The man gave a wooden smile and said, "I was just...I was just"—he glanced at the big revolvers aimed at him again and finished with—"I was just hossin' around, ya see, Mannion."

"Hossin' around."

"Yeah, I didn't mean nothin' by it."

"You didn't come here for the loot."

"Me? Nah. What loot?" Trainor swallowed again. "I just came to be neighborly. You know, drink a cup of coffee with the girl."

"You weren't going to rape her?"

Trainor's long cheeks mottled red above his mustache. "Oh, hell, no. I was just—"

"Hossin' around," Mannion finished for him.

Ilsa said softly, "Please, Marshal Mannion..."

"Get out of the way, girl."

Again, Ilsa glanced over her shoulder at Trainor. Turning back to the lawman, she said, "You can't..."

"Kill him? Why not?"

"Because..." She didn't seem to know how to finish that.

Mannion said tightly, his voice taut as razor wire, "He was going to ravage you. He'd likely have killed me in my sleep and taken the loot."

"Me?" Trainor appeared flabbergasted. "I wouldn't have done no such thing! Like I said—"

"You was just here to be neighborly."

"That's right!"

"Step aside, girl!" Mannion ordered. "Some men just plain need killin'."

"But you're a lawman!"

"Like I said..."

"Marshal Mannion...*please!*"

"Listen to her, Mannion. You can't kill me. My hands are raised!"

Mannion looked at the girl staring up at him, her eyes grave. "If I don't kill him, there's gonna be hell to pay."

Slowly, she shook her head. "He has a family."

"What about your family? You an' the boy?"

She just stared at him. The skin above the bridge of her nose wrinkled and then tears glazed her eyes. She didn't say anything. She just stared at him like that, at a loss for words until Mannion depressed the hammers of both Russians, lowered the weapons—both of which seemed inordinately heavy—to his sides.

To Trainor, he growled, "Get the hell out. Don't ever come back here. If I ever see you again, even from a distance, I'll kick you out with a cold shovel. No questions asked."

Trainor lowered his hands and fairly lunged at the door.

In seconds, he was outside, leaping onto his horse, and galloping off through the pines, King barking at the horse's scissoring feet. As the horse clomped across the wooden bridge, Mannion saw through the open door a horse and rider trotting along the trail toward the cabin. It was the kid on a black horse. When he saw Trainor, the boy reined up suddenly and reached for the rifle in his scabbard. Trainor yelled something at him then galloped past him.

King gave up the chase, turned to the boy, and began wagging his tail. The dog's barking switched to a greeting, an excited pitch.

The boy turned to follow the fleeing Trainor with his gaze then looked toward the cabin and booted the thoroughbred across the bridge and into the yard. Ilsa saw him through the open door.

"Sam!" she yelled with relief and ran out onto the porch.

Mannion backed into the bedroom. His knees quivered with weakness.

He sat on the edge of the bed, rested the Russians on the bed to each side of him. He could hear the girl and the boy talking in the yard, the dog barking happily. Mannion looked at the bulging saddlebags hanging over the back of the chair in the corner and wished the kid had left him where he'd been lying in the wash.

He drew a deep breath, fighting to remain conscious. He needed to get out of here. He'd poisoned these kids' lives enough already. He needed to be on the trail back to Del Norte. He placed a hand on the burning wound in his side and bowed his head as though in prayer.

"Going...to be...hell to pay!" he said, then sagged back on the bed, out like a blown lamp.

CHAPTER 12

MANNION WOKE WHEN THE GIRL BROUGHT HIM FOOD —more bone broth and a small elk steak fried in butter and wild onions. He forced the food down despite his lack of hunger. His body needed it. Occasionally as he ate, spooning the broth into his mouth and forking the steak the steak girl cut for him, he glanced at her sitting in the chair beside the bed.

Her eyes were hard with a brooding resentment.

Mannion didn't blame her a bit.

He ate until he couldn't force down another bite, despite how good it was, then handed her the tray. He saw the boy standing in the partly open doorway. Sam was wrapped in a blanket, and he was shivering. His longish blond hair was damp. The shepherd-collie dog sat beside him, staring guardedly at the big man in the bed.

"What happened, boy?" Mannion croaked out. "Where were you?"

"Ran into a little trouble, s-sir." His lips quivered as he shivered.

"What kind of trouble?"

The girl answered for her brother, her tone crisp. "He

went out to wipe out the tracks of your bay and ran into the men after you. He might've died." She'd said that last bit with increased hardness, narrowing her eyes and flaring her nostrils.

Mannion wasn't normally a blancher, but he felt himself blanch under the pretty girl's hostile gaze, her dark, Scottish eyes hard with ancestral anger. She above all else wanted to protect her and her brother, to maintain their quiet, independent way of life.

Mannion didn't blame her. Guilt racked him.

He frowned up at her, curiously. "My bay?"

"He followed you here," the boy said through the two-foot gap in the door, between the curtain quilt and the door frame.

Mannion sighed and lay back against the pillow. "Ah, hell."

It was the first time he'd ever regretted Red's loyalty.

He glanced up at the girl. "I'll be gone first thing in the morning."

She did not respond to that. Holding the tray with the empty bowl and empty plate, she turned and kicked the curtain quilt open wider with her foot then strode out the door past her brother. The boy walked into the room. He wore heavy wool socks and continued to shiver. The dog remained in the doorway behind him, mewling softly, sensing the anxiousness filling the cabin.

Likely knowing it was due to the stranger.

Sam stopped beside the bed. His lips were nearly blue.

"Don't mind Ilsa, Marshal. She's hotheaded. Pa always said so. He told me as he lay dyin' that she'd give me more trouble than rustlers." The boy glanced over his shoulder at his sister working in the kitchen then turned back to the lawman. He gave a weak smile. "And, boy, was he right!"

"Should've left me in that wash, boy."

"Couldn't do that, sir."

"You don't know me. Don't owe me a damn thing."

"It's not about knowin' or owin'." The boy paused, stared down at Mannion. "You got family?"

"A wife...daughter."

"Really don't matter, though, does it?" Sam said. "I reckon I'd never have slept a wink if I'd just left you there. Truth to tell"—he glanced over his shoulder again then turned back to Joe—"Ilsa wouldn't, neither. Some things are just meant to be, I reckon."

"I apologize," Mannion said.

Sam frowned. "I told you—"

"Not for bein' a burden...a risk...to you and your sister. For callin' you 'boy.' You're a man...way ahead of your time."

A proud flush rose in Sam's cheeks.

"I'm gonna sleep now," Mannion said, glancing at the night-dark window flanking him on his left. "Long ride tomorrow."

"You sure? You lost a lotta—"

"I'm sure."

"All right."

"Scribble me a map, will you? How to get down out of these mountains. I got no idea where I am. Leave it on the dresser there."

Sam nodded. "I'll show you a way that avoids the canyon where them vipers are."

"No."

Sam frowned. "Huh?"

"I want to go back through the canyon." Before the boy could object, he continued with: "Wake me if there's trouble. Any at all. Those jackals might have followed you here."

In fact, he knew they had.

"I know. There was no way to wipe out my own trail back. The ground was too wet."

"Good night, Sam."

"Good night, sir."

The boy shuffled out and drew the quilt closed behind him.

Mannion drew a deep breath, hoping no trouble would come before he could leave the boy and the girl to their previous peaceful lives.

————

THE LAWMAN COULD HAVE SLEPT MOST OF THE NEXT day, but he willed himself awake at the first flush of dawn and the first chirp of a morning bird.

He had a clean change of clothes in the saddlebags Sam had taken off of Red when he'd stabled him—long-handles, socks, dark-red corduroy shirt and black denims, just like he always wore—and put them on, careful not to strain the wound that had tightened up on him and that still ached like blazes but that he was going to have suck it up against to head for home. He stepped into his boots, set his hat on his head, and shrugged into his canvas jacket against the morning's mountain chill. The boy had set a crudely penciled map on the dresser. Mannion gave it a quick study and shoved it into a pocket. His saddlebags draped over his left shoulder, his Yellowboy in his right hand, he slid open the quilt.

The dog, King, lay on the hemp rug in the middle of the parlor part of the cabin. Now the dog rose to a sitting position with a grunt. He pricked his ears, lifted his long snout, sniffed and, gazing threateningly at Mannion, growled, showing his teeth.

Joe had anticipated such a greeting and had fished a couple of old chunks of jerky out of his saddlebags. He tossed them to the dog, who caught one out of the air then lay belly down, jerky between his paws, chewing. Mannion gave a wry snort and crossed the near-dark cabin to the front door.

Behind him, he sensed movement. He saw the boy's diminutive silhouette standing in the open doorway of the middle bedroom, clad in only his longhandles.

"Marshal Mannion?" he said, quietly.

"Yes?"

"Leavin'?"

"High time. All quiet last night?"

"Musta been or King woulda kicked up a fuss."

He glanced at the dog still busily chewing the jerky and snarling as though it were a rabbit he'd stalked and killed himself.

Mannion pinched his hat brim to the boy. "Take care of yourself."

He went out, looked around carefully. He spied no threat, but his sixth sense told him trouble was about, likely staying just out of range of the dog's sniffer. He hiked the saddlebags higher on his shoulder and strode around the side of the cabin to the stable in the back.

He and Red had a warm though short-lived reunion. Joe gave the horse some oats in a bucket, and Red ate as Mannion saddled and bridled him. He led the horse to the doors, peered out cautiously, then opened both doors, noting the sky had turned just a little bluer that it had been only ten minutes earlier. Enough light now to steer by.

Joe hoped he could find his way down out of the

mountains. He'd never journeyed into the Stalwarts before. To him, they'd merely been an isolated, mysterious range humping up in the west when he'd followed desperadoes out of southern Colorado Territory and into western New Mexico, between the San Juans and the Black Range. Now he found himself in them and, since he'd been unconscious when the boy had brought him here, he was badly disoriented.

The boy's map would help.

He closed the stable doors, reached up to grab the horn with his left hand, and winced at the fire in his side as he swung up into the leather. Feeling the hair rise on the back of his neck, he looked at the pines around him slowly clarifying in the growing light. Birds piped and winged this way and that in the rookery for breakfast. The cold hand signifying danger was splayed across his back, between his shoulder blades.

He could see monsters staring at him from the darkness lingering in the forest surrounding the cabin. They blinked slowly, watching him closely.

Of course, no real monsters were there but only in Mannion's brain.

But he knew monsters stalked him just the same. They'd followed the boy or the thoroughbred's tracks here. They were keeping just out of sight, waiting for the right opportunity to make their move. To shoot Bloody Joe off his horse and to take the sixty grand in cold, hard cash.

Joe said through gritted teeth, "I'm ready to end it if you are," and touched steel to the stallion's flanks and galloped around the rear corner of the cabin and out onto the trail that led into the valley beyond it. As he'd passed the cabin, he'd glanced to his right to see the pale, oval shape of the boy's face as he'd stared out through the glass. A light was on in the kitchen. Behind Sam, the girl was crouched to stoke the stove for breakfast, the dog sitting beside her, watching her, ears pricked with interest.

As Red's galloping hooves clomped across the bridge spanning the creek, Mannion spied movement in the brush in the corners of both eyes. He heard the rustling of brush as his sudden appearance and hasty travel caught them by surprise and they were scrambling around to mount their horses.

The pines drew back behind Mannion. He grinned as, following the trail, Red angled toward the south, the forested ridges standing tall on each side of him, the creek threading through the shallow draw on the right. A lone coyote stood on the bank of the draw, its shaggy, gray fur looking nearly white as the dawn light intensified. Something dead dangled from its jaws as it turned to glance over its shoulder at the galloping horse and rider. It dropped the dead thing from its jaws and lurched forward with a start and disappeared into the draw and out of sight.

It wasn't the only predator out here, Joe knew.

A single glance over his own shoulder showed two predatory riders just then emerging from the pines along the creek to converge on the trail behind him. Two more riders emerged behind the first.

As Joe had anticipated, they'd been waiting for dawn to make their play on the cabin. Mannion had taken them by surprise.

He swung his head forward, grinning in wolfish delight.

As he'd intended, he was luring his stalkers away from the McDowells' ranch.

He held Red to a hard gallop. The bay put his head

down and flattened his ears back against his skull. The black mane flashed silver in the growing light. The wind was cool against Mannion's face. He drew it in deep, wanting to gulp down large drafts of it, suppressing the grinding ache in his side.

Ahead the canyon narrowed.

He and Red galloped through the narrow gap between stone outcroppings. Then the trail dropped, and the walls of the valley drew back once more—wider than before. Mannion kept the bay galloping for another hundred yards. In a broad bowl, he reined in Red then looked back the way he'd come. The riders were just then galloping out of the narrow gap between the stony dikes. Bowdrie was in the lead, then the Southerner in the gray campaign hat, then the Mexican, then the big blond bear with the shaggy beard. The Southerner had one arm in a sling.

Joe galloped up a low rise, stopped, curveted Red, and stared back the way he'd come, the rising sun a bloody crescent behind him.

The riders drew back on their own reins, stopping their horses a hundred yards from where Mannion sat atop the rise, grinning back toward them, his gray eyes narrowed wolfishly, the red sun behind him silhouetting him against it but glinting orange in his eyes.

The sunlight revealed the men before him thoroughly as the shadows receded around him. The dust catching up to them billowed like a salmon-colored curtain.

Mannion raised his gloved hands to his mouth and shouted, "You fellas want that sixty grand?" He leaned back and patted one of the bulging saddlebags behind him.

His deep baritone echoed off the ridges.

Crows cawed in the distance.

The sun climbed higher behind him.

Blue Bowdrie glanced at the former reb, Winslow. Then he encircled his own hands around his mouth and shouted, "You know we do!"

His voice echoed. More crows cawed distantly.

Again, Joe raised his hands to his mouth and, grinning, bellowed, "Then come and get it, you damn tinhorns!"

CHAPTER 13

GAZING OUT THE CABIN'S WINDOW, SAM SUCKED A sharp breath through his teeth.

"What is it?" Ilsa said. The stove door squawked as she closed it.

Sam stared out as two riders rode along the inside of the pines along the creek to the right of the bridge, heading toward the bridge itself. Two more riders were riding along the edge of the pines to the left of the bridge, also heading toward the bridge. Sam recognized the four as the men who'd confronted him in the wash and who'd been looking for Mannion.

The very same riders who'd chased him late yesterday afternoon until he'd nearly ended up crowbait on that ledge above the canyon.

As Blue Bowdrie put his horse into a trot, the tall, lean former rebel fighter close behind him—the former reb had his arm in a sling, Sam noted with satisfaction—he cast a dark gaze toward the cabin then turned his head forward as he led the others across the bridge and down the trail toward where Mannion had just galloped off on his bay.

"They were out there, all right," Sam said, his voice hushed with awe. He looked over his shoulder at his sister standing on the other side of the table. Ilsa was fully dressed in her skirt and blouse and wearing her wool-lined elk hide vest against the morning chill. She was wrapping a white apron around her waist and tying it behind her as she prepared to start mixing biscuits for breakfast. The bowl, flour, sugar, and baking powder were in sacks on the table.

King had moved to the door. He sat whining in front of it, working his nose. He'd winded the outlaws as the dawn breeze had picked up from the south. "All night, most likely," Sam said. "I led them here...to Marshal Mannion."

Ilsa's cheeks turned pale and she hurried around the table, giving a tug on her brother's left arm as she crouched to peer through the window while trying to draw Sam away from it. "Sam, get away from there—they'll see you!"

Sam jerked his arm back and continued to look out the window. "They done already seen me. But it's Bloody Joe they're after!"

"Bloody Joe! Bloody Joe! Will you forget about him, Sam?"

Sam turned to his sister glaring at him through her Scottish dark eyes, black hair hanging loose about her shoulders. Now her fine, smooth cheeks were flushed with trepidation. "They'll kill him!"

"Better him than us!"

"But then they'll win. They kill him and take the loot! I gotta go help, Ilsa!"

Sam grabbed his hat off a hook and tried to move around his sister to get to the door. Ilsa stepped in front of him. "You'll do no such thing! Sam, aren't you one bit scared of those men? They'll kill you?"

Sam gazed up at her. "I used to be afraid of everything, Ilsa. Every odd sound I heard out on the range I thought was made by some still half-wild Injun come for my topknot or another rustler out to shoot me off my horse the way they did Pa. But after I climbed out of the canyon, I lost that fear." He shook his head slowly, bunching his lips. "And it sure feels good to not be fearful no more, Ilsa."

"Oh, you're some tough guy now!" Ilsa gritted her teeth, flung her right, open hand forward. It *cracked* sharply across Sam's left cheek, turning his head sideways. "You're not going anywhere, young man. I'm your elder, and I'll—"

Sam grabbed his cheek and glared savagely up at his sister. "You go to *hell*!"

Ilsa gasped. "How dare you. I'm going to wash your mouth out with—"

"You'll do no such thing. I'm gonna go help Bloody Joe!"

Left cheek still burning from the slap, Sam stepped quickly around his sister and picked up the sheathed Spencer repeater leaning against the wall near the door.

"You don't owe him a thing, Sam!"

Sam grabbed the door handle and turned to her. "Like I told him—it's not about the owin'. It's about bein' brave an' doin' the right thing and right now that right thing is helpin' a lawman against four cutthroats who aim to kill him when all he's tryin' to do is lead them away from us!"

"You're not him, Sam!"

Sam opened the door. "No, I'm not. But I'll never be half the man he is if I don't help him!"

"What about me?" Ilsa cried, bent slightly forward at the waist, sobbing, tears streaming down her cheeks.

King sat between them, swinging his head back and forth, regarding them both curiously, anxiously, whining.

"Keep King here," Sam said.

He went out, pulled the door closed behind him, and broke into a run as he made for the stable flanking the cabin. He gathered his tack from the stable and carried it out into the corral where both Lightning and Honey stood staring in the direction Mannion and the outlaws had ridden, testily switching their tails and flicking their ears. Sam had just set the blanket on Lightning's back when he heard panting and quick footsteps. He turned to see Ilsa and King just then making their way around the cabin's rear corner.

Ilsa had her double-barrel shotgun clamped under one arm while she pulled on a pair of black gloves.

"Ilsa, what're you doing?" Sam called to her as he flung his saddle with a grunt onto Lightning's back.

"If you're going, then I'm going with you," Ilsa flung back at him, tightly.

King hurried eagerly along beside her, panting with excitement.

"Forget it," Sam said. "This is no job for a—"

As she opened the corral gate, Ilsa cast him a hard, caustic glare. "No job for a what? A *girl*? But it *is* a job for a thirteen-year-old *boy*?"

"Ah, heck," Sam said, gritting his teeth as he tightened the saddle cinch. "*Girls!*"

"*Boys!*" Ilsa said as she stomped into the stable for her saddle. She cast another hard glare over her shoulder at her brother. "Boys! Little *boys* who think they're *men!*"

She turned her head forward and disappeared into the

stable's deep shadows, ignoring the excited dog as he leaped up against her.

"I'm a *man*," Sam countered, strapping his Spencer's scabbard to the side of his saddle. "Bloody Joe said so!"

———

MANNION SHUCKED BOTH OF HIS BIG RUSSIANS FROM their holsters, held them barrel up in front of each shoulder, his reins also in his left hand, and gazed toward the cutthroats, grinning challengingly. He clicked both hammers back.

The four cutthroats glanced around at each other.

Blue Bowdrie turned toward Mannion, poked his concho-studded hat up off his forehead, and said, "A man's dead a long time, Marshal. Why don't you leave those bags and ride on out of here? Your life—especially yours, *Bloody Joe Mannion's* life—ain't worth sixty thousand dollars!"

"Are your lives worth sixty thousand dollars?" the lawman fired back.

Bowdrie and the others glanced at each other. They grinned and chuckled; Mannion could see their shoulders jerk while their horses anxiously tossed their heads.

Then Bowdrie shucked his rifle from his saddle boot and his pistol from a holster on his right hip. The others followed suit. They spread out in a line across the trail, sitting their horses five feet apart, staring toward Mannion.

"Come an' get 'em, you chicken-livered coyotes!" Mannion bellowed.

He booted Red into an instant gallop, tearing up the trail in the direction from which he'd come.

Bowdrie lowered his head and bellowed, "*Hy-yahhh!*"

into his horse's ear and rammed steel against the mount's flanks. The horse whinnied shrilly and lunged forward into a ground-chewing gallop, heading straight toward Bloody Joe who, quickly closing the gap between himself and the outlaw leader, aimed his right-hand Russian straight out from his right shoulder, and fired.

Bowdrie's face acquired a shocked look as he jerked back in his saddle, triggering his own extended revolver far wide of Mannion. The bullet spanged off a rock somewhere off Mannion's right flank. Joe lined up the second Russian's sites on the chest of the Mexican galloping with his head low, gritted teeth showing beneath his bushy, dark-brown mustache. The man flinched as Mannion's bullet, nudged high by his rocking platform, blew the man's low-crowned sombrero off his hat to dance wildly behind him in the wind, tethered to his neck by its chin thong.

Mannion kept galloping and firing, his own bullets flying wide as bullets fired by the other two riders caromed about his head.

And then they galloped past him, one wide off his left stirrup, the other wide off his right stirrup. Bowdrie, still sagging back in his saddle, sat his own edgily prancing mount off the trail's right side as Mannion approached still at a full gallop. Blood pumped from the ragged hole high in the left breast of the man's red shirt. Bowdrie grimaced while, holding both his Colt and his rifle as well as his reins, he fought to remain seated in his saddle while also trying to hold his frightened horse in check.

When Mannion was nearly parallel to the man, still galloping hard, he extended his left-hand Russian and shouted, "This is what sixty grand's worth, you cork-headed son of a two-legged sow!" and calmly drilled another round into the man's heaving belly.

Not wanting him dead yet. Wanting him to ponder the folly of his ways.

Of endangering the lives of two innocent kids and of trying to separate Mannion from the loot he had the responsibility of returning to its rightful owners.

Bowdrie gave a fierce yell and triggered his rifle into the air just before his horse pitched sharply, clawing at the sky with its hooves and throwing its rider off its back and onto the ground beside the trail. Then the mount wheeled and galloped straight up the trail toward where the other three outlaws were just then reining their own mounts around sharply and galloping back toward Mannion.

Mannion reined Red around and galloped toward the three men galloping toward him. He returned fire with both Russians, one at a time, as smoke and flames lapped from the barrels of the three men sending lead his way to screech through the air around him. The reb had flung off his arm sling and gritted his teeth as he fired both his six-shooter and carbine.

One bullet tore through the lobe of Mannion's right ear half a second before he fired his right-hand Russian and galloped past the Mexican just as the man screamed shrilly and flew off his own galloping mount's left hip. The man hit the sage-stippled ground and rolled dustily, his sombrero flying wildly around his head and shoulders.

He came to a stop on his belly, ground his knees into the ground beneath him, trying to rise, then fell flat, jerked, and lay still in death.

The other two riders—Winslow and Anderson—had galloped on past Mannion and were wheeling their own mounts once more.

Mannion stopped Red, holstered the Russian and crouched in his saddle, closing his gloved hand over his right ear—or what was left of it. Judging by the burn and all the blood on his hand, not much.

"Look out, Bloody Joe!" came a boy's shrill cry as both Winslow and Anderson galloped back toward him, grinning and extending their own revolvers and rifles.

A rifle to Mannion's right thundered.

The big, blond bear triggered the carbine in his hands toward Joe then grunted loudly, dropped the rifle, and sagged straight back in his saddle, a look of shock washing over his round, bearded face. A quarter second earlier, Mannion had seen blood and viscera geyser out of the left side of the man's head, from just above that ear. The big man's inexplicable demise had caught Winslow's attention. As the former reb turned toward the man just as Anderson flew back off his horse's rump and rolled heavily, pinwheeling his arms and legs, Joe lined up the sights of his left Russian on Winslow's chest, and fired.

Winslow was only ten feet from Mannion when Joe's bullet knocked the Southerner sideways from his saddle and down. Winslow screamed when his left foot got caught in its stirrup. Horse and rider went flying past Mannion, Winslow bellowing as he bounced along the trail, arms thrust up above his head, beside the galloping mount. The horse whinnied shrilly, making Red, who'd been turning sharply, jerk with a violent start.

Joe wasn't ready for the move.

He was favoring both his burning left side and burning right ear—or what was left of it. He gave a yowl and flew off Red's right side, striking the ground on his right shoulder and hip and rolling onto his back.

In the distance, a girl yelled and a dog barked wildly.

Mannion grimaced and lifted his head to look around.
What in blue blazes?

The boy, Sam, lay on the crest of a hill on Mannion's

right, smiling over the barrel of his Spencer repeater. His sister was just then galloping up behind him, her hair blowing in the wind beneath the billed wool immigrant's hat she wore. The shepherd-collie dog was running along beside her, barking excitedly. The black thoroughbred stallion, Lightning, stood several feet behind the boy, reins dangling.

"Sam!" Ilsa cried, staring down in horror at her brother.

Sam turned his delighted smile to her and yelled, "I got him. I got one o' them nasty buggers, Sis. He woulda shot Bloody Joe!"

He turned to smile down at where Mannion was propped up on his elbows, feeling blood leak from his burning right ear. The lawman stretched his lips back from his teeth in frustration. When he turned his head forward, he spied movement on a bald spot on a distant, dome-shaped ridge—several riders crossing the top of the ridge and riding down into deep timber.

Five, six—more like seven—though they were a long way away.

Definitely heading this way, though. Toward the sound of the gunfire they'd heard. They were riding with too much purpose to merely be cowpunchers checking on summer herds.

"Ah, hell!" Mannion said. "Is there anyone who *doesn't* want my loot?!"

CHAPTER 14

MANNION SCOWLED UP THE HILL ON HIS RIGHT, DOWN which the boy was now riding the black, his sister following, that look of deep trepidation paling her pretty, oval-shaped features. The dog ran along beside the boy now, ears pricked, tail arched, eyes glinting its excitement. Same as the boy's.

The boy and the girl reined up ten feet from Mannion, the boy leaping out of the saddle and running over to Joe, dropping to a knee beside him, concern now showing in his gaze. "You all right, Bloody Joe?"

"Stop calling me that, goddammit, boy!" Mannion yelled, fury racing through him. "You know what, kid? I was wrong about you. You're not a man at all. You're still just a kid. A man would have stayed home with his sister and left the fight to the professional!"

The boy's lower jaw hung, crestfallen. He glanced toward where the big blond bear of a man lay inert. "He woulda...he woulda..."

"Shot me? Maybe. But you two would be home with your dog and your horses—safe!"

"He's right, Sam," Ilsa said from the back of the

calico, who turned its head to sniff the breeze no doubt laced with the scent of the approaching riders. The girl was staring in the same direction, toward where the new batch of riders were just then reaching the bottom of the distant, dome-shaped ridge and were putting their horses down the valley in hers, the boy's, and Mannion's direction.

She turned her anxious gaze to Mannion. "That's Zeke Trainor."

"I figured as much."

"How bad you hit, Joe?" the boy asked him.

"Never mind." Mannion heaved himself to his feet then stooped with a grunt to retrieve the Russian he'd dropped. He returned it to the holster on his left hip and turned to the boy and the girl, who both grimaced when they saw his ear.

Or what was left of it. Likely not much. The blood had run down Mannion's neck and under his shirt collar. He stared off toward where Trainor rode at the point of the arrow-shaped group of men loping their horses toward him over the sage-stippled valley floor.

He turned to the boy and, wide-eyed with anger, said, "Mount up. You're both riding with me. He's seen you here, and if he gets his hands on that loot, which he fully intends to do, he won't leave any witnesses."

Mannion ripped off a glove, stuck two fingers between his lips, and whistled.

Sam stood staring stiffly toward the oncoming riders.

From her perch atop the calico, Ilsa stared toward them as well. "Mount up, Sam," she said quietly but firmly. Remembering the previous afternoon, she turned to her brother and said more sharply, dark eyes glinting anxiously, "Mount up, Sam!" She cast her angry gaze to the lawman and said, caustically, "We're riding with your Bloody Joe!"

That jerked Sam out of the trance he'd fallen into, having realized their trouble wasn't over and that he'd only gotten him and his sister right back into the thick of it.

"All right," he said, grabbing the black's reins, leading it over to a rock upon which he stepped before swinging into the saddle. "All right." He glanced down at the lawman just then pulling his Yellowboy from its scabbard, his loyal horse having come to his whistle. His lips quirked a smile of barely bridled excitement. "We'll ride with Bloody Joe!"

Mannion rolled his eyes and turned to the girl. "Ride! Straight up the valley! I'll catch up!"

Ilsa reined the calico around and batted the heels of her ankle boots against its flanks, calling over her shoulder, "Come on, Sam!"

Sam looked down at Mannion. "Sure you don't want help, Marshal?"

Mannion bunched his lips and smashed his open hand against the black's rump, yelling, "*Hyahhh!*"

The black's eyes widened as it lunged off its rear hooves and shot up the valley after the girl and the dog running along barking beside the calico.

Mannion racked a live round into the Yellowboy's action.

He rested the barrel on his saddle, aiming down canyon toward the seven men galloping toward him. The lead rider drew back on his reins with one hand, raising the other hand, and the six others followed suit, checking down their mounts and curveting them, casting their anxious gazes toward the lawman.

Mannion held fire. They were just out of the Yellowboy's accurate range. Besides, he was racked with so much pain, he doubted that even using the saddle as a prop he'd be able to hold the Winchester still. He'd only wanted to slow them. He'd done that. They'd think twice or three times about getting into range. They didn't know how feeble and frustrated he felt—with the ear wound, the tearing pain in his side, his fury at the boy for endangering himself and his sister once more, when Mannion had wanted so desperately to keep them both safe at home.

Now they'd seen Trainor coming for the loot.

Trainor knew they'd seen him. If he got the loot, which it appeared he fully intended to do, maybe give up ranching for good and live the good life down in Mexico —yeah, Mannion had looked into the man's eyes; they'd told him who he was, the kind of *man* he was—he'd have killed Sam and Ilsa and likely burned their cabin to rid the valley of any trace of them. Making it appear as though rustlers had done it.

The girl should have let him kill the bastard.

Mannion shoved the Yellowboy into its boot, pulled his weary, aching body into the saddle, cast one more look at the men gazing back at him from just over a hundred yards away, then swung Red around and put the steel to him. He galloped off across the valley, heading toward the boy and the girl and the dog, three small, jostling figures heading toward a distant pass.

"Dammit!"

———

"WHAT DO YOU WANT TO DO, BOSS?" ASKED TRAINOR'S foreman, Walt McClory.

Trainor stared off toward Mannion galloping to catch

up to the girl and her kid brother. Trainor spat a wad of chaw down the left side of his dun gelding, wiped his mustached mouth with the back of his hand, and said, "We follow 'em. Slow. Make our move when the time comes. That Mannion's a devil. No point in takin' him by the tail."

He spied movement in the shade roughly a hundred yards ahead.

"Come on," he said, leaning forward to slide his Winchester '79 into his saddle boot and spurring the dun ahead, toward where he saw a dark-haired man in a red shirt flopping around, lifting his head and arching his back as though in great agony.

As Trainor approached the wounded outlaw, his lips formed a grim smile. He recognized the man. Blue Bowdrie, his own damnable self.

Bowdrie lifted his head again. His eyes found the rancher in the checked wool shirt, black vest, and black chaparreras riding toward him. His brown-eyed gaze widened slightly then darkened. Even though the man lay helpless, Trainor felt the cold touch of evil evoked by Bowdrie's gaze in his loins. Bowdrie had a bloody wound in his upper left chest, just above where that lung would be. He held a brown-gloved hand over the wound in his belly, trying to hold the blood and viscera inside him but not having much luck.

"Good Lord," Trainor said, chuckling dryly as he and his six men reined up in front of the hard-dying outlaw. "You look a little worse for the wear, Blue."

The smile left the outlaw's mouth as well as his eyes. But only for a second. They returned as the man said, "I beat this long enough, I reckon. My long overdue note was called due's all."

"That's one way of lookin' at it." Trainor looked at his

foreman—a short, stocky, granite-faced man, clean-shaven save for long muttonchop whiskers. McClory was totally bald save a band of light-brown hair above his ears. It was the same color as his slate-gray eyes. His square-crowned, pea-green hat covered it and the pale bald crown of his head. McClory chuckled as he, too, stared down in subtle jeering at the hard-dying outlaw.

"He don't look near as tough now as he did yesterday." McClory drew the long-barreled Smith & Wesson from the holster tied low on his right thigh and clicked the hammer back. "Want I should finish him?"

Bowdrie slid his devil's gaze toward Trainor, hopefully.

Trainor smiled back at him despite the chill the man's gaze kept locked in his bowels. "Nah." The rancher shook his head slowly. "Don't do him any favors."

Bowdrie's eyes turned mean. Trainor could see those two, small, inner, amber eyes glaring at him now, too, from deep within the man's skull. He braced himself against that devil's glare as Bowdrie said, "I'll be waitin' for you, Trainor." He glanced at the six other well-armed cowpunchers surrounding their boss. "I'll be waitin' for the rest of you."

With that he let his head flop down against the ground and continued grunting and writhing as the two bloody holes in his torso continued to leak blood. He stared up at the sky and gave a grim smile. "Yep," he grunted out as Trainor glanced at McClory and reined his horse away from the dying outlaw, "I'll be waitin'."

"You see his eyes?" McClory asked Trainor when they were twenty feet away, heading up canyon, the other fiver riders flanking them.

"You seen it, too?" Trainor asked him.

"Yeah." McClory shuddered. "He ain't from this world."

"Yeah, well," Trainor said. "Mannion ain't, neither. From some other world, for sure—ol' Bloody Joe. But"—he tipped his head back to indicate the dying outlaw behind them, "he'll end up the same way as Bowdrie as long as we play our cards right, don't get in a hurry."

"I hear ya, boss."

"Joe did us a favor. Eliminated the competition."

"That's for sure," McClory laughed, glancing behind him once more.

They were approaching a horse standing roughly a hundred yards north of where they'd left Bowdrie. While the others reined in, Trainor walked his dun around to the horse's far side. He stared down at the sandy-haired man, Reb Winslow, who lay on the ground, one badly swollen, booted foot hung up in the stirrup. Blood oozed from a wound in his shoulder.

Winslow stared dreadfully up at the rancher staring down at him.

Winslow's holsters were empty, his coat badly torn. Trainor could see that his ankle was broken, the man's right knee dislocated, the bulge of the knee itself not where it should be. The former rebel fighter was bathed in sweat and his features were pale.

"You fellas didn't have what it takes to take on Mannion, looks like," Trainor noted with a look of grim self-satisfaction.

Winslow glared up at the rancher, flaring one nostril. "You do?"

"We'll see." Trainor shucked his Colt from its holster, cocked it, and aimed down at Winslow's forehead. He narrowed one eye.

Winslow closed his eyes.

The Colt roared.

Trainor flicked the loading gate open to pluck out the

spent shell and to replace it with fresh. He clicked the gate home, spun the cylinder, holstered the gun, and said, "I want that loot and the girl. See you don't shoot her when you're trying to shoot Mannion. I don't care about the boy. Shoot him all you want. I want the loot and the girl."

He turned his craven eyes on his men. "We'll split the loot evenly." He smiled. "But not the girl. She's all mine."

"Havin' seen her," McClory said with a lusty grin, "I can see why."

"Best damn piece o' tail in these mountains," Trainor said.

He reined his dun around and booted it into a trot.

CHAPTER 15

MANNION CAUGHT UP TO THE BOY AND HIS SISTER when they slowed their horses down to trots to rest them, as they were climbing through harsh terrain now— a shelving country of rocky dikes and steep, forested ridges. Mannion stayed back, giving the boy and the black their heads.

The dog, King, was running along beside Sam, often leaving the boy's side to chase a rabbit or a fox but returning soon after.

Sam knew these mountains. Mannion did not. Mannion assumed the kid was leading them—or would lead them eventually—down out of them to the north-east, for that's the direction they seemed to be generally headed. Several times Ilsa glanced questioningly back at Mannion, conveying her incredulity about where her little brother was leading them on such a circuitous, seemingly willy-nilly route.

Mannion wasn't worried. Obviously, Sam knew the country.

The route he was taking was one in which their horses left few tracks, as the ground was hard even after the previous day's storm, and flinty. Trainor would have a hard time following them. Over the past hour and a half that they'd been riding away from Mannion's encounter with Bowdrie's men, Joe hadn't spied anyone on their back trail.

So, maybe the kid's ploy was working.

He wasn't going to question it, just sit back and enjoy the ride—as much as he could with one ear shot up and blood spotting the bullet wound in his side.

He'd wrapped a long, white handkerchief from under his jaws to the top of his head, covering that ear—or what was left of it. Dabbing at it with a cloth had told him a good part of the appendage including the lobe was gone.

Oh, well. What were earlobes for, anyway? In his line of work, he was bound to get one shot off sooner or later.

By noon, Mannion felt a few hunger pangs despite his aches and pains.

If he was hungry even in his downtrodden condition, he knew his trail guides must be, as well. He doubted they had any food in their saddlebags. They hadn't known they'd be taking to the trail. Mannion had some jerky in his saddlebags, maybe a can of beans. That would do. When they'd crossed a pass that was beginning to look more and more like the desert, which meant they were descending the Stalwarts, he reined up behind the pair riding single file ahead of him and said, "Hey, you two—hold up."

They both reined in, turned their horses around to gaze back at Mannion.

"Did you have breakfast?"

They glanced at each other, shook their heads.

The girl looked past Mannion to regard their back trail. "I'm too scared to be hungry. Trainor's a bad fellow. I've had an encounter with him before yesterday."

Sam, sitting up trail from her, scowled curiously at his sister. "You *did?*"

Ilsa kept her eyes on Mannion. "It's not important. It's just that—well, he's bad, that's all."

"He wants you, don't he?" Sam asked, his face flushing with brotherly anger. "I've seen the way he looks at you."

Still keeping her gaze on Mannion, Ilsa said, "I just want to be away from him."

Mannion looked past her at Sam. "You hungry?"

"I'm as empty as a dead man's boot," Sam said without an ounce of irony.

Mannion glanced at a cluster of boulders up a rise on his left and ahead about two hundred feet. "We'll build a fire up there. Wood should be dry by now."

Ilsa kept her concerned gaze on their back trail. "Do we dare stop?"

"We don't have any choice," Mannion said, booting Red up toward the boulders. "These horses are blown, and we have to eat. Even you, young lady."

Brother and sister followed him up the rise and into the boulders which would offer a modicum of privacy. Any passing wayfarers would likely smell a fire, but Mannion had a feeling that Sam's choice of route had effectively—at least, for the meantime—scoured their stalkers from their trail. When he was feeling better and had more of his strength back, he'd lay back along the trail and try to pick their pursuers off one by one or two by two. If he could at least kill Trainor he might discourage the others, though from a distance Trainor's men had appeared as hungry-eyed and venal as the rancher himself.

Like Trainor himself, they likely wanted the girl as much as the loot.

He could tell by the stiff way Ilsa carried herself as they dismounted and unsaddled and tended their horses that she knew it was true. She looked pale and drawn and kept casting her dreadful, dark-eyed gaze toward the craggy peaks from which they'd come. Mannion wished there was something he could do to comfort the girl. If only she would have let him kill Trainor the day before.

If she had, the killing would have haunted her, however. Now, it likely would not. Now, she'd likely welcome the idea.

When he'd tended Red and Sam and Ilsa had tended their own mounts, Mannion fished his coffeepot out of his war bag. Sam took it from him, saying, "You sit tight, Marshal." The boy placed a hand on his shoulder. "You don't look so good." He grimaced when he looked at the bloody cloth over Joe's ear, the streams of blood that had dried on his neck. "Ilsa an' me'll build a fire. We don't have anything to eat, but—"

"There's some jerky and a can of beans in—"

He stopped when he heard a whining sound. He and Sam turned to see the shepherd-collie, King, move into the camp between two rocks. Mannion just now realized he hadn't seen the dog in a while. Now, he realized why. The dog had slipped away from the trail to track a jackrabbit. A big one, too. The beefy, gangly jack hung by its neck from the dog's jaws.

King dropped the jack and looked at Sam and Mannion and wagged his tail.

"Well, I'll be hanged!" Joe said.

"Ilsa," Sam said, looking toward where the girl was gathering dry branches down the slope. "Look—King brought us stew meat!"

The girl brightened. "Good boy, King!"

The dog mewled and wagged his tail.

Chuckling, Mannion sat back against his saddle as Sam went over, picked the jack up off the ground, shucked a Barlow knife from a small sheath on his belt, and went to work dressing the rabbit on a flat rock. Soon, coffee boiled on a low fire and Ilsa was working on putting a stew together with Mannion's beans, a can of stewed tomatoes he also found in his war bag, and the rabbit Sam had chopped into bite-sized chunks.

Joe sat back against his saddle, taking a badly needed breather, lacing the thick, hot, black coffee with the bottle of "medicinal" whiskey he'd had in his saddlebags. He had to be careful. He had a weakness for the stuff, and he had to keep his head clear. He had to stay alert. While he sipped the flavorful brew, his spirits lightened by the flavored java and the succulent smell of the stew simmering on the iron spider in the fire, he cast his gaze through a gap between the boulders and to the trail winding back toward the higher ridges behind him.

No movement back there but the occasional hunting hawk or golden eagle.

So far, so good. Part of him hoped Trainor would pick up his trail again, so Mannion could complete the job he'd started the day before. Sooner or later, the man had to die. He was too much of a threat to the girl. Mannion had found himself feeling right protective of Ilsa McDowell and her brother Sam.

When the stew was done, Ilsa filled a bowl for each of them. She passed one to her brother, who looked down at it, his face acquiring an odd expression before he passed it on to Mannion. Ilsa handed her brother his own steaming bowl of stew and a fork then sank back against her own saddle to eat. She looked at Sam, who was staring down at his own stew with much the same, odd expression he'd acquired when he'd seen Mannion's bowl. She cast a curious look across the fire at Joe, who returned his gaze to Sam who sat with his bowl of stew resting on one thigh while he rubbed his other thigh with his left hand, fidgeting.

"What it is, Sam?" Ilsa said, frowning at him. "Don't like my cooking anymore?"

Sam looked at Mannion. The boy, too, seemed vaguely puzzled.

Mannion could read the boy's mind through the cast in his eyes. "Strange thing, killing a man—isn't it, boy?"

What he was feeling just then seemed to dawn on Sam then, too. Slowly, keeping his eyes on Mannion, he nodded. He said, "I...I shot plenty of birds...wild turkeys...deer...elk. Never a man."

"Oh, Sam," Ilsa said.

"It's different," Mannion said.

"For you, too?"

"Yes."

"For Bloody Joe?"

Mannion gave a dry snort. "Bloody Joe's just a man, boy. Like any other."

Sam looked down at the stew again. He swallowed, set the bowl aside, and climbed to his feet, tucking one arm across his stomach. "I reckon...I reckon I ain't as hungry as I thought!" He swung around and ran off through the rocks, stumbling as though drunk. "Sorry, Ilsa!"

The dog followed him, looking concerned, as he disappeared around a rock. There followed the sounds of dry retching.

Mannion started to fork some of the stew into his mouth but stopped when he saw Ilsa staring at him from across the fire, a dubious look in her eyes. An accusing look, Mannion thought.

"I know," he told her. "Some hero ol' Bloody Joe is. Endangers your lives, introduces your brother to killing."

Her expression the same, she shook her head. Her untouched stew bowl steamed in her lap. "That's not what I was thinking."

"Oh?"

She looked at him directly. "I was thinking I wish I'd let you kill him."

Mannion winced a little at that. He was the gift that didn't stop giving.

He'd finished his stew and set it aside when Sam came back into the camp, looking a little better than before, brushing his shirtsleeve across his mouth. "Boy," the kid said, shaking his head.

He picked up his canteen, took a drink, then sat back down on his saddle. King sat down beside him, looking up at him, still concerned.

Mannion said, "Just hope it doesn't get any eas..."

He let his voice trail off. Tied just outside the camp with the boy's and the girl's horses, Red gave a warning blow. Mannion followed the horse's gaze to the high ridge on his left. Three riders were just then coming down out of the timber to walk their horses along a trail on a slight shelf protruding from the belly of the slope maybe fifty yards up from its base, maybe a hundred yards from Mannion's camp.

Sam and Ilsa looked at Mannion curiously then followed his gaze to the three strangers, who'd just spied Mannion and his two campmates in the rocks below them. They had the wild, rugged, bearded looks of market hunters. Or maybe they hunted for some nearby mining camp. One of them nudged one of the others, and all three drew rein, stopping their horses.

One extended his hand to one of the others. The second man reached back to pull something out of a saddlebag pouch and handed it to the first man. Brass glinted in the sunshine as the man, wearing a black immigrant's hat from which long, stringy blond hair hung straight down to his shoulders, raised the spy glass to his right eye.

The man brashly studied the camp.

Mannion stared up at him, unease building inside him.

What had the man so interested that he studied the camp for a good minute, maybe longer?

Then Joe looked at Ilsa, who stared up the slope at the three strangers, as did her brother.

"Ilsa," Joe said.

She turned to him, frowning curiously.

"Don't look at them."

"Why not?"

"Don't—that's all."

Sam turned to him then, too, and Mannion could see by the expression in the kid's eyes he knew what Joe was thinking.

When the man handed the spyglass to one of the others, who also trained it on the camp in the rocks, Mannion reached over for his Yellowboy. He held it up high, so the three strangers could get a good look at it. He made a big show of cocking it one-handed then resting it across his thighs.

When the second man had lowered the glass and returned it to his saddlebags and the three rode on along the shelf and out of sight behind Joe's left shoulder, back into timber, Mannion rose, pulled the spider and coffeepot out of the fire, and kicked dirt on the flames.

"Time to break camp."

He glanced back up the ridge, at where the three strangers had disappeared.

Something told him that wasn't the last he'd seen of them.

CHAPTER 16

MANNION'S PARTY CAMPED THAT NIGHT AT THE BASE OF the Stalwarts.

They'd had to feel their way down the mountains' northeastern flank, for the boy's precocious explorational adventures, previously made when he'd been hunting or looking for stray cattle, had taken him only so far in the mountains. That was all right. He'd led Mannion to his own familiar country now, back on the relatively flat desert floor with the San Juans humping up before him in the north, the Black Range flanking him in the east.

He could take it from here.

He figured he was roughly three days out of Del Norte now, which lay ahead and slightly east, to the right of the San Juans, between that range and the Sangre de Cristos, which were a sawblade shadow to the north and east, a hundred miles away as the crow flew.

Now Mannion studied their back trail through his field glasses. He gave the mountain canyons now behind him a good scrutiny then lowered the glasses, returned them to their case, and made his way back down the rocky bluff he'd climbed, to where Sam and Ilsa waited for him at the bottom with their horses.

"Any sign of 'em?" Sam was letting his black draw water from his hat.

Ilsa was taking a conservative sip from her own canteen.

"Nothing," Mannion said, and dropped his field gasses into his saddlebag pouch. "I think you lost 'em, kid."

Sam smiled as he tipped his hat over to empty it.

Mannion caught Ilsa giving him a critical, speculative look.

She was an observant one; Joe would give her that.

He sighed as he swung up into the leather and started out, at the head of the two-man, one-girl, one-dog procession. King stayed with them for only another half mile before taking off after another rabbit. He'd caught several over the past day since he'd caught the one they'd put in the stewpot, and hadn't shared.

He must figure he hadn't gotten enough of the first one to go to the trouble to continue to feed these humans. The previous evening, Sam had set three rope snares, two of which had proven fruitful. So, they'd dined on rabbit again early that morning, before setting out before sunrise. They needed supplies to get them the rest of the way to Del Norte. Mannion knew a road ranch out this way. If he could find it—he'd never taken this route before, having stuck to old Indian trails and freight roads farther to the east—they'd stock up on what they needed.

A half hour after he'd scanned their back trail, Ilsa gigged her mount up beside Mannion and fingered breeze-tossed strands of her long hair back from her cheek.

"I read that look on your face, Marshal," she said with vague bemusement in her voice.

"Oh? Which one?"

"The one you had when you climbed back down that butte. After scanning our back trail...?"

"Oh, that one."

"You were disappointed not to see Trainor back there."

Mannion hiked a shoulder. "Oh, not really."

"Really?"

"Really. For your sake and the boy's."

"But to your mind, he needs killing. So you wish he was behind us."

"I have a feeling he still is. Just keeping his distance. There's too much loot for him not to continue. He likely knows I'm heading for Del Norte. He'll catch up to us soon enough."

"Yes, there's too much loot. And there's me. Am I right?" She looked at him again and pulled her mouth corners down.

"Yes."

Ilsa shook her head. "Why are men the way they are, Marshal Mannion?"

"Good question."

"What if he doesn't show?"

Mannion reined Red around the left side of a rock then turned back to ride with the girl once more. "If he doesn't show before we make Del Norte, I'll ride back into the Stalwarts ahead of you and Sam."

"And kill him?"

"Yes."

"Why?"

Mannion stopped his horse. She stopped hers and turned to face him.

"He'll never leave you alone. He won't have the loot. But he'll make damn sure he has you."

Ilsa gave a dry laugh. "Am I all that much?"

"Yes."

The bluntness of his response seemed to take her aback. She paled again, then flushed and looked down at her saddle horn. She looked up at him again, fingered more hair from her face, and said, "He has a family."

"You have Sam."

"I know, but..."

"Besides," Mannion added, "do you really think his family is going to miss him all that much?"

She seemed to think about that for a time. She glanced at her brother sitting Lightning behind her and Mannion, King sitting beside Sam. The boy and his dog regarded Mannion and the girl curiously. She turned back to Joe, gave a wan smile, shook her head, and said, "No."

Mannion pursed his lips, nodded, and booted Red on ahead.

Late in the afternoon, he pulled Red to another stop.

"Whoa...whoa, boy..."

He turned toward where he'd spied movement out the corner of his right eye. Three horseback riders were making their way out from behind a tabletop mesa roughly two hundred yards away. They followed the shadowed base of the mesa out into the brassy sunlight then swung straight north, disappearing a minute later behind a high, flat-topped bluff.

Mannion was not surprised.

He'd spied them skirting his, Sam's, and Ilsa's trail the previous evening, just before they'd stopped for the night. He'd spied a distant campfire after good dark last night, as well. He couldn't see them clearly from this distance, but he recognized the immigrant cap of the lead rider and the buckskin jacket of another. He knew their horses now, too—two pintos and a claybank. They were still at it, all right. Shadowing Mannion and the McDowell kids.

He glanced at Ilsa stopped on the trail ten feet behind him.

She stared toward where she, too, had seen their three stalkers. Her eyes were dark, fearful. Her long, straight, nearly black hair danced in the breeze around her pale cheeks. Instinctively, she drew the flaps of her elk hide vest across her breasts and turned to Mannion.

"Them again."

"Yeah," Joe said. "But not for long."

He clucked Red forward.

———

Since it didn't look like rain anytime soon, Mannion stopped for the night in a shallow wash sheathed in mesquites and cottonwoods. A spring-fed stream trickled along the east side of the wash—pure, cool water gurgling over its sandy bed. Horse, riders, and King had their fill; Mannion, Sam, and Ilsa filled their canteens then settled back against the bank on the wash's west side, heating what was left of their rabbit over a low fire over which they'd also brewed coffee from Mannion's fast-depleting stores. He hoped he could find the road ranch sometime tomorrow or there were going to be three hungry riders riding into Del Norte the day after next.

King was doing just fine hunting, however. And not sharing so much as a single bite. As the dog now snapped and snarled and tore at the meat just beyond the edge of the firelight, Ilsa returned from where she'd cleaned the dishes in the stream. When she'd stowed the utensils in Mannion's canvas war sack, she produced the cloth and bar of soap that had been in her saddlebags since the previous year's fall gather and turned to Mannion.

"I'm going to prepare for bed," she said.

Sam was eating the last of the rabbit he'd roasted on a sharpened stick. His and the lawman's face showed bronze in the light of the flames flickering across their faces—Mannion's old and craggy one, showing the weight of his years and current aches and pains; Sam's young and smooth one but with eyes that suddenly appeared much older than they'd had only a couple of days earlier.

"Don't stray far, honey." Mannion lifted his steaming coffee to his mustached mouth and sipped.

Behind him, King's eyes glinted copper in the firelight.

Ilsa walked out into the darkness, to where the spring-fed stream glinted in the starlight at the base of the opposite bank. She looked around apprehensively, afraid to be alone out here. No telling where those men shadowing them from a distance might be. But Mannion had scouted the area thoroughly just before dark and had seen no sign of them.

Ilsa looked at the dark water glinting at her feet, which were bare.

It looked so cool and refreshing. She wanted so badly to scour the trail grime from her body.

She stepped into the water, wincing a little at the sting of the cold water against her tender flesh. The water soothed her, though, too, as it slid down its sandy bed, over and around her feet. She lifted one foot and ran her hand over it, digging her fingers in, cleaning between her toes. She did the same with her other foot and then she went to the edge of the narrow, shallow stream and dropped to both knees. She looked around again, cautiously.

No one out here but herself, she deemed.

She had a blanket wrapped around her shoulders. Now she removed it to reveal the thin chemise she wore beneath it. Again, she looked around. Then she slid the chemise's left strap down her left arm, then the right one. She cast the garment aside and cupped water to her breasts, lifting her head and taking a deep draft of the cool night air.

So refreshing...

She soaked the cloth and rubbed it across her bosoms, shivering with the chill as well as with sensuous delight. As she did, she looked down into the water and saw her bare-breasted reflection as she leaned out from the shore, her breasts sloping toward the water, pale and full. She knew a moment's abhorrence at what she saw. A pretty girl with bosoms that had become large and full... and a detriment to the welfare of her and her brother. She reflected suddenly as she stared at her reflection in the glinting, sliding stream that she was as much a danger to Sam as Mannion had been.

It had been since she'd started filling her blouses and skirts out a couple of years ago that the men she'd met on the range and when she rode to town for supplies had started lingering their gazes on her...started talking to her more and in jocular and insinuating tones. That was when Zeke Trainor had started riding over to the ranch now and then. He made the excuse he just happened to be in the valley looking for herd-quitting calves or tracking a wolf or a puma, and he sure could do with a cup of coffee and a slice of that pie Miss Ilsa was so well known for baking and keeping on hand for weary, passing wayfarers.

Or maybe just a glass of the milk Ilsa bought from a neighbor who grazed a couple of milch cows and kept cool in the stream near the cabin...

And then he'd ridden up on her when she'd been wading in a stream very much like the one she was bathing in now. Again, she shuddered, feeling his hands on her hips sliding slowly up her sides, feeling his scraggly, sweat-damp mustaches rubbing against her neck.

She saw her reflected figure shudder in the water before her.

Chicken flesh rose on her arms.

Quickly, she scrubbed under her arms then gave a gasp when a sudden breeze rose out of nowhere, jostling the branches of the mesquites and cottonwoods on the low bank on the other side of the stream from her. A cottonwood branch slid to one side, revealing the pointed, yellow light of a distant fire.

Again, she gasped, crossed her arms over her breasts as she stared in mute terror at that guttering light.

A footstep crackled behind her and Mannion's deep voice said commandingly, "Get back to camp, girl." He held the chemise out to her.

She gasped with a start then grabbed the garment, dropped it over her head, and slid the straps up onto her shoulders.

Mannion stood tall beside her, staring out across the stream and through the breeze-jostled branches on the bank toward the fire.

Ilsa cleared her throat. "It's...it's them...isn't it?"

"Yes." Mannion cocked the Winchester in his hands. "You and the boy stay by the fire."

She rose slowly, frowning up at him. "What...what...?"

"Stay by the fire. I'll be back."

He walked across the shallow stream, climbed the low bank, pushed through the branches, and was gone in the night.

CHAPTER 17

MANNION HAD WORKED HIS WAY AROUND THE THREE stalkers' camp to the downwind side, so the men's horses wouldn't scent him.

Now he followed another shallow wash toward that guttering fire growing more and more distinct before him, with every step he took. The three figures sitting around it grew more distinct, as well, so that he could see that two wore Stetsons, both battered and weathered, while the third man with the long, pale blond hair and beard a shade darker than his hair wore the black, wool immigrant cap.

He sat Indian style near the fire, chewing on a bone and wiping his greasy fingers on his fringed buckskin trousers. He wore a blue shirt under a deerskin vest trimmed with Indian beads and what appeared talismans fashioned from the bones of small animals sewn into the hide.

There was one—the bleached skull of some rodent— on the front of the black immigrant cap, as well.

Another man sat to his right, resting back against his saddle propped against the base of a slender cottonwood.

Black-haired and black-bearded, possibly owning some Indian blood, he held a smoking coffee cup on his chest. He was talking; Mannion could see his mouth opening and closing. He could hear only bits and pieces of what he was saying between breeze gusts and the scratching of the leaves in the trees surrounding the men's camp, just ahead now and roughly twenty feet from the bank of the wash Mannion stole down, crouching, holding the Yellowboy low so the light from the men's fire wouldn't reflect off the brass receiver.

The third man was short and thickly built. He sat with his back to the wash but stopping now at a cleft in the bank, Mannion could see the man's square head in profile. He had a long, red beard and a thick neck. He wore a checked shirt, buckskin jacket, canvas trousers, and suspenders. Indian-style moccasins were pulled up to his knees, so badly worn Mannion could see part of one grimy sock through the frayed seams. An old-model Winchester rested across the man's thick thighs. He was slipping cartridges from the double shell belt encircling his thick waist and thumbing them through the rifle's loading gate.

As he did, Mannion now picked up pieces of what he was saying between breeze gusts and leaf whispers: "... purty as a speckled pup...prob'ly virgin...when we're done...get a good price for a piece like that...Mexico..."

"Nogales," said the man in the immigrant cap, chewing an end of the deer bone in his hands.

The camp was roughly twenty feet from Mannion's position in the wash.

Now he stepped up out of the wash and onto the bank, aiming the Yellowboy straight out from his right hip. "Halloo, the camp!"

"Shit!" the man loading the Winchester said with a

start, levering a round into the action and swinging around to face Mannion, who triggered a round into the bole of the tree, just left of the man's head.

The Yellowboy's roar echoed, tearing open the otherwise quiet night and making a night bird screech.

"Don't get excited," Mannion said, moving slowly forward. "Getting excited will get you a bullet faster than otherwise."

The man in the immigrant cap froze with his arms crossed over his belly, each hand on the grips of a pistol holstered for the cross-draw on his hips. The man to his right, having sat up so quickly he'd sent his coffee cup flying, the coffee now steaming on the ground beside him, froze with a snarl on his own, black-bearded face, teeth showing between his parted lips, eyes dark beneath the brim of his funnel-brimmed, cream Stetson.

The thick-set man sat half turned toward Mannion, also gritting his teeth inside his own, red beard, the rifle angled toward the ground. His lumpy chest rose and fell heavily. "Who the hell are you?"

Mannion stopped at the edge of the firelight, gloved right hand closed around the neck of the Yellowboy aimed out from his right hip. The fire snapped and cracked; a coal just then popped, sending up sparks. That made all three men jerk with slight starts as they cast their gazes from the wolfish gray eyes of the tall, middle-aged man before them aiming the cocked Winchester at them.

"The man you're shadowing," Mannion said. "The one with the boy and the girl."

They continued to stare at him darkly. Finally, the big man sitting just ahead and to Mannion's left glanced at the other two then returned his gaze to Mannion and chuckled. "What you talkin' about, mister? We ain't followin' nobody."

"Shut up." Mannion tracked the Yellowboy from left to right, aiming at each man in turn as they gazed at him, fear-bright eyes glinting orange and yellow in the fire-light. "Now," he continued, "I would just leave you with a warning and orders to clear out..."

He shook his head and blinked his eyes once, slowly.

"But that wouldn't do any good—now, would it?" He shaped a knowing smile. "You'd just keep following and wait for an opportunity to make a play. And, if truth be told, I just can't afford the distraction. You see, I have other men on my trail. Smarter and deadlier men than you three cork-headed tinhorns."

The three men before him glanced around darkly at each other.

The man with his greasy hands still closed around the grips of his cross-draw six-shooters narrowed one eye and said, "So...what're you sayin'...?"

"I'm sayin' you're dead men. I just wanted you to know why."

Again, they looked around at each other, their eyes despite the reflection of the fire in them even darker than before.

The black-bearded man, ahead and to Joe's right, scrunched up his eyes with exasperation, and said, "Who the hell *are* you, mister?"

"Joe Mannion, Del Norte town marshal."

That rocked the man sitting straight across the fire from him back on his proverbial heels. Then he yelled, "*Bloody Joe!*"

And started to pull the twin hoglegs from their holsters on his hips.

He didn't get them even half out of the leather before

the Yellowboy flashed and roared.

Mannion ejected the spent, smoking round, seated fresh, and quickly but calmly shot the man to his left, an eyeblink before the man triggered his own rifle wide. Mannion slid the smoking Winchester to the black-bearded man on his right.

The man threw his arms high above his head. "No! No! No! I wasn't in with them two. I wanted to no part in—"

The Yellowboy drowned him out, drilled a neat, round, puckered hole through the dead center of the man's forehead. He flopped straight back against the ground with a dull thud and lay still.

————

HUDDLED CLOSE BESIDE HER BROTHER, BY THE snapping, popping fire, a blanket around both her and Sam, Ilsa gasped and jerked at the distant rifle pop.

She jerked again with the next one...and the next.

Sitting nearby, staring out into the night, King whined.

When the echo of the last shot had dwindled to silence and the quiet night closed down around the camp once more, Ilsa and Sam shared a dark, knowing look.

She turned her head to stare straight out into the night again, toward where the distant campfire suddenly went out.

Ilsa's heart thudded with an inexplicable excitement.

She felt a warmth deep in her belly. Goosebumps rose on her breasts.

Sam stared at her. She turned away.

————

"HOLD ON," MANNION SAID MIDMORNING OF THE next day.

He reined Red in and stared into the brush off the right side of the old freight trail he and his young trail mates had picked up roughly an hour earlier. Since then, the terrain had grown more and more familiar to the Del Norte town marshal. No near landmarks but distant land formations—large mesas and dikes.

"What is it, Marshal?" Sam asked.

"Not sure." Mannion swung down from his saddle, dropped the bay's reins, and moved into the brush.

He crouched to pick something up off the ground. An age-silvered sign nailed to a four-foot-high cedar post. He turned it over and saw the badly faded, ancient lettering:

GLASS'S CASTLE.

The sign was shaped like an arrow.

Mannion saw where the sign had been broken off its base likely by a passing stage or freight wagon. It had been pointing up a trail that angled off to the right of the main one only fifteen feet beyond where the sign had been standing.

Sitting astride the calico mare, Honey, Ilsa frowned at the sign. "Glass's Castle?"

"Sure enough." Joe propped the sign against a mesquite. "That's the name of the road ranch I've been looking for. Fella named Glass owns it. Or did last time I was through here—two, three years ago now. Clayton Glass."

Mannion stepped back into the leather. "We'll head up that trail. Once I get to Glass's place, I'll be able to find my way back to the old freight road I usually take through this country." He glanced at Sam and Ilsa. "And we can stock up on a few supplies, maybe have a bowl of chili. Ol' Glass is famous in these parts for his chili. Said it once quelled and Indian uprising."

Joe chuckled and spurred Red off onto the secondary trail heading northeast. "He never did explain how it managed to do that, but that was Glass."

Again, he chuckled.

He reined Red in again twenty minutes later, atop a rise that looked down on the road ranch itself. Sam and Ilsa rode up to sit their own mounts to Mannion's right.

"That it?" Sam said.

"That's it," Mannion told him.

"Don't look like much."

"It's not much," Mannion said. "Just an old bunkhouse—all that remains of a ranch some Texan established down there in that bowl. Indians wiped out the house and all the outbuildings except that bunkhouse. The rest of the buildings were built of pine from the surrounding ridges. The rancher thought to build the bunkhouse of adobe."

The ancient adobe was cracked and showed black charring from the fire the Lipan Apaches had lit. The roof of the long, low, L-shaped place was rusted, corrugated tin. A corral and stable lay on the other side of the building, out front of which was tied a single, buckskin horse just then lifting its snout from a stock trough to turn to stare up the ridge at Mannion and his trail mates. The buckskin wore a fancy, Texas-style saddle with a large, silver-trimmed horn. The bridle was studded with hammered silver disks. The horse's tack looked far spiffier than the horse itself, which appeared old, knock-kneed, and slightly swaybacked.

"Only one customer," Mannion said.

Good.

In the corner of his right eye, he saw Ilsa glance at him from where she sat on the other side of Sam and Lightning. King was taking a break from chasing rabbits and gophers and was lying across the back of her calico, atop her saddlebags and blanket roll.

Mannion turned to study his back trail.

He'd spied no sign of Trainor over the past two days. At least, nothing to soundly confirm Trainor was on their trail. Early that morning, however, he had seen something in the distant flash of sunlight behind him. The sun possibly reflecting off a bridle bit, gunmetal, or a spur. If Trainor was following, he was holding well back, biding his time, possibly hoping Mannion would forget about him and let his guard down.

Well, Joe wouldn't. But he and Sam and Ilsa had to stop here for enough supplies to get them the rest of the fifty-mile ride into Del Norte, and to pad out their bellies here and now. They'd had no breakfast and the previous night's supper had been damned meager.

Mannion would have plundered the possibles of the trail wolves he'd killed, but there'd been little to plunder but a single, wrinkled apple and some half-rotten venison. He'd freed their horses from their picket line and left the men to molder where he'd shot them.

"Come on, children," Mannion said now, his stomach growling at the anticipation of a bowl of spicy chili. "Let's see what ol' Glass has on the range...if he's still on this side of the sod, that is. In this country, even in these more civilized times"—he laughed ironically—"you never know."

As he and the McDowells rode on down the ridge toward the road ranch, Mannion did not see yet another glint of sunlight off something shiny back along his trail.

CHAPTER 18

WHEN MANNION REACHED THE BOTTOM OF THE HILL and was riding into the hard-packed yard fronting the old former bunkhouse, he called, "Hey, Clayton! I say, Clayton Glass, you old sidewinder! You still kicking, you fat son of a bitch?"

Joe glanced quickly at the two young'uns flanking him. "Um, pardon my French, children. When I ride in here, I'm usually alone..."

Sam grinned.

Ilsa gave him a schoolmarmish look. Not a man easily cowed was Bloody Joe Mannion, but this girl could cow him.

He reined up a few feet from where the old buckskin eyed him and his trail mates dubiously and regarded the building's closed door. A badly age-silvered board above the door had the establishment's peculiar named burned into it:

GLASS'S CASTLE.

The ground in front of the door was badly worn, the

small boardwalk over it partly sunken into it. A rusty washtub rested back against the wall to the right of the door while a ladderback, hide-bottom chair sat to the left of it, as did an upright log atop which sat an ashtray over-filled with cigar stubs and ashes. A lurid-covered dime novel lay open and face down on the chair. A little, red-headed, yellow-breasted desert warbler just then lit on the chairback. It looked around then settled its little dark eyes on Mannion before rising on its spidery feet to give a screech and wing up and over the building's rusted tin roof.

Nothing from inside the place but silence.

Sam and Ilsa looked at Mannion, a growing concern in their own gazes.

Mannion glanced toward the rolling, creosote- and sage-spiked hills of his desert back trail then started to inch his right hand down toward the walnut grip of the Russian holstered on that thigh as he filled his lungs and started to yell once more, "I say—"

Suddenly the front door burst open, and a big man clad all in smoke- and grease-stained buckskins and a filthy red apron ducked out with a wooden bucket of soapy water in both roast-sized, brown hands. The Indian-dark man's baby blue, watery eyes found Mannion and the two youngsters sitting their horses near the hitchrack, facing him, and he stopped dead in his tracks, eyes widening in shock and surprise.

"Well, I'll be hanged!" he said, getting his moccasin-clad feet set beneath him once more, twisting to one side and tossing the soapy water into the yard to the left of the boardwalk before setting the bucket down. "If it ain't Bloody Joe Mannion, his own cussed self! Why didn't you tell me you was here, Joe, an' I'd have rolled out the red carpet for you? Liable to get yourself shot, ridin' in without announcin' yourself. I'm gettin' spooky in my old age an' I keep my double-barrel primed and ready to go!"

The big man, broad through the shoulders and chest but slightly stooped and craggy-faced with age—Mannion didn't know for sure but he thought Clayton Glass was somewhere in his late seventies; he'd been a sergeant when Mannion had been a private in the frontier army—cackled a horsey laugh.

His long, salt-and-pepper hair hung down well past his shoulders and his matching beard hung nearly to the considerable paunch that bulged out his deerskin tunic trimmed with Indian beads. Glass wore his customary necklace of died porcupine quills. He was originally from England and still had a touch of an accent at times, but before, during, and after his stint in the army, he'd married several Indian women and lived the life of a hide hunter, fur trapper, mule skinner, saloon owner, and about everything else a man needed to do to survive when he had more wives and kids than he could count on both hands.

He was a survivor, was Clayton Glass.

Mannion had spent a year hunting buffalo with him and three other men from the army before Joe had secured his first job as town marshal and deputy sheriff and began his storied career wrangling Texas cowpunchers and pistolero gunfighters between Hayes, Kansas, and Nacogdoches, Texas. That had been before his first wife, Sarah, had hanged herself when their daughter had been only a few months old.

Now Joe snorted a dry laugh and said, "Clayton, if I'd shouted any louder, I'd have awakened the ghosts of the dead Indians and white cowpunchers whose bones litter these grounds!"

Glass's thick brows stitched over his eyes. "You did?"

"I sure did." Mannion frowned and canted his head to one side. "You haven't gone deaf in your old age, now, have you, Clayton?"

"Ah, heck," Glass said. "Every Saturday night I get drovers from two competing ranches in here, and sometimes the gunfire gets as furious as when we met up with them Lipans down along Hanged Woman Creek—you remember, over by Socorro, Joe?"

"That was awful loud, Clayton."

"Then when I get to haulin' out my double-bore and started blastin' away my ownself, tryin' to quiet things down...well, I reckon that don't do my hearin' no good, neither, in such close quarters." Glass grinned suddenly and then strode off the sagging, splintering boardwalk and into the yard, gesturing with both big hands, "Get down off the cayuse, Joe, and give your old friend a big hug!"

Mannion swung down and then Glass's bear-like arms and hands were around him, squeezing him tight against him and lifting him clear off the ground—not an easy task with a man of Mannion's size. But then, Glass was no slouch either. He stood nearly as tall as Mannion's six four and Joe could still feel the strength in the man's body.

"Good to see you, Clay!" Mannion said, chuckling as his old friend set him back down on the ground but also wincing at the pain the maneuver had kicked up in his side.

"Where you been keepin' yourself, you ol' scudder. Say, what'd you do to your ear? That looks nasty!"

"Cut myself shaving."

"Ha! You best use a duller knife, Joe! Ain't seen you in a month of Sundays. That last wife o' mine didn't run ya off, did she? She had a temper!"

"Nah, nah. Nothin' like that. I reckon no owlhoots have ridden down here over the past two years. Leastways, not till a few days ago."

"You don't say!" Glass turned to Sam and Ilsa still on their horses. "This ain't them, is it? If so, the owlhoots are not only gettin' younger these days, but they're gettin' purtier, too!" He slapped his thigh and laughed then slid his appreciative gaze from Ilsa to Mannion. "Is that Vangie?"

"No, that's not Vangie," Mannion said. "She's home in Del Norte. With her husband."

"With her *husband?*" Glass said with another bout of shock and surprise. "Why, she can't be old enough to get hitched."

Mannion chuckled. "The years roll on, Clay. That there is Miss Ilsa McDowell and her brother, Sam. We're headed for Del Norte." He narrowed one eye to give his friend a direct, warning look. "Not sure, but we might have men on our trail. They're not circuit preachers either."

Glass wrapped an arm around Mannion's broad shoulders. "Well, it wouldn't be like you, Joe, to not have men on your trail. Either before you or behind you or hangin' belly down over their saddles!"

Glass guffawed again then turned to the youngsters.

"You folks hungry?"

Sam raised a shoulder. "I reckon I could eat a bite."

Mannion was pretty sure the boy's appetite had, indeed, returned.

Ilsa smiled at the big, old codger. "We heard your chili was right famous around here, Mister Glass."

"Now, I wonder who told you that," Glass said, scratching his neck with manufactured thoughtfulness before rolling his gaze to Mannion. Then he laughed and said, "All three of you look hungry as coyotes durin' a drought. Come on in, an' ol' Glass will set you up!"

King, who'd leaped down from Ilsa's horse to stand up against the stock trough by the buckskin, drinking the murky water inside, looked at the big, buckskin- and apron-clad man and barked his own demand for grub.

They all laughed and went inside, King barking at their heels.

———

GLASS SET THEM UP, ALL RIGHT.

He had them take a seat at a table in the middle of the low-ceilinged, earthen-floored room. They had their pick of tables, but Glass knew that Mannion would want to be positioned so he had a good view out the door, which Clayton had propped open with a rock, and out the windows to each side of it. He'd want to get a look as soon as possible at any visitors.

There was only one other customer—a rangy, elderly Mexican dressed in the colorful garb of the vaquero and who obviously belonged to the old buckskin with the smart-looking Texas saddle outside. He'd smiled and nodded at Mannion as Joe and the two McDowell children had entered the place and raised his clear glass of tequila in salute. Sitting against the rear wall, he'd enjoyed his meal and now, sitting sideways in his chair, with his back against the wall and one arm hooked over the chairback, one long, skinny leg crossed over the other, he was dreamily enjoying the tequila and the sun bathing the left side of his ostenta-tiously mustachioed face through the window flanking him.

He wore a high, broad-brimmed, silver-gray sombrero, flare-legged charro trousers and the brush-scarred chaparreras of one who has spent many years in the saddle...and likely many nights on the hard, cold ground, following cattle from one pasture to another, likely having worked at half the old Spanish ranches from deep in Mexico to the Montana border.

Mannion touched two fingers to his hat brim in return greeting and a warm smile. He was a hard man, but he respected the old ones—men of honest, hard work and experience.

Mannion and Sam and Ilsa hadn't been seated long before Glass returned from the kitchen with a big, wooden tray of three steaming, wooden bowls filled with chili, its steam rife with the smell of Mexican spices as well as jalapeño peppers. He set a big plate of cold elk meat on the table, another with a wheel of cheese on it, another of thick, crusty brown bread and then a white china bowl of fresh-whipped, dark-yellow butter. He made a trip back to the kitchen only to return with a meal-punctuating tray of pickled ham hocks and pickled eggs and a tall glass of creamy milk for each of the young McDowells and a thick, white mug of smoking coffee for Joe.

Sam and Ilsa stared at the food before them as though mesmerized, as though they'd never seen food before. Mannion had to admit he was probably guilty of the same thing because after it was all spread out before him, it took him a minute to lift his stiff arms, as all the blood seemed to have run to his belly to prepare it for the gift it was about to receive.

"Enjoy!" Glass said, laughing delightedly. A true drink-and food-slinger, the man took great pride in his cooking and the full satisfaction and admiration of his customers. "I'll be back in the kitchen if you need me. I'm canning a big batch of my homegrown tomatoes to keep me in chili for the winter!"

"Th-thank you, sir," croaked out Sam and Ilsa in turn.

Then they grabbed bread off the plate, slathered the slices with butter and went to work building themselves each a sandwich the thickness of which would do a hard-working mule skinner proud. When they'd had their turn at the secondary plate, Mannion took his, building a stout sandwich of his own, thinking that with a meal this size he and the McDowells might not need to eat again until well after they'd reached Del Norte.

While he, Sam, and Ilsa ate, Mannion could hear King lying out in the yard, snarling as he ripped and chomped on the meaty elk bone Glass had gifted him with. Joe was half done with his meal when the dog stopped snarling suddenly and commenced barking loudly, threateningly. As he did, the sound of approaching riders reached Mannion's ears.

He looked up to see five riders clad in range gear ride into the yard from the north. King pranced around them, tail and hackles arched, barking.

"Glass, when d'you get a dog?" yelled one of the men reining in out front of the cabin. "Get him to heel, dangit, or I'm gonna put a bullet in him!"

Mannion saw the man—blond, early twenties, wearing a low-crowned cream Stetson with a feather poking up from behind the band—pull a six-shooter and click the hammer back. Mannion and Sam were already to the door. As Sam ran out to rein in his dog, Joe narrowed one eye threateningly and said, "Pouch that hogleg, son. If you put a bullet in that dog, I'll put two in you."

He hadn't realized how much he'd become partial to the shepherd-collie. In fact, he realized now, as the blond cowboy eyed him owlishly, he felt nearly as protective of the dog as he did of the boy and the girl.

Thankfully, Mannion's point turned out to be moot. Sam managed to grab the dog by its rope collar and got him settled down and back to work on his bone at the cabin's far end.

Holstering the hogleg, the blond cowboy cast Mannion another hard stare and said, "Well, well, well— if it ain't Bloody Joe Mannion!" He turned his sneering gaze to his partners, all six of whom were swinging down from their sweaty, dusty mounts. They'd apparently ridden a long way that morning, likely tending herds scattered here and there around this neck of the desert just over the line into Colorado Territory.

The others looked at Mannion, then, as well. He didn't recognize any of them, including the blond with the stubby nose, close-set, brooding eyes, and three days' growth of sandy beard stubble on his sunburned cheeks.

"I know you?" Mannion asked him, waving Sam back inside, in case lead started to fly. With him, he never knew.

"Collie Vernon," the blond drover said, tossing his reins over the hitchrack while his partners filed up to the roadhouse and brushed past Mannion as they made their way inside, thankfully appearing hungrier than they were eager to mix it up with the Del Norte town marshal. Walking up behind the others now, Vernon said, "You had me roomin' for two nights a little over a year ago at your notorious flophouse, Hotel de Mannion."

"Ah," Mannion said, still not recognizing the flinty-eyed younker. "I hope the amenities weren't none too crude. I put in an order with the town council for cloth napkins but the jury's still out on that one."

Collie Vernon stopped in front of Mannion and

pointed at the bulge and short scar high on the bridge of his nose. "You give me that right there. My eyes were swelled shut for two weeks."

Mannion raised an admonishing finger. "Makes me wonder if you *might not* have been on your best behavior."

Vernon chuckled. "I hope that ear hurts mighty bad, Joe."

"Don't worry—it does."

Vernon laughed again then stepped past him into the roadhouse. Mannion followed him in, seeing that the firebrand's trail mates were already seated at a long table running along the front wall to his left. Clayton Glass was already scribbling their orders in a soft, pasteboard-covered notebook as old and worn as ancient leather.

When Mannion retook his chair, again facing the open door as well as the seven dusty, sunburned newcomers, he saw that the bright, oily eyes of a couple of the punchers had already found Ilsa. She sat at the table to Mannion's left while Sam was on his right.

When Glass had trundled on back to his kitchen, all seven of the drovers had their goatish gazes riveted on Ilsa, who calmly spooned chili into her mouth. Mannion wasn't sure she noticed the drovers' attention—she did not so much as even glance at them—until she lowered the spoon from her mouth and cast him a dark, weary look.

Mannion sighed and slid his hand down under the table to unsnap the keeper thong from over the hammer of his right-hand Colt.

CHAPTER 19

Mᴀɴɴɪᴏɴ ᴄᴀsᴛ ʜɪs ꜰʟɪɴᴛʏ-ᴇʏᴇᴅ ɢʀᴀʏ ɢʟᴀʀᴇ ᴀᴛ ᴛʜᴇ drovers.

That seemed to cow them for a bit, but after Glass had delivered their chili and they were building their sandwiches, their interest in Ilsa appeared to grow again. They cast her lusty glances, elbowed each other, and giggled like schoolgirls. Mannion was going to suggest that he and his two charges leave but just then Glass came out of the kitchen with two large pieces of dried peach pie buried under miniature mountain-sized dollops of rich whipped cream.

Ilsa looked none too hungry anymore, but Mannion doubted he'd be able to cart Sam away from that table with two teams of stout Missouri mules.

Glass replenished Mannion's coffee cup and supplied the boy and Ilsa with fresh glasses of milk. Still, the drovers were giving the girl unwanted attention. But then three more men in range gear galloped up to the road-house. These three had come from the south whereas the others had come from the north. King, likely having been distracted by a rabbit and having left the yard, didn't let out a peep.

Mannion was not happy to have three more men in the roadhouse. They, too, would likely fall under the girl's spell, and that might very well erupt into something not only unseemly but downright dangerous.

The men dismounted, tied their horses, beat their dusty hats against their chap-clad thighs, and filed up and into the roadhouse, ducking through the door. Mannion was sure their eyes would find Ilsa, who sat maybe ten feet just inside the door. She must have figured their eyes would find her, also, because her own eyes dropped to the piece of peach pie she'd only picked at.

But as the first man entered—tall and dark and wearing a low-crowned black hat—he glanced at the first batch of men at the long table to his left. He looked away then stopped in his tracks and turned back to them again, his dark-brown eyes clouding up suddenly and appearing about to rain.

The blond-haired rider in the first batch, Collie Vernon, had already seen him. Flaring his nostrils distastefully, he said, "Well, if it ain't Blackie Dawson of the Six Bar Cross!"

"And Cap Bringham and that scrawny little coyote, Jasper Reed," said the hound dog-faced drover facing Vernon.

Jasper Reed stopped just inside the door. He really did look like a coyote, Mannion silently, absently opined. All he needed was a gray coat and a bushy tail. Reed screwed up his own face in sudden antipathy and shot back with: "Well, if it ain't that big sissy, Carol Granger— foreman of the Goose Creek Outfit who can't keep his wife to home!"

Jasper Reed clapped his hands and gave a coyote laugh. If coyotes laughed, that was.

Granger turned his thick, square head to the human coyote and balled his small, freckled hands on the edge of his table. "You know I don't go by Carol. I'm Ham—*Ham Granger*, by God. No one but my mother calls me Carol. Leastways, does so and lives to crow about it!" He jerked to his feet, closing one of his small, freckled hands around the handle of the six-shooter hanging low on his left thigh. He was short. Mannion guessed not five seven. But he was as broad as a barn door.

Mannion was about to intervene, try to settle things down, but just then the man sitting to Granger's left wrapped his right hand around the foreman's left one. "Come on, boss. No cold-steel work in such tight quarters. Besides, they're just Six Bar Crossers. They ain't worth a shallow grave."

Granger just snarled as the three Six Bar Cross men laughed and sauntered on past Mannion's table toward a long table on the other side of the room. As they did, the old vaquero polished off his tequila, untangled his long legs, rose from his chair, dropped some coins down beside his empty chili bowl, and strode with strained nonchalance across the room and out the door, keeping his sombrero brim pulled low. Galloping hooves thudded, dwindling quickly to silence.

As the Six Bar Cross men took seats and Glass came out to take their orders, Mannion saw the men from the Goose Creek Outfit casting them the woolly eyeball from their table just ahead of Joe, to the right of the still-open door. There was no love lost between the two outfits, obviously. That was all right. A dustup had been averted and now the men's attention was on each other and not on Ilsa.

The girl, too, seemed relieved.

Suddenly, she was no longer picking at her pie anymore but chowing down on it with nearly as much vigor as her brother, following up every few bites with a large sip of the milk. The milk gave her a white mustache and she turned to Mannion, grinned shyly, and licked it off.

Joe chuckled.

He stopped chuckling when one of the Goose Creek men, a tall drink of water in a black hat and red shirt, glanced over his shoulder to yell at the Six Bar Cross men behind him, "Too bad about your brother, Blackie. Heard he got caught long-loopin' out on the Triple Eight, stretched some hemp, and danced until he kicked out of both boots!"

Red Shirt lowered his head, snickering.

The other Goose Creek men laughed with glee.

Mannion's spine tightened.

While the Goose Creek men chuckled and laughed like schoolboys with a dirty secret, the Six Bar Cross men sitting behind him sat in stony silence.

Oh-oh...

Sensing that Red Shirt might have touched the proverbial match to the proverbial fuse connected to the proverbial black powder keg, the Goose Creek riders let their chuckles and insinuating laughter boil down to silence.

And what a pregnant silence it was, too, filling the room.

Mannion thought he could hear the heart of each man before and behind him tattooing his breastbone with a war rhythm.

It was so quiet that Mannion could hear the screech of a hunting hawk from far in the distance, hear Glass boiling jars in the kitchen behind the counter to Joe's right, and humming softly.

Sam and Ilsa sensed the danger. They'd stopped eating. Each holding his or her fork above his or her plate, they stared at Mannion, the cast of imminent danger in their eyes. Joe didn't blame them. He sensed it, too—sensed that he and his young trail companions were about to get caught in a whipsaw of fast-moving lead.

He turned his head to one side and glanced behind him.

Good thing he did, too, because just then the Six Bar Cross rider whose brother's demise had been made ghastly fun of by the red-shirted Goose Creek rider just then leaped to his feet so quickly that his chair went flying back against the wall behind him.

"How dare you malign my brother, you gutless orphan of a moaning whore!" he screamed.

"*Down, children!*" Mannion bellowed, slamming both his hands palm open on the table before him then hurling himself to his right, throwing out one arm to hook it around Ilsa's shoulders, driving her backward to the earthen floor.

In the corner of his left eye, he saw Sam, giving a horrified yelp, throw himself from his own chair an eyewink before Blackie Dawson brought up two long-barreled six-shooters and began blasting away at the Goose Creek men, his bullets slicing through the air where Mannion and his two young charges had been sitting a half a second before.

Screaming and shouting and the thunder of more guns filled the room until Mannion, covering Ilsa's head and shoulders with his own upper body, felt as though open palms were being slammed against both his ears, making them ring painfully. The earthen floor reverberated beneath him with each room-jarring blast. He glanced up to see a heavy curtain of smoke billowing. Through the smoke, at each end of the room, men were doing bizarre death dances, screaming and cursing, gun flames stabbing through the smoke with each thundering report.

There was a screech of breaking glass, and Joe peered to his hard left to see one of the Six Bar Cross riders—Blackie Dawson himself, he thought—fly backward through the window at that end of the room, both black eyes wide in shock and exasperation as he fired his left-hand Colt into the floor just before he dropped out of sight and was gone, bullets barking off the window frame and adobe wall around him.

The shooting continued for another ten or fifteen seconds, but it was quickly dwindling to sporadic bursts accompanied by the thumping of heavy feet, agonized groans and sighs, and the thumps of bodies striking the floor.

"Ah, hell..." a man sobbed.

One more shot and one more thump and then...silence.

The rotten egg odor of gun smoke was heavy in Mannion's nose.

He lifted his head and looked down to see Ilsa staring up at him in horror, her mouth half open.

Mannion looked to his left. Two bodies lay in twisted, bloody heaps under the heavy cloud of billowing smoke.

He looked to his right. More bodies lay twisted in bloody heaps under the heavy cloud of billowing smoke at that end of the room, as well. Some lay on the floor. Others lay slumped on the table or over chairs. One man lay over an overturned chair just behind where Sam had been sitting at Mannion's table. The man held a gun in the hand hanging over the seat of the chair. The gun just then slipped from dead fingers to drop to the floor with a heavy thud.

The man who'd been holding it gave a deep, final sigh and slid off the chair to the floor.

Outside came the quick, light thumps of padded feet. The thumps grew louder until King stood in the open doorway, peering in, ears pricked, whining.

Heavier thuds rose from the direction of the bar.

Mannion saw black boots moving toward him, the cuffs of deerskin trousers jostling around the boot tops. The boots stopped before Mannion, who looked up to see Clayton Glass scowling down at him from his Indian-dark, craggy face framed by long, stringy, salt-and-pepper hair. The road ranch proprietor's long-barreled, double-mawed Greener rested on his shoulder.

"Now that," he said, jerking his head to indicate one side of the room and then the other, "is a god-awful waste of good chili!"

———

HOLDING BLACKIE DAWSON BY HIS ANKLES STILL peppered with glass from the window he was shot out of, Mannion helped Clayton Glass carry the dead cowboy over to the side of the roadhouse and dropped the man down with the others they'd dragged out from inside.

Sam and Ilsa stood nearby, holding their horses' reins, watching the two men dubiously, scowls of revulsion tugging at their mouth corners. King stood between them, edgily shifting his weight between his two front paws.

Mannion glanced at them and sighed.

He wondered if the sister and brother would ever get

over the carnage they'd seen since Sam had made the gargantuan mistake of saving Bloody Joe Mannion's raggedy hide.

He looked at Glass who, breathing hard from exertion, stared at the dead men lined up along the side of the roadhouse, some of their eyes open, some half open, some closed. Already, the flies had found them, swirling around the fresh blood on their clothes.

"That accounts for a good quarter of my clientele, right there," the roadhouse proprietor complained. "Just last weekend, three others from two other outfits went down."

"You need to pick up and move to friendlier range, I reckon," Mannion suggested, lifting his hat and running a hand through his sweat-damp hair. They'd hauled nine men out of the roadhouse and another, Blackie, from around back. That was a job of work for a man his age, and with that bullet-torn side kicking like a mule.

He couldn't have refused his old friend the help, though. Glass was older than he was, and he didn't have anyone else to help. Since his last wife had run out on him, he'd been working alone out here. Business was not good, however, Mannion silently, vaguely, bemusedly opined, staring down at the line of bloody cadavers. No business was good when its customers kept shooting each other.

Glass shook his head and spat to one side.

"Well, Clayton," Mannion said, setting his hat back down on his head, "I'd best get a move on." He cast one more cautious glance along his back trail, wondering if Trainor had heard the shooting and was on his way to investigate. If so, he'd likely have shown by now, but Mannion didn't want to linger. He and his charges needed to get on up the trail and find a sheltered place to hole up for the night. There weren't too many more hours of good light left.

At least their horses were rested.

Glass stuck out his hand to him. "Farewell, Joe. Like you always say, keep a finger on your trigger and one eye..."

"On my back trail," Mannion said, smiling. He pinched his hat brim to his friend and began striding over to where Red was still standing at the hitchrack with the ten other, now-riderless horses. Glancing over his shoulder at Glass, he said, "What're you gonna do with all that horse flesh, Clayton?"

"I reckon they'll go back to the ranches they came from...as well as this fresh beef out here." Glass looked down at the dead men. "Eventually, someone will miss 'em...come lookin' for 'em." He kicked a foot of one of the dead and added, "Even these cork-headed tinhorns will be missed by someone."

Mannion removed his reins from the hitchrack and swung up into the saddle. He couldn't quash a droll chuckle. "Until next time, my frie..."

He let his voice trail off.

He'd just seen a sun flash atop a near ridge not far away on his back trail. It was the kind of glint you see off a lens. Maybe off a pair of binoculars or a spyglass. His pulse quickened. "Until later, my friend," he said quickly, then glanced at Sam and Ilsa and said, "Let's ride, you two!"

He reined Red around and put the steel to him. Sam and Ilsa glanced at each other with concern then, casting cautious glances over their shoulders, booted their own mounts after Mannion and the bay. As all three riders galloped out of the yard and King went running and barking after them, Glass turned his own cautious gaze to the south. Not seeing anything, he shrugged and strode back into his roadhouse and closed the door.

Not long later he opened the door again, this time only about a quarter way. He peered out as seven riders galloped on past the roadhouse and continued up the trail toward where Bloody Joe and his two young charges had gone.

Glass sighed and wagged his head. "Go with God, Joe. Children. Go with God..."

He closed the door and set to work mopping up blood.

CHAPTER 20

PEERING BETWEEN TWO ROCKS WITH HIS FIELD GLASSES,
Mannion watched the two sets of riders converge in the
wash below him and roughly sixty yards away, nearly
straight west. Zeke Trainor and another man, thickset
and with muttonchops sitting astride a black and white
pinto, conversed as dust rose around them. Both men as
well as the five others looked around; their expressions in
Mannion's field of magnetized vision were of deep frustration.

Mannion glanced at Sam lying flat against the ridge
beside him, and then at Ilsa lying just beyond her
brother. "We confused them," he said, then lifted the
glasses to his eyes once more. "Let's just hope they stay
confused."

He watched as the riders rode around, some
appearing to argue, one man speaking forcefully to
Trainor then swinging an arm up and out, pointing
directly north. Trainor looked at the other men then
booted his dun north, beckoning the others to follow,
which they did. All seven riders disappeared behind a
sloping, rock-littered, cedar-stippled escarpment, and

then they were gone, only their dust settling behind them.

Through the field glasses, Mannion grinned.

"They took the bait."

Earlier, when he was sure that it was Trainor on his trail, Mannion, the boy, and the girl had split up, converged, then split up again, riding in circles and then taking separate routes to the ridge they were now perched on. Mannion had ridden a good half a mile north before swinging west toward the ridge on which Sam and Ilsa had been waiting for him. The land around here was rocky; it did not take a track well.

That was why Trainor had followed Mannion's more legible trail to the north. When Joe had swung west, he'd covered his route by tying a pine branch to his saddle and letting it drag along the ground, wiping out his tracks.

Sam looked at Mannion hopefully. "Maybe that will be the last of those son of—"

"Sam!" Ilsa admonished him, her dark eyes cast with the warning of a bar of soap stuffed in his mouth.

Sam looked at her then back to Joe and amended his phraseology to, "Sons of...sinners." He gave a weak, nervous smile.

Mannion chuckled. He peered back through the glasses, spying no more sign of the wolves on his trail. "Let's hope," he said. "I need to get you both to Del Norte safe and sound."

He really did. He had to admit to an earlier reluctance to totally scour Trainor from his trail, when the man needed killing in the worst way possible. But now he only wanted to get Sam and Ilsa to safety. When he accomplished that task, he would ride back, track Trainor down, and kill him.

It was the only way he could be sure he'd no longer harass the McDowells.

Besides, a man like that—more goat than man, who'd abandoned his family to go after stolen loot and a girl he had no claim to and who wanted nothing to do with him, one he'd tried to rape only days before, no less—just plain needed killing.

Mannion peered west. They were in the southeastern foothills of the San Juan Range. He wanted to climb a little higher, ride into more rugged country, making it even harder for Trainor to trail him. Of course, since the man knew that Joe was heading for Del Norte, he might just ride ahead and wait for him, maybe make his play before Joe and his charges could reach the safety of the town itself.

A possibility Mannion would have to deal with when the time came.

For now, he wanted to concentrate on keeping Sam and Ilsa away from the man and the six devils he had riding with him.

He cased the glasses and rose. "Come on," he said. "We'll stop soon, but I'd like to get another hour of riding in while we can."

Wearily, for it had been a long day made even more trying by the shootout and carnage at Glass's Castle earlier, the three of them climbed into their saddles. King ran along beside them as Mannion led the way through a crease between two haystack buttes, heading for a darkening, forested slope dead ahead, to the northwest. On the other side of that slope were several old mines, one of which he'd holed up in when he'd been in this neck of the country chasing three men who'd escaped a jail wagon after murdering the two deputy U.S. marshals driving the contraption. One of the lawmen had made it to Del Norte and to the stoop of Mannion's office to report the incident before expiring on Doc Bohannon's leather-covered operating table.

A rocky trail curving between steep ridges led to the mines. It was along this narrow trace, filled with cool, early evening shadows while the ridges high above were still carpeted in sunshine the copper of newly minted pennies, they rode a little over an hour later, heading toward the crescent-shaped mine sitting atop a long mound of slag—rock that had been hacked and torn out of the mountain until the veins the miners had been following had apparently pinched out. A steeply sloping mountain littered with rocks and boulders and spiked with pines loomed far above the mine. There was an old mine office shack at the bottom of the ridge, but Mannion remembered the board walls were nearly as thin as paper.

If Trainor should happen to follow him, those walls wouldn't keep his bullets out.

The mine a hundred feet above it would be a safer place to spend the night, and the rocks around the mouth of the mine should conceal a fire. They were high enough in altitude that they'd need one. It got cold up here at night even in summer. Several other mines had been carved out of the canyon walls, but Mannion was heading toward the largest and easiest one to get to.

He led his charges around behind the shack and then up the switchbacking wagon trail as shadows bled out from the canyon's west wall and a cool breeze picked up, moaning softly up among the higher crags overlooking the chasm. Rusty picks and shovels with splintery gray handles littered the rocks along the trail. So did shattered brown bottles and rusted food tins as well as one old, hobnailed miner's boot.

Mannion had heard the canyon had been called Dead Man Canyon by the miners who'd toiled here. They'd believed the men the canyon had claimed—and apparently there had been quite a few due to cave-ins and rockslides as well as mishaps with wagons and mules— still lingered here at night, singing their death songs up among the fluted rocks and natural stone pillars that formed the crags jutting from the circular top of the ridge.

Mannion, not normally the superstitious sort, could believe it.

That breeze did sound like the soft wails of grieving men—dead men grieving for the lives that had been taken from them prematurely.

Ilsa, too, heard the grief in the breeze. As Mannion stopped Red and the girl checked her calico down beside him, she looked around and up toward the ridges jutting above them and down from which the wails caromed. Fear touched her gaze.

"It's all right," Mannion said. "Just the wind."

He had no intention of telling her or her brother what the miners had called the canyon. They had enough to think about.

With a couple of lit matches, Mannion checked out the mine to make sure no other wayfarers were calling it a temporary home. On his previous visit, he'd seen the tracks of wildcats in the area. Deeming it empty, nothing but rock and the rusted rails of the ore cars trailing straight off into the mine's stygian depths, and the stench of the coal oil coating the ancient timber framing, he went out to where Sam and Ilsa waited, holding the reins of their horses.

"We'll hobble the horses inside," Mannion told them, taking up Red's reins. "Plenty of room."

They unsaddled the mounts and gave them each a quick rubdown before draping feed sacks filled with oats over their snouts. Mannion had bought the oats along with a few other trail supplies from Clayton Glass. There was still some wood he'd gathered on his previous visit stacked along one wall of the mine, so they had most of what they needed except for water. Their canteens were empty.

"Sam, there's a spring-fed creek below to the east. Why don't you fill our canteens down there?" Mannion glanced at Ilsa, who stood at the mine entrance, gazing into the darkening chasm below, squeezing her arms as though chilled. "In the meantime, I'll get a fire going."

"You got it, Bloody Joe," Sam said, gathering up the canteens.

He headed out of the mine. Mannion stopped him with: "Best take your rifle."

Both Sam and Ilsa looked at him.

"I don't think we were followed in here, but no point being reckless. Shoot if you have to, son, but only if you have to."

"You got it, Bloody Joe," Sam said, unsheathing his Spencer. He rested the .56 on one shoulder, the canteens' lanyards hooked over his other shoulder, and strode on out of the mine, angling down the slope to the west. In seconds, he was a slender shadow in the gloaming.

In the dark-blue sky, stars kindled as bright as lanterns.

Mannion got a fire going quickly with the dry wood.

He sat down against his saddle, ready to rest after the long day's ride. Ilsa moved to him, holding his whiskey bottle in one hand, a white cloth in the other. He looked at her, frowning.

"I need to take a look at that ear," she said, dropping to a knee beside him.

"It's all right."

"The bandage is bloody. The ear needs cleaning, or it'll get infected."

Mannion grunted. The girl untied the bandage which he'd hastily knotted beneath his chin. Inspecting the ear, she sucked a sharp breath through gritted teeth, making a face.

"That bad?" he asked her.

"That bad."

"Funny, it doesn't hurt much anymore."

It started hurting again when she started cleaning it with the whiskey-soaked rag, despite her touch being gentle. He was more worried about her, however, than he was about his ear. She hadn't said much all day, and she had a faraway look in her eyes.

He reached up and closed his hand around her wrist. "You all right?"

She looked at him, feigned a smile, nodded. "Just tired."

"I'm sorry."

She frowned. "For what?"

"For everything."

"It's not your fault. I know that now."

"That's not what I meant," Mannion said, speaking softly, the moaning breeze doing its best to drown his words. "I'm just...sorry. For all you've been through...seen."

She gave him a dark, level, knowing look. "It's just the way of the world, isn't it?"

Mannion had to admit that it was.

She finished cleaning his ear then wrapped a fresh bandage over it, tying it beneath his chin. She'd just finished the task and was pulling her arms down when they both jerked with starts.

The loud crack of a rifle hammered up the slope from below and to the west.

Ilsa gasped and turned to gaze out the mine portal, where the night had turned nearly as dark as it would. "Sam!"

Mannion heaved himself to his feet and grabbed the Yellowboy.

"Stay here," he said, and took off down the slope, weaving around rocks and stunt cedars.

He stopped when a short, slender shadow moved before him. Fast-moving boots clacked on rock. The boy was breathing hard. As he approached Mannion, the canteens flopping against his side, the lawman said, "What was it?"

Breathless, Sam stopped before him. "Puma! Followed me up from the creek. Think I scared it off, though!"

Mannion winced and stared off across the nearly dark canyon. Only a little dark-blue light remained behind the craggy western ridges.

"Yeah, you likely scared him off," Mannion said, not as worried about the wildcat as he was about the human wildcats on his trail.

Sam stared up at him, reading the concern in his eyes. "You think they heard?"

Running footsteps sounded from upslope. Ilsa ran down from the mine portal, a slender silhouette against the dancing orange flames behind her, long hair blowing in the breeze. King was on her heels, yowling worriedly.

"Sam!" Ilsa cried. "Are you all right?"

"I'm fine, Sis. Just scared off a wildcat's all."

"Come on," Ilsa said, taking him by his wrist and leading him up the slope toward the mine. "Let's get you in by the fire." As she, Sam, and the dog climbed the slope, the girl cast a quick, worried gaze over her shoulder at Mannion.

She, too, was worried about the possibility that the shot might have called in their stalkers.

Mannion strode down the slope past the old mine company office and took a good, long look around. No movement down there. As far as he knew, there was only one way into the canyon, only one way Trainor could access it. But with the wind howling as it was up among the tall crags, he doubted anyone could have heard the shot beyond the canyon.

He was cold, weary, and he needed a cup of coffee.

He climbed the slope and sat down by the fire.

Ilsa had made coffee and poured a cup for her and her brother. They sat close to the fire, absorbing its warmth, King curled between them. The dog looked as tired as the kids did. Ilsa used a leather swatch to fill a cup for Mannion.

"Anything?" she said, handing him the steaming cup, worry in her eyes.

Joe took the cup and removed his hat, setting it down beside him. He sat back against his saddle. "Nah." He stifled a yawn. "I think we're fine."

He'd just taken his last sip of coffee, however, when a man's voice caromed above the wind from the canyon floor. "Hey, Mannion! You prepared to die tonight, old man?"

Laughter.

With a single swing of one foot, Joe kicked out the fire.

CHAPTER 21

MANNION GRABBED HIS RIFLE AND LEVERED A ROUND into the action.

"Oh, my God!" Ilsa said to Mannion's right.

"They heard my shot," Sam said.

"Stay here and stay down," Joe said.

He rose to a crouch, took two steps toward the mine entrance, then dropped to his belly, staring down the steep slope in the darkness. He could see nothing down there but the murk of night. Dark as the inside of a glove down there.

"Tell you what, Bloody Joe!" Trainor shouted up at him. "You send the girl down with the loot, we'll let you an' the boy live. What do you say to that?"

Mannion glanced over his shoulder. He could see the outlines of the boy and the girl sitting in the darkness around the fire from which pale smoke rose from a bed of orange ash. Their eyes were large and round. He thought he could hear their hearts beating above his own, above the spirits of the dead miners grieving on the wind.

Anger rose in him, burning up from deep in his belly.

He set the rifle down before him, cupped his hands around his mouth, and shouted, "*Go to hell!*"

He wasn't sure if Trainor had been able to hear him, with the wind blowing as it was, but then he heard loud, exaggerated laughter caroming up from below.

"Think about it!" the rancher shouted. "You have a few hours to mull it over! If we don't have the girl and the money by dawn, we're gonna come up there and kill you and the boy and *take* the girl and the money. This is the only way both McDowells get out of this alive, Mannion. And you, too, for that matter!"

More exaggerated laughter—Trainor and several other men yipping and yowling like moon-crazed coyotes.

"That tears it," Ilsa said behind Mannion.

She rose from where she'd been sitting by the fire, picked up the saddlebags bulging with loot, draped them over her shoulder and walked out of the mine. She was about to stride past Mannion when he reached up and grabbed her arm.

"What the hell do you think you're doing, girl?"

She glared down at him, dark eyes flashing with ambient light. "I'm ending this once and for all!"

"No, you're not!"

"This is the only way to keep my brother alive!"

"Ilsa, no!" Sam said, walking up behind her. "You can't throw yourself to those wolves!"

"It's the only way, Sam!"

Mannion rose and pulled her back into the mine, back beyond the fire, near where the horses were shifting on their hobbled feet and snorting anxiously. Mannion pulled the saddlebags off her shoulder and tossed them down against the wall.

"Forget it, kid!"

"You think that money is worth my brother's life? Hell, it's not even worth *your* life, Marshal!"

Mannion gave a caustic laugh, staring down at her. "Don't be a simple fool, Ilsa! It's not only the money they're after and you know it. You really think that if they get you and the money, they'll just ride on out of here? They won't! They can't afford to let any of us live. They know they'll be hunted for the rest of their lives!"

"As far as I'm concerned, it's worth the gamble. Even if there's a chance!" Ilsa glanced at Sam standing near the mostly dead fire.

"Forget it," Mannion said. "Not going to happen."

"So—what?" she said, defiantly crossing her arms on her chest. "You're going to shoot it out with them come morning? You're badly outnumbered. Even if you weren't, they're younger than you, and you're wounded. You can barely climb in and out of your saddle!"

"Oh, Ilsa," Sam said, slowly shaking his head.

"Look at him, Sam!" Ilsa threw out her open hand to indicate Mannion. "Your great Bloody Joe Mannion is old and beaten up. He's going to get both of us killed. He's going to get us *all* killed!" She glared up at Mannion. "You're right. My brother should have left you to die in that wash, because now...because of your muleheaded-ness...you're going to get both him and me killed!"

Her voice broke on that last bit. She covered her hand with her mouth then stumbled over to the side of the mine and slumped down against the wall. She raised her knees, tenting her skirt, closed her arms around them, and bowed her head, sobbing.

Sam looked up at Joe. "She'll be all right. She's just... she's just scared."

The boy walked over and sat down beside his sister.

The dog, who'd been taking it all in from the shadows, sensing the gravity of the situation, walked over and lay down beside Sam, curling himself into a tight ball, nose to tail. Sam slid his arm around Ilsa, drawing her against him as she cried.

Mannion gave a ragged sigh.

He walked over to the mine entrance, bent his creaky knees, and got back down on his belly.

He stretched his lips back from his teeth and shook his head.

The girl was right. Not only was he old, he was beaten up. His ear and his side burned like both were on fire. The wounds sapped his strength. He wasn't thinking clearly. As he stared out over the night-dark bowl of the canyon, he castigated himself silently. He'd led the McDowells into a box canyon.

There was only one way in or out.

And Trainor and his men would have it sealed off.

The creek running along the west side of the ridge came out of rock and disappeared into rock.

"Yep, Bloody Joe," he grumbled to himself aloud, removing his hat and running his hand through his hair, pulling at it painfully, "the girl's right. You're gonna get 'em both killed. Good goin', you stupid old fool!"

He slammed his hat down beside him in anger.

He stared down into the canyon. A light shone on the canyon floor, growing gradually. Trainor was building a fire.

He and his men would spend the night in comfort.

Mannion and the boy and the girl would spend the night up here in the chill, howling wind. He couldn't risk a fire. He needed his night vision lest Trainor and his men should steal up the slope and shoot him and the McDowells inside the mine. He had to keep his eyes sharp. He had to watch the slope for moving shadows.

Then what? he asked himself. *You going to shoot it out with seven men come morning, Bloody Joe? By then, after a sleepless, nerve-racked night, you're gonna be even worse off than you are now.*

Worthless.

Behind him, the girl's sobs faded to silence.

Between wind gusts he could hear the boy and the girl breathing deeply, evenly, sound asleep. Anxiety weighed heavy on them, finally exhausting them to the point of unconsciousness.

Something moved in the darkness behind Mannion. The dog gave a soft whine and came up beside him, brushed the tip of his cool, leathery nose against Mannion's cheek then lay down beside him.

"Hello, fella," Mannion said, giving the dog's head an affectionate pat. "You're not mad? Well, you likely don't know what I got you and the kid into—do you?"

He gave a wry chuckle, patted the dog's head again.

Then he turned his head back forward to stare down into the murky depths of the canyon and the lone fire burning down there, the flames dancing to the sway of the wind. He could see the vague shadows of a few men around it. The others were likely spread out, watching to make sure Joe didn't slip down the slope to ambush them.

He considered it but decided he couldn't chance it.

At least a few would stay on night watch, alert for just such a move.

No, Mannion had to hold his ground. At least, it was the high ground.

They'd work around him, though. Eventually.

Yeah, he'd gotten himself and the McDowells in a nice pickle.

He held the Yellowboy on the ground before him, tapping his thumb worriedly against the hammer.

———

ILSA LIFTED HER HEAD WITH A START.

She'd been dreaming that a man's arms held her fast. Long, sweat-damp mustaches rubbed revoltingly against her neck.

Her heart was racing. She drew a deep breath to quell it. Only, it wouldn't quell.

She turned to see Sam resting his head on her shoulder. The boy was breathing loudly through his mouth. His eyes moved behind his eyelids. Ilsa could see them moving because there was just enough light in the cave now. She looked out the mine entrance, over where the lawman lay belly down on the ground, peering out, holding his rifle in his hands.

King lay curled against Mannion's left side. The lawman's hat lay crown up on the ground to his right. His longish, salt-and-pepper hair hung down over the collar of his canvas jacket.

Ilsa looked at the saddlebags lying against the base of the cave floor to her right.

Her heart beat faster.

She looked at Sam. Sound asleep. Their recent trials as well as the long ride wore heavy on him. She turned toward him, placed her hands on his shoulders, supporting him while sliding away from him, easing him onto the cave floor. He murmured but did not awaken.

Good.

Ilsa looked at Mannion again. He lay as before, turning his head slowly from left to right then back again, watching the slope for a possible attack.

The sky to the east was turning light blue. It would be dawn soon.

Ilsa looked around, found a stone a little larger than

her clenched fist, and picked it up. She picked up the saddlebags, straightened slowly, wanting to make as little noise as possible. The breeze had fallen, and the night was quiet.

Ilsa glanced to her right. The hobbled horses regarded her dubiously.

She placed a soothing hand on the calico's wither then stole slowly around the dead fire to the cave entrance. She moved quietly; still, the lawman sensed her approach. He turned his head to stare up at her, frowning curiously.

"What...?"

"I'm sorry, Marshal," she whispered then gave a grunt as she pulled the hand holding the stone back behind her right shoulder then thrust it forward and down.

It smacked soundly against Mannion's right temple.

Mannion's head snapped to one side. He grunted and rolled onto his back, eyes closing, out.

King rose quickly, regarding the girl incredulously, whimpering anxiously. Ilsa glanced at where Sam still lay against the base of the cave wall, snoring softly. Ilsa dropped to a knee before the anxious dog, ran her hand over his head and down his back, trying to sooth him.

"You stay, King. Understand? You stay with Sam." She glanced at her brother. King did then, too, ears pricked. "Stay with Sam," Ilsa repeated, and pointed.

Understanding, the dog trotted over and sat down beside the slumbering boy, whining softly.

"Good dog," Ilsa whispered. She turned toward the steep slope turning gradually lighter as the dawn approached. It was still early. The birds weren't even up yet.

Fear making her knees quake, Ilsa stepped around the unconscious lawman and, adjusting the saddlebags draped over her left shoulder, started down the slope toward where Zeke Trainor and his men waited like silent monsters in the darkness.

———

MANNION SLUMBERED AT THE BOTTOM OF A DEEP WELL of unconsciousness, head aching. A hand nudged his shoulder.

Mannion groaned, then winced. Part of him wanted to awaken and confront what he knew had happened, that the girl had beaned him with the rock. Part of him wanted to stay down here at the bottom of the well and sleep, for sleep eased the pain if only a little.

Besides, the world at the top of the well had gotten far too complicated...

The hand shook him.

"Marshal?" the familiar voice said. Then, louder: "Marshal Mannion, wake up! You have to wake up!"

Mannion flinched as something cold and leathery pressed against his cheek. A dog's nose. The dog whined.

Mannion flung away the clinging arms of unconsciousness and opened his eyes. Sam and the dog stared down at him. Both regarded him anxiously, the dog's ears pricked as he canted his head from one side to the other, probing Mannion's eyes with his own.

"Marshal!" Sam said, giving Mannion another anxious shake. "Ilsa's gone!"

"Ah, hell," Joe said, remembering the determined, defiant look on the girl's face just before he'd seen the stone in her hand.

The one she swung forward with a grunt and smashed against his temple.

He remembered seeing the bulging saddlebags draped

over her shoulder in the half second before she'd brained him.

"Ah, hell," Joe said again, squeezing his eyes closed against the fresh batch of pain racking him, silently cursing his life.

"No," came a distant scream. "You promised!"

The girl's plea helped clear some of the fog from Mannion's brain.

Sam looked out of the cave entrance. The sun was just starting to peak through the gaps in the eastern ridges. "That's Ilsa!" he cried.

Mannion frowned as he stared down the slope toward the canyon floor.

"What the hell?" he muttered.

A rumbling sounded. Mannion felt the ground shudder beneath him.

King whined and backed deeper into the cave. Beyond him, in the mine's deep shadows, the horses stirred, restless, twitching their ears and rolling their eyes up to stare nervously at the cave ceiling above them.

The rumbling grew louder. The ground shuddered more and more violently beneath Mannion. He looked up at the cave ceiling, and a cold stone dropped in his belly.

Louder and louder the rumbling grew. More violently the ground shuddered.

Mannion heaved himself up, grabbed Sam, and flung himself and the boy straight back into the shadows. Both struck the ground and rolled just as rocks and boulders flew down over the cave entrance from above, quickly sealing it up as tight as a drum, filling it with shadows as dark as the darkest night.

The horses screamed.

CHAPTER 22

MANNION OPENED HIS EYES. AT LEAST, HE THOUGHT he did. It was hard to tell if they were open or closed. Either way, all he could see was darkness. Darkness so total it was like the darkness at the bottom of a grave. The darkness of death.

Close against his left side, the boy moved, groaned.

Mannion could hear the horses stomping around and breathing heavily and anxiously. The dog was running around, yipping.

"What...what happened?" Sam asked.

Mannion winced against the throbbing in his head and ear aggravated by his unceremonious meeting with the cave floor. He turned to stare back toward the opening. At least, he thought he was staring toward the opening. The darkness inside the cave was so total it was hard for him to get his bearings.

"Marshal?" Mannion felt the boy place his hand on his chest, just reaching out to check if he was here...and alive, no doubt. They were only inches apart, but they couldn't see each other.

"I'm here, boy." With a grunt and agonized groan,

Mannion pushed off a knee as he heaved himself to his feet.

Behind him, the dog was whining nervously, his claws clacking on the stone floor as he ran around, as frightened as the horses. Mannion couldn't blame him. He had to fight back the panic he felt rising in himself.

There was nothing like the panic evoked by the prospect of being buried alive.

Ensconced inside a mountain behind several tons of solid rock.

"Easy, King," Sam said. "Easy, boy. Come here, come here—can you see me? There you are." The clacking stopped. "It's all right. It's all right." A slight pause and then the boy's voice came again, thinner. "Won't it, Marshal?"

"Not sure." Mannion dug into a pocket of his denims for a lucifer match. He scratched it to life on his thumbnail, held it up and out in front of him.

As he moved forward, the weak sphere of flickering, watery matchlight revealed rocks of all shapes and sizes blocking the mine entrance. Not even a pinprick of daylight shown between the rocks.

Trainor and his men had somehow found a way up onto the ridge. Rather than chance climbing the slope to kill Mannion and the boy, they'd started a landslide from above. Mannion stretched his lips back from his teeth as he studied the rocks. Effective. Damned effective.

He felt as though he was staring at his and the boy's tombstones.

The match burned down to his finger. He dropped it with an "Ouch!" and lit another one. He turned to where he could see the boy's silhouette down on one knee beside the dog, who stood wagging his tail and whining anxiously. The horses flanked Sam and the dog, eyes glinting redly in the light from the match.

The boy said nothing. He was frozen, eyes large as 'dobe dollars.

Mannion knew how he felt. He felt the same way. The stones blocking the entrance were too large to move. Some were boulders. Some looked as though they'd been part of the solid mountain wall and had broken off during the slide to tumble down and turn the mine into a sarcophagus.

Mannion turned back to the boy and the dog. Then he looked at the horses. All three, including Red, appeared on the verge of panic. They couldn't do that. Panicked horses could very well smash Mannion and the boy to smithereens.

The match burned down again. Mannion dropped it, lit another, and stepped slowly forward, passing the boy and the dog, both now silent with shock and disbelief at their predicament. The dog seemed to know as well as Mannion and the boy and even the horses the direness of their predicament.

Mannion approached the horses. "Easy, now, Red. Easy, there, Honey. Lightning...let's just remain..."

He let his voice trail off. He'd seen something back in the mine behind the blowing, stomping horses. He moved forward between the horses, deeper into the mine.

"Well, I'll be..."

"What is it?" Sam asked as Mannion dropped the match and lit another, glad he'd laid in a fresh supply before leaving Del Norte.

"I think I see light back there." Ten feet from the horses, Mannion stopped, squinting into the shadows.

Sure enough, he was staring at a very small glimmer of blue light.

The dreadful beat of his heart was tempered by a faint hope. As faint as that shimmer of what appeared natural light. But it was a shimmer and it was hope, just the same.

He went back and gave Sam a few matches. "Keep one lit until I get back. I'm afraid these horses are going to panic in total darkness."

"You think there's a way out?"

"I'm going to check." Mannion lit another match while Sam lit one of his. The lawman walked back into the darkness beyond the restive mounts. "Keep your fingers crossed."

"Hell, I'm gonna keep everything crossed," Sam said quietly, holding the match in one hand, stroking King soothingly with his other hand.

Mannion's boots crunched on the mine's dirt and rock floor as he walked along the side of the old rails used for trundling out ore cars filled with rock. His spurs chinked softly in the deafening silence.

The light ahead of him grew.

When he'd walked maybe a hundred feet, he stood staring up through a crack in the ceiling. It was as though the mountain had split. Possibly during the landslide. Through the crack, a long way up, he could see the growing light of the morning sky. The crack was too narrow for him to be able to climb up through it. Possibly the boy could make it, but it ran nearly straight up, its sides too sheer for foot- or handholds.

That was all right.

Mannion still felt hopeful. He saw another light shimmer ahead.

Firing matches and holding them high and out before

him, he continued walking deeper into the mine, following a slight bend. More shimmers lay ahead. That meant more cracks. Maybe he'd find one large enough for him and the boy to crawl up through.

He didn't want to think about what would happen to the dog and the horses.

But if he and the boy could find a way out, they'd have to take it.

"Marshal Mannion?" he heard Sam yell behind him, the thin, frightened voice echoing off the mine's stone walls.

"I'll be back soon, Sam," Mannion called over his shoulder. "Keep a match going!"

Again, the mine curved. Then the floor dropped. There were enough cracks in the stone walls and ceiling that he no longer needed to light matches. Down he strode until he rounded yet another bend. More and more light shone before him.

His heart thudded hopefully.

When he'd rounded the bed, he stopped.

Straight ahead, pale blue light shone.

The air was distinctly humid. So humid that it was leaving moisture on his forehead and upper lip. He didn't think it was fear sweat. Also, he could feel a reverberation in the floor beneath his boots, like that caused by a train passing not far away.

"What in blazes?" Mannion muttered to himself, heading toward the light.

It grew before him. It kept growing as did the dampness in the air and the reverberations in the stone floor beneath his feet.

Hope grew in him.

The mine must have a back door!

He found himself chuckling to himself as the mine

walls drew back away from him on both sides. He stopped chuckling, however, when he found himself staring down into the stone bed of an ancient river. An ancient underground river. With the river still flowing through it...

The light came from an open dome high above him.

The mountain must be an ancient volcano. At one time it blew its top, creating the opening over two hundred feet above. Likely during that monumental explosion, the ancient river had shifted course to flow straight through the bottom of the volcano. It curved in through solid rock from Mannion's left and curved out through solid rock to his right.

Where it went, he had no idea.

Maybe deeper into the earth.

On the other hand, he'd heard that Silver Creek had its origins up here in this neck of the San Juans. Maybe this river flowed out of the mountain and into the open to become Silver Creek, one of the few creeks in this area that ran steadily all year long. Its water was notoriously cold, which meant it probably originated from deep underground.

The miners who'd tunneled all the way into the heart of the volcano must have had one hell of surprise. The ore core tracks ended near the chasm the river ran through.

Mannion scratched his neck thoughtfully. He studied the open dome of sky high above him. There was no way up those sheer, stone walls. Possibly no way out on the river either.

But it looked like the river might be his and the boy's only chance.

There was certainly no way out through the several hundred tons of rubble sealing off the mine entrance.

He walked back into the mine and started lighting matches when he got beyond the last crack in the ceiling. He saw a pinprick of flickering orange light before him, and then he saw the silhouettes of the horses. Beyond the horses, Sam knelt as before beside the dog.

"I might have found a way out," Mannion said. "Don't get your hopes up yet. I said *might*. And it's gonna be chilly." He walked over to Red and crouched down to remove the hobbles. "Bring your match over here."

Sam did as he'd been told, holding the light up so Mannion could see to remove the hobbles. When the lawman had removed Red's hobbles, he removed those of the other two horses, as well, while Sam held a lit match aloft.

"Ilsa..." Sam said, shaking his head slowly while Mannion removed the second hobble on the girl's calico. "She...she..."

He knew what had happened. He'd heard her scream. But it was too awful for him to give words to.

"Don't worry, boy," Mannion said, stuffing the hobbles into his saddlebags. "We'll get her back."

Sam held the match a little higher and sucked air sharply through his teeth, looking up at the goose egg rising on the lawman's left temple. "She gave you a good one, didn't she?"

"Yep," Mannion said, brushing his hand across the throbbing egg. "Yes, she sure did." He placed his hand on the boy's shoulder. "She was trying to save both you and me. She just didn't realize Trainor wouldn't keep his word and let us go."

He drew a deep breath. "Come on, boy." He handed Sam the reins of Lightning and Honey. "Let's see if we can find us a way out of here."

They kept matches lit as they made their way through

the darkest part of the mine then stopped firing matches to life when they saw the crescent-shaped slice of daylight growing ahead of them.

"Is that *outside*?" Sam said, voice pitched with astonishment and promise, pointing.

"Not exactly," Mannion said. "But it's close...I'm hoping."

And then they were standing on the lip of the canyon through which the silver-blue river coursed, ten feet below. The three horses and the dog settled down considerably, being out here in the open with the sky yawning overhead. King looked down at the river and barked and wagged his tail.

Sam looked at Mannion, frowning. "I don't get it. How we gonna get out of here?"

"The river, I'm thinking."

"I had a feelin' you were gonna say that."

Mannion chuckled dryly. He sobered suddenly and turned to the boy. "It's chancy. I'm thinking that river surfaces and becomes a creek above ground. On the other hand, I might be wrong."

"Meaning..."

"It might not surface but go deeper."

Sam looked down at the water and gulped.

King yipped worriedly, dropped to his belly, looked down at the water again, and panted. The horses were looking down at the water, too, twitching their ears and switching their tails.

Sam turned to Mannion. "That water looks mighty cold."

"Sam," Mannion said, not wanting to sugarcoat their situation. "We might not make it."

Again, Sam looked at the water then looked up at the

lawman again. "We don't have any choice but to try, though, do we?"

"No."

Sam sighed and shook his head.

Then he led Lightning over to a rock and used the rock to step into the left stirrup. He looked down at King and patted his left thigh. "Come on, King. You'd best ride with me."

The dog barked and leaped up into the boy's lap, settled himself across the pommel of the saddle.

Mannion climbed up onto Red's back, gigged the stallion up close to the lip of the canyon. Red looked down at the water then lifted his head and shook it.

"Oh, come on, boy," Mannion said. "We both need a little adventure in our lives!"

He laughed. Even to his own ears he sounded insane.

He could very well be leading both him and the boy, all three horses and the dog to a deep, watery grave.

He turned to Sam. "You ready?"

Sam stared dreadfully down at the silver-blue, churning water. "No."

"Yeah—me, neither." Mannion touched spurs sharply to Red's loins. The bay gave a defiant whinny then lunged ahead and over the edge of the canyon and into the river.

CHAPTER 23

THE COLD WATER CLOSED AROUND MANNION'S LEGS and over his lap, the bone-splintering chill instantly sucking the air out of his lungs.

He lifted his chin and gave a raucous howl which echoed off the arching stone walls that closed around him as the stream's insistent current shepherded him and the bay downstream and into the cavern the stream had carved out of the earth over the ages since the volcano had erupted.

Behind him, he heard a scream and turned to see the boy and the thoroughbred arc down off the stony shoreline and into the river. The water came up over Sam's saddle, and King rose to his feet, looking incredulously down at the water swirling around him, threatening to flood the saddle horn. The boy had led the calico down off the bank, and the poor beast hit the water, its eyes as large and round as silver dollars. Both it and the black whinnied shrilly as the current grabbed them and shoved them down to where darkness closed over and around Mannion as the stream took him into the earth's stony bowels.

"Oh, Christ...Oh, Christ," the lawman said, gritting his teeth against the cold that grew even more severe as he was swept under those low-arching walls.

Darkness enveloped him and for a long time he couldn't see Red's head only a few feet in front of him. Between and below his cold, numb legs he felt the horse's large heart beating quickly, powerfully, heard the poor beast snorting as he fought to keep his head above the waterline.

"You out there, Marshal?" Sam yelled somewhere behind Mannion.

"I'm here, boy," Joe returned, teeth clacking. "Just hold on tight and enjoy the ride!"

He could hear King yipping fearfully.

The darkness around him was complete. So complete and for such a protracted time Mannion was beginning to believe he had, in fact, killed both himself and the boy, consigned them to the earth's stony, watery bowels for the ages...until a dim light appeared ahead. The light must be coming from around a bend in the river channel because it shifted to the left and grew.

It continued to grow until Mannion and Red were swept right on through a slanting pillar of sunlight. The current swept them so quickly through it that, peering up, Joe got only a quick glimpse of sky far above, at the end of the natural flue carved through the ground.

Then he was in darkness again. That brief glimpse of sky had given him hope but that hope began to die again until more light shone ahead, just above the level of the water, as he felt the river slanting down ahead of him and Red, who was blowing hard now, frightened, cold, and exhausted. Behind Joe, he could still hear the tinny, frightened barks of King. The dog and the two horses and the boy were maybe thirty or forty yards behind Mannion and the bay.

Mannion glanced over his shoulder, hoping Sam was still in the saddle and hadn't been swept off. "Sam!" he yelled.

The response came several seconds later, in a voice quaking with the cold. "H-here! I'm...st-still here!"

"M-ore light ahead, s-son," the lawman said, his own voice quaking as badly as the boy's. "Hold on. There's...a lot...a lot more!"

It was true. The light was now dead ahead of Mannion now, maybe a hundred yards distant. It continued to grow as the current quickly closed the gap between horse and rider and the light. Sunlit ridge walls appeared on either side of the stream, also glistening with morning sunshine.

It was an exit into open air!

"Damn near home free, boy! Hold on!"

Sam gave no response.

The ceiling of the river channel pulled back behind Mannion and suddenly he was out in the raw sunlight, a blue sky yawning above him. If he hadn't been so cold, he would have laughed with delight.

As the river continued pulling him along its winding bed, the walls to each side spread out and lowered. Sagebrush and cottonwoods stippled each shoreline. There was a jarring as Red jerked beneath Mannion, who was nearly thrown forward over the horse's head. Grabbing the horn with both hands, the lawman realized the jarring came from the fact that the horse's hooves were on the bottom of the river; Red was fighting to get his balance and to stand.

He stumbled forward, shivering. He fell to his knees, whickered, then gained his feet again and clomped over toward the shore on the right side of the stream.

"Good boy, Red!" Mannion said, patting the horse's left wither. "Good boy!"

He was shivering so hard he thought he could hear his bones clattering, threatening to splinter. As the bay approached the low bank, Joe glanced over his right shoulder. Sam's thoroughbred was just then stumbling into the shallow water on this side of the river. The calico was about twenty yards behind them. Sam was slumped forward in the saddle, head down. He appeared unconscious. King stood on the boy's lap, gazing at the shallow water and yipping excitedly. The dog, too, was shivering.

Just then, King leaped down from the saddle, splashed into the river that came up to his shoulders, and ran the rest of the way onto the bank, where he turned and barked back at Mannion and the boy.

Red leaped up onto the bank that rose about two feet above the water.

Mannion was so wrung out, all his muscles seemed to give out at once and he stumbled down the stirrup of his saddle, hitting the ground on his right hip and shoulder before rolling onto his back and groaning. Shivering violently, he lifted his head. The black was just then climbing up out of the water. As it did, the horse lowered its head and shook, and Sam went flying out of the saddle to hit the ground with a yelp.

King ran around him, yipping anxiously.

Sam did not rouse or even open his eyes.

Mannion needed to get over to him, try to rub some life back into his near-frozen body. Try as he might, however, he could not move except to lay there and shake.

And cajole his foolishness.

He might have got them out of the mine but only to die from exposure.

While he lay there, shaking, and King sat beside the boy, staring down at Sam as though to will him awake, Mannion heard the drum of hooves and the rattle of what sounded like an approaching wagon. Teeth clattering, Joe turned his head to see a covered wagon approaching along a trail that ran parallel to the stream.

Two big, black birds with white rings over their foreheads appeared to be on the driver's seat.

Mannion blinked his eyes and shook his head as though to clear his senses.

Then he looked again as one of the blackbirds drew back on the reins of the cream horse in the wagon's traces, yelling in what sounded a like a female human's voice: "Whoa, there, Leo. Whoa! Whoa! Who-ahh! *That'sss* a boy!"

No, not blackbirds, Mannion realized now.

Nuns in black habits blowing out around them in the breeze, the black cloth glinting in the sunshine. Two plump, round-faced nuns—one younger, one older.

"Our mighty Father, Sister Agatha," exclaimed the younger nun riding to the left of the older one. "One looks dead and the other one looks *close*!" She shifted her gaze between Mannion and the still unconscious Sam and the dog, who had gained his feet to stand protectively over the boy, head down, eyeing the two women warily.

"Indeed, Sister Trudy," said the older nun, setting the brake and wrapping the ribbons around the handle. "I think we've a couple of bodies as well as souls that need saving. I'm a little out of practice with saving bodies, but it can't be any harder than saving souls—now, can it, Sister?"

"I guess we'll just have to find out!" said the younger

nun as each lady clambered down from the driver's seat, the older one on the side nearest Mannion, the other one on the opposite side. Both women were big, and the covered wagon shifted precariously.

Mannion glanced at the wagon itself.

On its cream canvas cover was stenciled in large, black letters:

SISTER AGATHA AND SISTER TRUDY'S HOLY BLESSING TRAVELING SHOW.

Beneath that, in smaller letters:

WINE BLESSED BY POPE PIUS THE VIII ON SALE!

"Grab blankets out of the box, Sister!" commanded Sister Agatha, hiking up her black skirt above her black ankle boots and black wool socks as she trundled heavily, huffing and puffing, over toward where Sam lay resting on his side, the dog standing over him. "Many blankets—the heaviest we have! Oh, this poor child!"

King raised his hackles and showed his teeth, at turns growling and barking.

Sister Agatha raised her stout arms and waved her hands wildly, palms out. "Away, you cur! Away!"

Sister Agatha appeared a right formidable foe—given her size and attire. Mannion could see her heavy breasts and round belly jiggling behind the habit. Apparently, King could, too. He gave only one more half-hearted bark then slinked away to sit in the brush at the edge of the stream, mewling.

"Oh, Heaven help this child!" Sister Agatha said, dropping to her stout knees beside Sam. "Dear Father on

His throne, bless this child. He has turned blue, and I don't think he's breathing!" She leaned down to press her ear to Sam's chest, lifted her head, and sighed with relief. "He's breathing! Oh, Father, you've heard my plea!"

Immediately, she started unbuttoning the boy's checked shirt that clung to his body like a second skin. She pulled the tails out of his black wool trousers, drew his suspender down his arms, and pulled the shirt off the boy's skinny body. As Sister Trudy clambered down from the wagon's open tailgate and ran, also huffing and puffing —she wasn't quite as large as Sister Agatha, but she was close—Sister Agatha said, "We must get them out of their clothes, Sister. They are soaked to the skin. We must get them out of their clothes, dry them with the blankets, and build a fire or the Heavenly Father will certainly have two new angels this day!"

She glanced at Mannion with a critical eye, her fleshy face acquiring a dubious look. "At least, the boy would be accepted into the Father's Kingdom. I'm not sure about that one. He has a questionable look about him and look at those two big pistols!"

"An outlaw, you think, Sister?" Trudy had dropped a pair of heavy blankets down next to Sister Agatha and was hurrying over toward Mannion, frowning down at the big, shivering man.

"If I was a bettin' gal," Sister Agatha said with a grunt and a shake of her head, making her jowls quiver, "I'd lay money on it."

Sister Trudy dropped to her knees beside Mannion, scowling down at him. "What on earth were you doing in the river? That water's so cold the fish you catch in it are half frozen into July!"

Mannion tried to answer but his teeth just clacked together.

"Oh, for Heaven sakes," intoned Sister Trudy. "Let's get you out of those duds, big man. You've nearly caught your death of chill!"

Like Sister Agatha had just done to Sam, Sister Trudy managed to skin Joe out of his clothes as though she'd performed the maneuver many times before. He wasn't much help because he was shivering too violently. All he could manage by way of helping was to sit up and then roll over as, standing at his feet, Sister Trudy gave a loud grunt and stripped him out of his denims and tossed them aside.

She had him down to his birthday suit a minute later and knelt beside him again, rubbing him brusquely with the blanket, starting with his hands and then his shoulders and back and chest and belly and sundry other areas. Mannion was glad to see that Sam stirred under Sister Agatha's ministrations. The boy pushed up on his elbows and looked around bewilderedly, staring incredulously from Sister Agatha to Sister Trudy to Mannion and then back again.

He was still shivering too violently to speak.

When Sister Trudy got Mannion dry and wrapped a fresh blanket around his shoulders, he managed to get out: "M-much obliged, ladies...er, Sisters," he amended, glancing at the wagon again.

"What were you doing in the river?" Sister Trudy asked him again. "Don't you know that's the coldest river on Earth?"

Mannion doubted it was that. But he had to admit it was damn cold.

"Long story," he said, holding the blanket taut around him.

"I'm sure a very interesting one, indeed," Sister Trudy said, sharing a dark, suspicious glance with Sister Agatha.

Both women returned those suspicious glances to Mannion.

He gave a grim smile and continued shivering.

"Sister Trudy," Sister Agatha said. The older nun was gathering wood among the cottonwoods standing along the stream. "Fetch the devil's elixir from the wagon. It is strictly for medicinal purposes, however," she said while shooting Mannion another castigating glance, "but should warm their blood if taken in sparing amounts." Looking at Mannion again, the older nun said, "I take it only when my rheumatism is acting up."

Mannion gave another grim smile, not having any of it. Something told him Sister Agatha swilled the "devil's elixir" like an Irish gandy dancer at End of Track on Saturday night. He glanced at Sam and winked. The boy, now holding King across his lap and using an end of his blanket to dry the chilly dog, gave a smile. His lips were still blue, but some color appeared to be returning to his cheeks.

Mannion's belly warmed when he saw Sister Trudy returning with a bottle from the wagon. It warmed him even more when the rotgut churned its way through his bowels, bringing at long last a flush to his face.

When the two nuns—he wasn't sure they were actually nuns, possibly con artists posing as nuns traveling around the territory selling supposedly wine blessed by the pope—had gathered wood and built a large, hot fire, he thought he'd died and gone to Heaven.

But by that time enough blood had run back to his brain that he cast his gaze back into the mountains from which he and Sam had come.

What of Ilsa?

CHAPTER 24

"No!" Ilsa cried. "You promised!"

Zeke Trainor closed his hand over her mouth and drew her fast against him. He laughed in her ear then nuzzled her neck. Her stomach churned with revulsion as she felt those long, scraggly mustaches slithering like large caterpillars against her neck.

She returned her gaze to the top of the mountain the mine was in. After she'd handed over herself and the loot-stuffed saddlebags to the vile rancher, he'd given some sort of unspoken signal to two of his six men who climbed into their saddles and rode off along the base of the slope to the west. Ilsa hadn't known where they'd gone. Now, she did.

There must be some secret route that Trainor and his men knew about that gave access to the top of the mountain, likely from the backside. Now those two men each waved their rifles high above their heads and stepped forward, kicking several large rocks off the lip of the ridge and down over its face. As those rocks rolled, they slammed into many other rocks perched precariously against that steep slope, and rolled, knocking even more rocks down ahead of them.

Soon there was the sound of near, rumbling thunder as more and more rocks were slammed free of the slope and went rolling until Ilsa found herself staring in horror at a landslide.

Not just a landslide but it appeared, before the billowing dust grew too thick for her to see through, chunks of the mountain's face gave way in large, jagged slabs, tumbling and rolling, hammering snapping pines and cedars growing out of cracks in the stone face as they did...

...and creating a larger and larger pile at the base of the mountain, piling up thick and high over the mine's black, egg-shaped entrance and scattering across the slope below, as well. Trainor's men had moved to the slope's far east side where a stone dike protected them from the tumbling rocks. Rock dust boiled up on the other side of that ridge.

Ilsa's heart raced, then fluttered.

She found herself sobbing into Trainor's rough, calloused hand.

Joe Mannion and her brother were buried inside that mountain. Forever.

She'd never see Sam again. Not King. Not the horses. But more importantly, Sam.

Ilsa's knees buckled, and Trainor pulled his hand away from her face as she dropped straight down to the ground. She lifted her chin and glared up at the horse-faced man with those long, revolting mustaches hanging down past both sides of his mouth. "You promised! You're a bastard and a liar and I hate you more than I've ever hated any man in my life, and if I get the chance, I will kill you, Zeke Trainor!"

Trainor stared down at her, laughing, showing his large yellow teeth beneath the mustache.

"Well, you're not gonna get that chance, darlin'." He glanced at the four ranch hands standing around him. "Fellas, we'll split up the loot as soon as Calhoon and McCluskey get back down off the mountain. In the meantime, I'd appreciate a little privacy."

He laughed again, grabbed Ilsa by an arm, jerked her to her feet, and half dragged her back into the rocks and brush beyond where the men's horses were hobbled. The mounts regarded her and the rancher with dark, dubious eyes. When Trainor dragged her back to where his men waited, smoking as they lounged around on their tack or on rocks, her right eye was swelling, and blood trickled from a burning cut on her lower lip. Her blouse was torn, and her skirt was badly disheveled and soiled.

The experience had hollowed her out. She was in too much shock to even cry for her brother...for herself. For what Trainor had so violently taken from her.

"We get turns, boss?" asked one of the rancher's men as Ilsa slumped down against a tree, keeping her eyes on the ground, feeling like a whipped dog.

"You know you don't," Trainor said, refreshening his coffee at the fire they'd built. He looked at Ilsa. "She's mine an' mine alone. We split the loot and vamoose, go our own separate ways," the rancher added.

"What about May?"

Trainor chuckled as he blew on his coffee. "What about her?" He sipped, chuckled again. "Me an' the girl are headin' to Mexico, see how things play out down there. You boys might want to figure on that yourselves. Bounty hunters are gonna be combin' this country for that loot." He kicked the saddlebags. "Especially after Mannion don't return to Del Norte."

"What's this I hear about Mexico?" asked one of the two riders who'd just ridden up, reining in a few feet from Trainor, Ilsa, and the rest of the men at the fire.

Trainor looked up at him—the ugly redhead with one unmoored eye whom Ilsa had heard called Calhoon. The short, broad-shouldered, ham-faced blond man sitting the pinto beside him was McCluskey.

"Nice work, boys. You just put an end to the life of the famous Bloody Joe Mannion. Climb down and pour yourselves a cup of well-deserved coffee. Then we'll split the loot."

"What about the girl?" the stocky man with bushy muttonchops asked, cutting a look at Ilsa. He was Trainor's foreman, Walt McClory. "Can we split her, too?"

He had to be forty, at least.

Trainor narrowed a peevish eye at him. "We done hashed that all out, too. We split the loot evenly, just like we agreed. Then we split up, go our own separate ways... or down to Mexico, which might be the smartest thing for all of us." He looked at Ilsa. "The girl's mine...till I get tired of her, that is."

"What if you get tired of her before you get to Mexico?" another man asked. He grinned as he blew out a plume of cigarette smoke.

"Then she goes to the highest bidder," Trainor said. He cast his goatish gaze to Ilsa again. "I done already had her and, truth to tell, she might be purty to look at it and fills out her blouse right well, but she wasn't all that much fun."

One of the men whistled. The others laughed.

Ilsa felt like a turtle, wanting to retreat into her shell. She drew her head and shoulders down, drew her elk hide jacket tighter around her, and ground a heel of one foot into the gravelly ground. She felt beaten down;

Trainor had savaged her soul from her. Still, she looked up at Trainor from beneath her brows. He was grinning, leering down at her. She vowed right then and there to kill him.

She hardened her jaws, narrowed her eyes in barely bridled fury.

Yes, Trainor would die. He would die hard, very painfully.

For Sam. For Marshal Mannion. For King and the horses.

And for her.

Her resolve almost made her smile.

"Oh-oh," said Calhoon. "Better look out for her, boss. She looks a tad angry." He chuckled and sipped his coffee.

Trainor stared down at her. There was a faint change in the cast of his gaze. Something besides goatish victory and the thrill of having humiliated someone weaker than himself in his eyes now. Apprehension? Yes, however vague. Apprehension. He'd have his guard up around her now.

As though to dismiss the uncomfortable feeling, Trainor chuckled then lifted his cup again to his lips and sipped.

Ilsa looked at the knife sheathed on his left hip and smiled inwardly.

———

MANNION TIPPED THE BROWN BOTTLE OVER HIS smoking coffee cup and watched the light-amber liquid pour from the lip to mix into the rich blackness of the coffee. He could practically smell the gunpowder and rattlesnake venom added to give a little kick to the rotgut. He swirled the cup gently to mix the coffee and the whiskey then held the bottle up to look at it.

No label on it, of course.

"Sister Agatha," he said, narrowing one eye suspiciously to gaze across the blazing fire at the older nun sitting directly across from him, sipping a cup of her own coffee mixed with the skull pop, "you don't distill this yourself, do you?"

He turned his head slightly to one side, challenging her truthfulness.

The flush that came to her smooth, plump cheeks gave him the honest answer he was looking for though she slapped a hand to her mouth, glanced at the younger Sister Trudy perched on the same log as she and exclaimed, "Oh, gracious Father in Heaven—certainly *not*, Brother Mannion! A Catholic nun, a Sister of our savior Jesus Christ, distilling *likker*?"

Sister Trudy's cheeks colored, as well, and she averted her eyes. She held a cup of coffee not "sweetened"— Sister's Agatha word—with the Who-Hit-John.

Mannion gave a wry snort then held the bottle over toward where Sam was still shivering beside him, as close to the fire as he dared get without risk of being turned to black ashes. The dog, King, sat a little farther back from the fire but very close to the boy, just off Sam's right elbow. The Sisters had wrapped a striped trade blanket over King and each of the three horses, grazing nearby where the nuns had hobbled them, also had blankets draped over them.

Bless the beasts and the children...as well as an irascible aging lawman.

By now, Joe and Sam had introduced themselves.

He and Sam had set their wet clothes on rocks

around the fire, which was so hot, the duds were already nearly dry.

"Here you go, boy," Mannion said, tipping the bottle over the tin cup of coffee steaming in Sam's hand, "let's sweeten your mud a little. It carries a wallop, but it will melt the frozen marrow in your bones." He chuckled as he added a liberal portion of the busthead to Sam's brew. "It's making mine as light as maple syrup on a warm June afternoon."

Both nuns gasped in shock.

"Praise be to the Father in Heaven, Marshal Mannion," Sister Trudy intoned. "Giving the devil's elixir to a mere *child?*" Then she looked at Sister Agatha and said, "Oh, well, I suppose since it's only medicinal. Though you use it, Sister Agatha—sparingly. And it will warm him."

Sister Agatha flinched a little at the insinuating, vaguely castigating tone in the younger nun's voice.

"Yes, yes, of course," said Sister Agatha, taking a sip of her own liberally sweetened brew. "As long as it's only medicinal and used sparingly," she told Sam with a commanding look in her brown eyes set shallowly in doughy sockets. "The operative word here is *sparingly*, young man." She cut a quick, furtive—sheepish?—look at Sister Trudy sitting beside her. "Don't let it take hold, though, or you'll come to nothing!"

She turned to Mannion and softened her tone. "Not that you've come to nothing, Marshal. I mean, well, Sister Trudy and I have certainly heard of your famous exploits, helping civilize the wild western frontier with a commanding hand…"

"And blazing six-guns," Sister Trudy added then instantly flushed as she raised her cup to her lips. She sipped her coffee and said, "I mean…that is what the novelists call it, is it not? I believe I might have read a story or two about you...over the long winter, of course. Just for something to do."

It was her turn to cut a sheepish look at Sister Agatha, who gave an ironic chuckle.

Mannion cut a quick look at Sam and smiled. Sam returned the smile over the steaming rim of his coffee cup. Neither nun was quite as innocent nor pious—should we say "sinless"?—as they let on. That much was obvious. But Mannion didn't doubt that they were nuns. Maybe three-quarters nun and one-quarter con artist, but their hearts were generally in the right place. He didn't doubt that Sister Agatha had a still somewhere in these mountains though he did doubt their wine was actually blessed by the pope.

Oh, well. They needed to bring in a few dollars now and then, just like everyone else. Nuns had to eat, too. He didn't doubt they preached a good sermon to the unwashed masses. At least, such sermons couldn't hurt. Everyone needed a finger shaken in their face from time to time.

Mannion sipped his coffee and, holding his blanket close about his shoulders that he was beginning to feel again, along with his fingers and even his toes at long last, cast his gaze to the nuns on the other side of the fire once more. "Tell me, Sisters, what brings you to this far-flung neck of the San Juans?"

Sister Agatha hooked a thumb to indicate the covered wagon sitting behind her. "Just like it says—we travel around the frontier, spreading the Father's word." She crossed herself and kissed the silver cross hanging down over her heavy breasts.

"As well as our patented elixirs," Sister Trudy

muttered, snidely, then quickly lifted her cup again to her lips.

Sister Agatha flushed again and cast the younger nun a look of growing intolerance.

Changing the subject quickly, Mannion said, "How did you get here, exactly? I didn't even know there was a trail on this side of that mountain." He jerked his head back to indicate the cone-shaped mountain looming behind them and out of which they'd spilled on the underground stream which apparently became Silver Creek in the San Juan's lower, southeastern reaches. On his many travels through the range, he'd never seen the stream before. He had not, in fact, ever even seen it on a map.

"We found it quite by accident," said Sister Trudy. "We were looking for a shortcut between Orion to the south and the mining camp at the base of Mount Eagle."

"We got lost one day a few years ago," said Sister Agatha, "and happened upon a rocky, two-track trail that climbs up out of the valley below and angles across the stream then nearly straight north to Eagle. It's shorter and easier, as we were happy to discover, than the newer freight road that crosses Picnic Gulch."

"Shaves a good day and a half off our trip," Sister Trudy said.

"We certainly never expected to find anyone swimming in the river!" exclaimed Sister Agatha with a dry laugh. "You never did tell us, Marshal, what on earth you and young Sam and your horses and that poor dog were doing in there!"

King gave a little whine, as though he'd been wondering that very thing, then dropped forward to lay flat on his belly, cozy beneath his red-striped, yellow blanket.

"Sisters," Mannion said, tapping his thumb against the brim of his cup, "we ran into a bit of trouble." He shared a dark glance with Sam. "Trouble that's going to pull us out of here just as soon as we both think we can ride!"

CHAPTER 25

"OH, DEAR FATHER," TRUDY SAID, CROSSING HERSELF and kissing her crucifix after she and Sister Agatha had heard Mannion's and Sam's story. "That poor girl!"

"What she must be going through right now," added Sister Agatha, dreadfully shaking her head. "Those jackals. I'm certain each one wears the sign of the beast!"

"That tears it," Mannion said, taking a deep drink of his lukewarm coffee and looking at Sam. "You ready, boy? Feel all your fingers and toes?"

King looked at him, wide-eyed, eager.

"I can feel most of 'em," Sam returned. "But it don't matter if I couldn't. We have to get on them toughnuts' trail. We have to get Ilsa back!" He set his coffee down and whipped his blanket off, giving a sudden, near-girlish yell when he remembered that under that blanket he was as naked as the day he was born.

He covered himself back up with the blanket and turned to the two nuns, flushing.

Mannion chuckled. "Ladies, uh..."

"No need to be bashful, boys," said Sister Agatha. "As you both know, we done already seen you both in"—she turned to Mannion and he could have sworn the smile that came over her face and the glitter in her eyes were the result of one of the seven deadly sins—"all your glory!"

She gave a ribald laugh, throwing her head back, then quickly covered her mouth with her hand.

"*Sister!*" Trudy admonished the older woman.

"Oh, all right," relented Sister Agatha. "Sister Trudy and I will head over to the wagon and pack you fellas some food for later. Sister Trudy shot a deer yesterday. We roasted the whole thing up and have far more than we need, so we will be happy to share with our traveling brothers...and the girl, young Ilsa. I do hope you track those animals down and get her back safe and sound!"

"You two ladies are far more than generous," Joe said. "We appreciate everything you've done for us—Sam and me."

"We sure do," Sam agreed.

King rose and barked across the fire at the two nuns. They laughed, heaved themselves to their feet, and trundled off toward their wagon.

When they returned with a small burlap food sack, Mannion and Sam had dressed and were saddling their horses.

"This should do you for both supper and breakfast tomorrow morning," said Sister Agatha, handing Mannion the pouch, which he accepted and stuffed into his war bag.

He turned to Sister Agatha, placed his hands on her shoulders, and pressed a tender kiss to her forehead. "Ladies," he said. "Again, we can't thank you enough."

He stepped over to Sister Trudy whose pasty cheeks turned crimson when he gave her the same treatment he'd given Sister Agatha.

"Thank you, Sisters," Sam said. He led Lightning over to a rock which he used to assist his climb into the saddle. He pinched his hat brim to the nuns, who each blew him a kiss and said they'd be praying for all three of them.

Mannion swung up onto Red's back. The marrow in his bones was still chilled, and his temple still ached where Ilsa had brained him. Still, his physical ailments were paltry compared to his concern for the girl. His own daughter, Vangie, had been kidnapped by savage men led by one who had a bone to pick with Mannion, so Joe knew what she was probably going through at that very moment. He couldn't reach her fast enough and kick each one of her assailants out with a cold shovel.

He waved one final farewell to the nuns, swung around to get his bearings, intending to ride up onto the south side of the mountain the mine was—or *had been*—in and try to pick up Trainor's trail. He and Sam gave their mounts the steel and they and Honey rode off toward the rough country rising in the southwest, King running along behind them, barking.

It was already late in the day, the orange ball of the sun was starting drop in the west, but Mannion wanted desperately to pick up the jackals' trail before dark so he and Sam could get an early start after them in the morning.

———

LATE IN THE AFTERNOON, ILSA LOOKED BACK OVER HER shoulder toward the mountain that had claimed the life of Sam and Marshal Mannion. Farther and farther, it fell back behind her as Zeke Trainor's coyote dun chewed up the trail. Ilsa rode behind the gutless killer, her hands firmly tied behind her back. His six men—six flat-eyed, soulless accomplices to murder, including the stocky, granite-faced Walt McClory—rode behind her and Trainor. They'd been on the trail for several hours now, after the men and Trainor had divided up the loot. They spoke casually, sometimes boisterously, their moods buoyant now with so much filling their saddlebags.

It was likely far more money than any of them had ever seen at one time in their lives. They were ranch hands no more. Now they were free, moneyed men heading to Mexico to cool their heels, as the saying went. Following their former boss who had the crowning trophy—Ilsa herself.

How long Trainor would keep her for himself was anyone's guess.

During the long ride, Ilsa had occasionally heard them muttering furtively behind her. Their tones had been menacing and she'd caught them glancing at her sharply, pointedly as they'd spoken, making her believe they were plotting to get her away from Trainor.

She'd never felt more miserable. More desperate.

More filled with anguish at the death of her dear little brother.

It wasn't Mannion's fault. At least, she no longer blamed the lawman. It wasn't Sam's fault either. Sam had done the right thing by saving Mannion. If it had been her in that wash where Sam had found the injured lawman, she'd have done the same thing. There'd been nothing else she could have done, just as there'd been nothing else Sam could have done.

At least, not done and been able to live with himself.

Of course, he'd still be alive, most likely, but what kind of living would that have been—knowing he'd let a defenseless man die to save his own hide? And his sister's hide.

No, Sam had done the right thing.

What a good, sweet boy he was. *Had been.*

Ilsa lowered her head now as sorrow exploded in her once again, and tears again streamed from her eyes. She convulsed, sobbing.

"Shut up," Trainor said.

Anger nudged aside the grief and she stared at his broad back. Sweat basted his shirt to his skin across his shoulders and down along his spine nearly to the small of his back. She could smell the revolting odor of the man. She'd had to smell it for hours now, had had to endure it while he'd ravaged her earlier, chuckling in delight as he'd humiliated her, rubbed those sweaty mustaches against her cheeks and neck.

"Why?" she said. Then, louder: "Why?"

Keeping his head forward, Trainor chuckled. "Why what?"

"This. All of it. Why did you kill my brother and the lawman? You didn't have to do that. You promised you wouldn't do it. And you did it even after I turned myself and the money over to you!"

She could barely restrain the fury inside her. She clenched her tied wrists behind her back and hardened her jaws, staring up at the back of the rancher's neck. She hated herself, though, as much as she hated Trainor. She'd been a fool. She was the one who'd gotten Sam and Mannion killed. There it was. The clear, cold thought that had been lurking in the murk of sorrow and horror inside her.

She was a simple fool. There was no other way to look at it.

If she'd stayed in the mine, not struck Mannion with

that rock, they'd have at least had a chance. But she'd taken all chances away from them, gotten her brother and the lawman killed in the bargain.

"Your mistake," Trainor said as though reading her mind. She could hear the grin in his voice.

"You have a family."

"They'll get along fine without me."

"What kind of a man are you?"

"A tired one. Tired of riding the range from sunup to sundown. Tired of brushpopping stupid calves. Tired of digging post holes. Tired of every damn thing about ranching and listening to my kids fight and whine, tired of a wife who maybe...just *maybe*...will say six words to me throughout one whole day!"

They rode in silence for maybe ten of the coyote dun's strides and then he added, testily, "She lost her looks after the kids were born. Was never any damn fun even before." He gave a caustic chuckle.

"Earlier was better? Taking me by *force*?"

Again, he laughed. "Yeah. Kinda was."

"You really are an animal, Trainor."

"Stick an' stones, girl."

Ilsa glanced behind her. The six other men rode easily in their saddles, chatting, occasionally glancing at her with goatish glints in their gazes, making her skin crawl.

"Better watch your back, Trainor."

"What's that?"

"Better watch your back. That's all I'm saying."

Trainor turned his head to cast a glance at the wolves flanking him. A dark cast passed through his eyes. He turned his head forward again with a nervous chuckle and kept riding.

"Keep your mouth shut or I'll pull you off this hoss and slap you silly."

Ilsa smiled as she stared up at the back of his neck, red behind his suntan. She'd gotten to him. He'd be nervous now, his attention diverted.

Again, she looked at the big knife sheathed on his hip.

She tried pulling her wrists apart, but they were firmly tied. If only she could work them free.

What then? she asked herself.

Again, she glanced at the six wolves trailing behind her and Trainor. One of them glanced at another one and laughed. Trainor turned his head to peer behind him again.

I best be careful, Ilsa thought. *Or I might just find I've leaped out of the frying pan and into the fire.*

But then she spied movement on a low ridge on her left.

She turned to see a half dozen men, silhouetted against the sky over there, sitting horses at the top of the ridge, staring toward Elsa and her captors.

"Hey, boss," said one of the men flanking her and Trainor.

Trainor glanced behind him. The man who'd spoken turned to the riders silhouetted atop that distant ridge. "Take a look," he said.

Trainor turned his head to stare east. Softly, he cursed.

"Law, you think?" asked one of the others.

"Or bounty hunters, maybe," Trainor said.

"By now, news of the loot and Mannion's disappearance has likely traveled far and wide," said yet another man, darkly.

"And now they see we got a girl with us," remarked another man, insinuation if not cold accusation in his voice.

One of the others cursed.

Several glanced at Ilsa. If she'd been a turtle, she would have pulled her head into her shell. She had no shell, however. Nothing. And her hands were tied.

She hadn't thought she could be anymore terrified than she already was, but she'd been wrong.

But then the six riders turned their horses and dropped down out of sight on the other side of the ridge.

"Hmm," said a man named Hawkins. "Maybe they're just cowpunchers."

Hope lightened Ilsa's heart. But just a little.

"Maybe," Trainor said. He glanced at the men behind him. "Keep your eyes skinned. They might try to work around us, set up a bushwhack."

He booted the dun ahead.

Ilsa held a silent vigil, sitting there behind Trainor, grieving, tending her fear, and keeping a close watch on the cactus-stippled desert around her. The six men did not show before Trainor and his men stopped for the night on a low ridge from which they could keep watch on the country around them and which was partly sheltered by cottonwoods and rocks.

Trainor hauled Ilsa down off the dun's back and shoved her down against a tree. He produced a length of rope from his saddlebags and moved back over to her, paying out the rope between his hands and scowling owlishly down at her.

"You're going to tie me to this tree?" Ilsa said, disgust in her voice. "My hands are tied behind my back. How far would I get if I tried to run away, and where would I go, anyway?" She looked around and gave a dreadful shudder that was only partly feigned. "There's likely wildcats out there...and those men."

Trainor stared down at her, his eyes dark beneath the

wide brim of his weathered Stetson. His men were unsaddling their horses behind him, regarding him and Ilsa with mute interest. The appearance of those six other men had done one thing for her—they had taken her from the center of Trainor's men's attention. For the last two hours, they'd been focused more on the terrain around them and a possible ambush than on her. Those six possible bounty hunters seemed to still be foremost in their minds.

Trainor spat to one side and nodded. "All right. You're a smart gal. You run off an' you won't last more than a couple of hours on your own." Especially with her hands tied behind her back, he did not have to add. "When we get the horses tended, I'm gonna free your hands. You're gonna cook." He glanced at Walt McClory, grinned, and said, "Since we got us a girl now, she might as well cook— eh, boys?"

He seemed to be trying to get back in their good graces. That comment of Ilsa's earlier had shaken him, she was glad to see. He'd keep his men away from her and think more about them...of possibly getting a bullet or a knife in his back...than her. That might give her an opening to stick his own knife in his back if they were far enough away from the others and she saw a possibility of getting away.

Tall odds, as a gambler would say, but she had to find some way to survive.

She'd bide her time. When she made her move, it had to be a good one, with a good chance of getting free of these killers. She couldn't outrun these men or their horses, of course, but she might be able to hide and then slip away when they gave up on her. How much time would they waste trying to hunt her down?

They were wealthy men now, and they were eager to

get to Mexico. She was nothing special. Trainor might have thought she was and had coveted her but now that he had her, he would tire of her quickly. He'd enjoyed raping her, because that was the kind of man he was—more animal than man—but how long could that last?

Certainly, he realized she couldn't ever feel anything for him. He'd killed her brother and abused her terribly. But who knew how men thought? Certainly not her.

The others chuckled as they laid out their tack in a slight clearing in the cottonwoods and rocks.

When they'd laid out their gear, ambled off to tend nature and returned, Trainor posted three pickets to keep an eye out for the possible bounty hunters. They'd picketed the horses close, and the mounts would give the alert to possible trouble. Trainor and two men gathered wood and built a fire. Then the rancher cut Ilsa free and ordered her to get to work cooking supper even though their stores were sparse, mainly fatback and beans.

Ilsa didn't care. She wasn't hungry.

Besides, as she cooked in front of these men, she grew more and more nervous.

Trainor tried to keep up a playful tone with the men. But she sensed a growing tension between the rancher and his former hands, who couldn't keep from eyeing her lustily. It didn't help that they passed a bottle.

Sooner or later, Ilsa knew, the tension was going to snap.

Trainor's men were going to make a play on him. She could tell that he knew this, as well, because all night he constantly followed his men's glances to the target of their obsession—her. They might have been concerned about the six men they'd seen earlier, but now they were drinking and sitting comfortably around the fire, and their minds were straying back to the young woman Trainor wanted for his own.

Ilsa doubted he would relent and turn her over to them.

He was far too stubborn for that, and prideful. By relenting, he'd give up his position as their leader. Besides, he genuinely wanted her for his own. At least, for now.

Ilsa only picked at her food. She knew she needed to eat, to keep her strength up, but could not. Just looking at the food made her sick to her stomach.

After it was good and dark, Trainor got up from where he'd been lounging against his saddle, drew more rope from his saddlebags, and walked over to where Ilsa sat back against the tree.

"Time to tie you for the night," he said.

She dreaded saying it, but she had to. Her bladder was splitting at the seams. She feared he'd use the opportunity to drag her off and ravage her again. On the other hand...

She glanced at the knife on his hip.

Her nerves were stretched thin.

She had to make her play. She doubted that she would survive the night amid these barbarians. Trainor's men would kill him, and then they'd kill her, though they'd likely take their sweet time doing it...

Panic grew inside her.

She had to make her play.

"I have to make a nature call," she said.

CHAPTER 26

TRAINOR SIGHED. "THAT AGAIN."

He glanced at Walt McClory sitting by the fire just then adding some whiskey to a cup of steaming coffee. "Take her out. Not far. And keep an eye on her. But not *too* close an eye." He narrowed one of his own eyes, threateningly.

The thickset, stocky McClory frowned up at Trainor. The order surprised him as it did Ilsa.

"You sure you want me to do it?" McClory said, glancing at the other two men sitting around the fire, firelight and shadows dancing across their sun-seasoned features.

"I'm sure," Trainor said, tossing the rope down beside Ilsa. "When you get back, tie her good and tight to the tree."

He removed his hat and ran a hand through his hair as he walked over and sank down against his saddle. He lifted his coffee cup and took a sip. He looked off into the night. He was more concerned about keeping his guard up than taking his pleasure with his captive. That disappointed Ilsa. Again, she looked at the knife on his belt. What she wouldn't give to slide that blade up between his ribs. Then run like hell. She knew not where, but she had to run or she doubted she'd make it through the night. If she would happen to make it through the night, she doubted she'd make it through another one.

Standing awkwardly, she regarded McClory. He was only a little taller than she was. She gave him her back, showing her tied wrists. "Untie me."

The foreman glanced over at Trainor. "Do it," the rancher said, and took another sip of his coffee. "Then tie her again...tight."

"You got it, boss." McClory slid his own bowie from the sheath on his belt. The blade glinted in the firelight. He slid it between her tied hands and sawed through the rope. Her wrists came free. Rubbing the blood back into her hands, she glanced at Trainor then started moving off through the trees, McClory following.

"You mind your p's and q's, girl," Trainor said. "If you try anything...and I mean *anything*...what's happened to you so far is gonna seem like a Fourth of July rodeo."

Again, Trainor sipped his coffee. The others chuckled.

Ilsa moved through the rocks and trees, descending the slope toward the dark plain opening below the ridge. She was starting to wonder if maybe Trainor wanted her to try something, so he'd have an excuse to give her to his men for the punishment he'd threatened. To throw them the meat they so desired so he wouldn't have to keep looking over his shoulder. She wouldn't put it past him. Now with bounty hunters possibly shadowing him, he had more important concerns than slaking his lust with her. She was becoming unwieldy baggage.

"That's far enough," McClory said. "Get down to it."

Ilsa stopped, glanced behind her, past the silhouette

of McClory toward where the fire flickered in the rocks
and trees at the top of the ridge.

"If you don't mind," she said, testily, "I'd like to go a
few more feet. You stay there."

"Only a few more. Like Trainor said, don't try
anything."

"Oh, please...what would I try?" she said.

She moved off down the slope for a few more feet
then stepped behind a large rock. Her heart was beating
like a war drum against her breastbone. Her hands were
sweating.

Now was her moment of truth. Could she do what
she needed to do even though her chances of success
were nearly nil?

She had to try.

Before sundown, she'd seen a small canyon angling
along the base of the ridge. If she could reach that ravine,
she might be able to run and hide. Surely Trainor
wouldn't spend much time looking for her. Not with
those other men possibly shadowing him. No, he'd leave
her to the wolves.

The thought made her shudder. She'd rather be killed
by actual wolves than at the hoggish hands of her wolf-
like captors. The latter would take too much pleasure
with the task, and they'd take their own, sweet time. She
might not die for hours.

As she looked around nervously, Ilsa peered into the
darkness around her. Once she'd finished with McClory,
she'd have to avoid the three men Trainor had sent out to
keep watch. She'd work around behind McClory, slide his
knife from its sheath, stick it between his ribs, and...

The crunch of a stealthy footstep sounded
behind her.

A shadow slid across the ground on her left.

She gasped but before she could turn around, a rough, thick hand was pressed across her mouth from behind. She was thrust harshly forward. She struck the ground on her belly, the full weight of the man on top of her. Her nose filled with the rancid stench of the man's breath as McClory said, "Cry out and I'll gut you like a pig. You just lay there an' enjoy it—understand? Then not one word—"

He gave a startled cry, and then his head rose up and away from Ilsa's left cheek.

"No!" he chortled. "Boss, I'm sorry, I didn't—"

That sentence was cut off by a strangling sound. Ilsa twisted around to see McClory on his knees, straddling her. Trainor stood behind him, holding his head up by pulling back the collar of the man's shirt. Stray light from the fire on the ridge glinted on something in Trainor's right hand, down low by his side. It glinted redly. Then, as McClory continued to choke and strangle, Ilsa saw the oily black line of the cut curving across his throat. The man held both hands to his neck, as though trying to stem the flow. Elsa felt the warmth of it spurt across her cheeks.

A horrified scream exploded out of her.

Slowly, McClory lowered his hands to his sides. His eyes rolled back in his head so Ilsa could dimly see their whites. Trainor pulled him back by his collar and released him. McClory flopped back down on the ground beyond Ilsa's outstretched feet, quivering as he died.

"Oh, my God!" Ilsa cried, kicking, trying to get away from the dying man.

She didn't realize she'd heard footsteps down the slope on her right until a man's shadow appeared in the darkness and the man's voice said, "What the hell happened?"

Other men were running down from the top of the ridge.

Trainor casually reached down to clean the blade of his bowie knife on McClory's canvas trousers. "Our cuts of the loot just got bigger," he said and gave his sardonic laugh.

Ilsa stared at him in exasperation.

He'd anticipated McClory would try to attack her. He'd even wanted him to. Killing him was Trainor's way of reestablishing his position as cock of the walk—a man not to be messed with.

And, like he'd said, now he and the others would split McClory's share of the loot.

———

A LITTLE AFTER NOON OF THE NEXT DAY, MANNION lay belly down at the crest of a ridge and adjusted the focus wheel on his field glasses.

When the field of magnified vision became one clear circle, in that circle the images of six horseback riders clarified as they made their way at an angle down a low, rocky ridge roughly three hundred yards away, ahead of Mannion and Sam, slightly east. They were a roughhewn, motley collection of men on good-looking horses. Well-armed men. Rifles jutted from saddle scabbards on their tall, rangy horses.

"Bounty hunters," Mannion said as he continued staring through the glasses. When the riders reached the bottom of the ridge, they swung straight south, heading toward a trough between two more desert ridges. "They're shadowing Trainor."

"You sure, Bloody Joe?" Sam asked, lying belly down to Mannion's left.

Mannion nodded. "I recognize the lead rider. I'd bet the seed bull he's Milo Philpot. The man riding behind him is Hedrick Gregoire. Broad as a bard door, red-haired son of a...scoundrel. Somehow, they got on Trainor's trail. Six men riding south with well-filled saddlebags. They're thinking Trainor has the loot."

"He has the loot and my sister," Sam added, darkly.

"Don't worry—I haven't forgotten about Ilsa, boy."

Sitting on the other side of Sam, King cocked his head, pricked his ears, and whined.

Sam turned to Mannion. "I hope we can get Ilsa away from those savages before they come up against the bounty hunters. Don't want Ilsa takin' a bullet...if she's even still alive," he added, his tone filled with dread.

"She's alive," Mannion said. Philpot's men had just disappeared from sight, so he lowered the glasses. "One of Trainor's men, likely Trainor himself, is riding double. I can tell by the deeper impressions of that horse's shoe prints. As of a couple of hours ago, anyway, she was still alive."

Mannion and the boy had picked up Trainor's trail at the base of the ridge Trainor had caved in on the mine, believing they'd literally sealed the fates of Joe and Sam. They believed Mannion was dead, so they hadn't bothered covering their tracks. Mannion had followed them for the past day and a half. He believed he and Sam were only an hour behind them.

They were close.

He had to make his play for the girl before the bounty hunters did.

Philpot didn't appear all that much in a hurry. He and his fellow man hunters were likely going to let their prey get well into southern New Mexico, out on more open ground, before making their play. Here they were in the rough country off the flanks of the Black Range quartering on Mannion's left—all dikes, mesas, haystack buttes, and canyons. Too hard to keep their prey in sight and try to get ahead of them. They'd wait for open ground and then swing around them, try to get ahead of them, and ambush them before Trainor's men even knew what was happening.

Philpot was an experienced man hunter, known for his savagery, and that's what Mannion would do if he didn't have a girl to rescue from Trainor's clutches. Tonight, the lawman would make his play. Trainor was down to a total of six men. Earlier that morning, swirling turkey buzzards had led Mannion and Sam to where one of Trainor's men lay on the side of a ridge, near their previous night's cookfire, with his throat cut, eyes picked out by the carrion eaters.

Mannion had wondered what had gotten the man killed.

He still wondered.

He had an unpleasant feeling Trainor's men were fighting over Ilsa.

He'd try to get her out of Trainor's camp tonight. How he'd do that without getting her killed, he had no idea. He hoped something came to him soon.

He crawled back down away from the crest of the ridge, cased his glasses, donned his hat, and rose.

"Come on, boy," he said. "We're gonna close the gap between us and your sister. Tonight, we're gonna get her back."

"Yes!" Sam said.

King must have understood. At least, he understood the boy's excitement and no doubt figured out what it was for. The dog likely missed the girl every bit as much as the boy did.

Wagging his tail, he followed Mannion and Sam down to where they'd ground tied their horses. Mannion dropped the glasses into a saddlebag pouch, mounted up, and reined Red back toward the southwest, where he and Sam had left the kidnappers' trail. They picked it up again without problem. A couple of hours later, as the sun sank low in the west, hovering just above the Arizona desert and darkly limning the sprawling formation of Black Mesa, Mannion stopped Red.

He left the horses and the dog with Sam, shucked his repeater, and scouted ahead on foot.

There was only an hour of light left. He was betting that Trainor had stopped for the day. He wanted to find out where the man had set up camp without riding right into it.

He followed their horse prints to within view of a clearing in sycamores and cedars along the bank of a shallow wash. A high mesa rose on the left of where Mannion spied the faint, orange glow of their cookfire. The wash lay to the right. It was broad with little cover, so anyone approaching from that direction would be in danger of being seen.

The mesa made approach impossible from the left.

Mannion studied the layout from the lip of a canyon that made approach from his current position also impossible. He'd have to backtrack, circle around, and follow the wash.

Trainor likely knew the bounty men led by Philpot were on his trail. He'd likely have posted pickets, and all six of the kidnappers would sleep with one eye open.

Mannion cursed under his breath and squeezed the Yellowboy in his hands.

He had a job of work cut out for himself this night.

He had to try to steal into the camp as quietly as he

could and free the girl without any of Trainor's men knowing. He couldn't go in shooting at risk of getting Ilsa drilled.

He had to get her back. He owed both her and her brother that much.

Anxiety tightened the muscles between his shoulders. The last time he'd been as nervy about a situation was when Vangie had been kidnapped by cutthroats led by the son of rancher Garth Helton and Mannion and his oldest deputy, Rio Waite, had tracked them to the road ranch they'd held her in.

Dangerous. Damned dangerous.

It didn't help that Philpot was out here somewhere, too.

Mannion looked around, hoping the bounty hunters hadn't spotted him. No sign of them, though. Philpot was experienced. He was likely keeping well out of sight. Joe just hoped the bounty men hadn't spied him and Sam on the kidnappers' back trail the way Mannion had spied them, the bounty hunters.

"Yep, damn dangerous," Mannion said, crabbing back between two rocks. He'd lay low until more darkness had settled over the desert. Then he'd make his move.

"Damn, damn dangerous."

CHAPTER 27

WHEN THE SKY WAS SPRINKLED WITH A MILLION glittering stars, Mannion made his move.

He'd been lying belly down on the ground for over an hour, so at his age he was stiff as a board when he finally rose and, moving quickly, staying low, holding the Winchester low so the breech wouldn't reflect the starshine, he headed in the direction of the wash. He skirted the canyon's southern tip, walked through relatively flat, rocky ground then up and over a low knoll. The stars gave enough light to see where he was going and to avoid kicking rocks and possibly giving himself away to the bounty hunters.

He had no idea where they were camped. They likely had no fire, just as Mannion ordered Sam not to light one either. Trainor had a fire. Either he didn't know the bounty hunters were trailing him or he was confident in his ability to fend them off if they should come calling. Likely, he'd posted those pickets Mannion had to be concerned about.

Once over the knoll, the lawman had to cross a hundred-yard stretch of open ground. Being out in the open on such a starry night made his skin crawl. He could walk up on the bounty hunters' camp at any moment. He strode quickly, purposefully, casting his cautious gaze around him, often snitching the air for the smell of horses, possibly cigarette smoke.

Thankfully, he found no sign of Philpot's men.

When he reached the lip of the wash, he heaved a relieved sigh though he knew the danger was far from over. The wash wound up near Trainor's camp. He should be able to see the fire soon. He slipped over the lip of the wash and cursed when his left boot struck soft ground. Part of the bank of dirt and gravel gave away. He lost his balance, fell on his left shoulder and sighed, and rolled twice, losing the Yellowboy, which struck ground with a clatter.

He gritted his teeth against the pain in his left side.

He rose quickly to a knee, castigating himself with: "You old, lumbering son of a bitch!"

He picked up the Yellowboy, held it across one knee, and looked around, pricking his ears, listening. The night was silent. Not even a hunting nightbird's shriek.

When he was as sure as he could be that he hadn't been heard, he rose and moved south along the broad wash, clinging to its left bank and keeping his head low, just below the lip of the bank. He moved slowly now, one quiet step at a time, wincing when he heard the grating of sand and gravel beneath a boot. He had a good half a mile to cover. Impatience nettled him, but he kept his tread slow and quiet, casting his gaze far ahead, probing the darkness with his gaze then looking toward each bank, then behind, making sure he hadn't been flanked.

From ahead came a sour stench. Mannion stopped.

At the same time, there was a growl and a snarl and then the quick tread of padded feet. Something moved ahead of him, sliding out from behind a rock hugging the base of the left bank. There were quick, raking breaths then two yellow lights appeared maybe fifteen feet ahead. Around the lights, which were the animal's eyes reflecting the starshine, he could see the gray-brown fur of either a coyote or a wolf. The outline of the beast's large, square head and the stiff triangles of two pricked ears shone in the darkness.

Ah, hell, Joe thought, instinctively aiming the Winchester out in front of him. *This could be over right here and now if this beast attacks me...*

The animal—likely a wolf, judging by the size— raised its lips. The white line of the teeth shone. Mannion was about to lever a live round into the Winchester's action when the wolf growled, gave a mewling yip, then turned and dashed off across the wash. It was a shadow climbing the far bank and disappearing into the brush.

Joe heaved another relieved sigh and removed his hand from the Yellowboy's cocking lever.

The wolf had smelled human and decided it didn't want to tangle tonight.

Mannion was about to continue forward but stopped when footsteps sounded ahead along the wash. Joe dashed forward and quickly dropped down behind the rock, pressing his left should against the bank, sort of half sitting on it, his boots in the wash.

"What the hell was that?" a man's voice said, quietly, as though to himself.

The crackle of gravel under boots grew louder.

The smell of cigarette smoke touched Mannion's nostrils, faintly.

It grew stronger as the bootsteps grew louder.

They stopped suddenly on the other side of the rock.

"Ah," the man said. One of Trainor's pickets. "Dead deer. Pee-*you*!"

More cigarette smoke. Then the crunch of footsteps came again but dwindled gradually as the picket drifted back up the wash.

Joe heaved himself up off the side of the wash, stepped to his right, and cast his gaze around the rock. The picket's shadow moved in the darkness, heading around a rightward bend. Mannion stepped out from behind the rock and moved quickly forward, wanting to catch up to the man. He passed the dead deer—he couldn't see it but he sure could smell it—and quickened his pace, following the curve in the wash, staying very close to the left bank, hoping the thick shadows there would hide him from view.

He stopped suddenly.

He could see a yellow, pulsating glow just ahead and up the bank on his left.

Trainor's camp.

The picket had stopped where a thumb of rock jutted out from the wash's left side. A scrawny tree grew up from the base of it, partly concealing the figure of the picket outline silhouetted against the fire's distant glow. Mannion could see the starlight reflecting off the breech of the man's rifle, which he held close against his right side, maybe clamped under that arm.

Pale smoke wafted around the man's head.

The man gave a luxurious sigh. There was the sound of water trickling onto the ground. The man sighed again.

Quickly, Joe took his boots off and moved ahead in his stocking feet, wincing against the string of gravel and thorns against the soles of his feet. He moved up to the rock bulging out from the bank. He leaned his rifle against the rock, unsheathed the bowie knife on his left hip, took in his right hand, and stepped out from behind the bulge of rock and the scrawny tree.

The man was so close, Joe could smell the sour odor of his water.

The knife slid smoothly into the man's back, skidding off a rib. Mannion lowered the hand and shoved the blade up into the man's heart while at the same time thrusting his left hand forward and closing it over the man's mouth, muffling his groan. He removed his hand from the knife just as the man's rifle began to slide out from under his right arm. Mannion grabbed the rifle as he stepped back and eased the man's spasming body down to the ground.

He set the rifle down on top of him.

The man stared up at him, blinking frantically, and then he gave a soft groan and lay still.

Mannion looked around. Seeing no one else near, he grabbed the Yellowboy and continued walking up the wash, the fire's glow growing brighter ahead of him and to his left. When the glow was directly to his left, he doffed his hat and peered up over the lip of the wash.

The fire was in a clearing surrounded by trees maybe sixty yards away from the wash. He couldn't see much from this vantage.

He donned his hat and climbed up out of the wash, immediately lying flat and inching his way forward through gravel and tufts of wiry brown grass and sagebrush. The fire's glow grew in front of him, reflecting off the mesquites and cottonwoods surrounding it. He crawled to within fifty feet of it, doffed his hat, and peered around the side of a gnarled cedar. There appeared to be three people in the camp. He couldn't be sure. He was still too far away.

He left his hat on the ground and grabbed forward, quartering slightly to his right for a better view into the camp. When he'd moved another fifteen feet, he drew up behind a large cottonwood. Yep, there were three people in the camp. Mannion's heart quickened when he saw that one of them was Ilsa. She sat back in the shadows on the far left side of the fire, which had burned down now to three small, dancing orange flames nibbling at two half-burned logs.

There were more shadows than light, which was good.

One man sat back against his saddle and a tree straight across the fire from Mannion. His legs were crossed at the ankles, gloved hands entwined on his chest, hat pulled down over his eyes. Another man lay to Mannion's right, curled on his side inside his bedroll, his hat on the ground beside his head, obscuring his face. Mannion didn't think either man was Trainor, which meant Trainor must be out away from the fire, on night watch.

Him and one other, since the group was down to five including Trainor himself.

Mannion could see the eye glow of a couple of horses off in the shadows ahead and to his right. Good. They were picketed away from Ilsa.

Mannion looked around, pondering his options.

He had to move fast, before the picket he'd killed was discovered.

But he had to be careful. Somehow, he had to get Ilsa out of here without alerting the men, who'd surely start shooting and ask questions later.

Mannion crabbed straight back on his belly, moving as silently as possible in the silent night, and then crawled to his left, toward where Ilsa sat back against a cottonwood, chin hanging low as she slept, hands tied behind her back. Her long, tangled, nearly black hair obscured her face. More rope held her fast to the tree.

Mannion crawled around behind the tree she was tied to. He crawled more slowly than before, not wanting to startle her awake. She might gasp or scream and alert the others. When he was within a few feet of the tree, moving with painstaking slowness and quiet, he gained a knee, leaned forward around the tree's right side, and clamped his hand over her face and nose, drawing her head back against the tree. She gave a muffled cry into the palm of his hand. Glancing at the two sleeping men, making sure they didn't awaken, Mannion slid his face up close to Ilsa's, giving her a good look at him.

Her dark eyes met his and held there. At first, she appeared to think she must still be asleep and dreaming. She just stared back at him, blankly. Then her eyes widened, the pupils contracting, the wan light from the fire flickering in them. Mannion pulled his hand away from her mouth and pressed two fingers to his lips.

Her mouth opened in shock, and she just stared at him, eyes wide and glassy with the realization he was not a ghost. That he was, indeed, alive.

He glanced at the two sleeping men. One snored softly. The man on the far side of the fire moaned, dreaming. Mannion slid his lips up close to Ilsa's right ear and said, "I'm going to cut you loose. We have to be very, very quiet. Understand?"

Her dark eyes glued to his, she nodded twice, slowly.

Her throat moved as she swallowed.

Mannion slid his bowie knife from its sheath and sawed through the ropes tying the girl to the tree. Then he reached around the tree, between the tree and Ilsa, and sawed through the ropes binding her hands together.

When the ropes dropped to the ground in pieces, Mannion looked at her, reminding her with his eyes to be as quiet as she could.

He sheathed the bowie knife, picked up the Yellowboy, looked around him, feeling the presence of Trainor and the other picket but not seeing either man. He looked at the two men by the fire. Still asleep. Holding the Yellowboy across his knees, Mannion glanced at the girl and nodded. She stretched her lips back from her teeth, tensely, and set her hands on the ground to either side of her. Very slowly, she leaned forward, drew her feet toward her, beneath her torn skirt, then turned slightly to her right, placing the bulk of her weight on her right hand and continuing to draw her feet toward her body.

Mannion kept one eye on the girl, one eye on the sleeping men while pricking his ears, listening for the approach of one of the two pickets.

Ilsa turned to place her left hand on the ground to her right and began to hoist herself up.

One of the horses whickered.

Ilsa froze.

Heart quickening, Mannion cut his gaze toward the horses tied to a picket line in the darkness on the far side of the camp. He could faintly see the dimming fire's glint in one eye back there. One of the horses was eyeing him and the girl suspiciously.

"Keep going," Mannion whispered very softly.

Bunching her cheeks in dread, Ilsa pushed herself up off her hands, placing more and more weight on her feet, slowly rising. As she did, Mannion heard the faint crackle of sand beneath her feet, heard the faint rustle of her clothes. Keeping his attention on the two men sleeping by the fire, Mannion stretched his own lips back from his teeth.

With her feet under her now, Ilsa straightened, lifting her hands off the ground. She continued straightening her back, her eyes now glued to Mannion, who again looked at the faint light in the eye of the horse giving him and the girl the woolly eyeball.

"Quiet, boy," he silently bid the mount. "Easy, now... quiii-ett..."

Ilsa finished straightening.

Hope rose in Mannion. He canted his head in the direction of the wash, intending to retrace his route back to where he'd left Sam. He took one step in that direction, moving very quietly. He glanced over his shoulder. Ilsa was taking one slow step at a time behind him, holding her hands out to her sides for balance. Mannion saw his hat, paused to pick it up then, setting it on his head, glanced back again to give the girl an encouraging look.

He'd taken one more step when a man's voice thundered up out of the wash straight ahead of him, *"Trouble, boys! Thiel's dead! Someone's here!"*

The voice echoed around inside Mannion's head like the boom of a .45 inside a cave.

One of the horses whinnied shrilly.

Mannion whipped around and rammed a live round into the Yellowboy's action. Both men before him sat up with startled grunts, widening their eyes and opening their mouths. The hat of the one on the other side of the fire tumbled off the man's shoulder as he reached for the Winchester carbine leaning against the tree to his right.

Mannion's Yellowboy roared, plunking a .44-caliber round through the man's cheek and knocking him straight back against the tree. The other man turned to Mannion as he snatched a revolver from the holster on the ground beside him. Seeing Joe eject the spent round from his Winchester's breech and lifting the rifle to his cheek once more, taking aim, the second man screamed, "*Nooo!*" at the same time the Yellowboy spoke again, flames lapping from the barrel.

As the second man grunted and slammed back against his saddle and piled tack, Mannion lurched to his feet, turned to Ilsa standing frozen in shock behind him, and yelled, "Run! That way! *Run!*"

He gave her a hard shove to his right then fired two quick rounds into the darkness ahead of him, toward where the picket had yelled from the wash. Then he lowered the Yellowboy and took off running after the girl, a vague shadow retreating into the deeper darkness beyond the camp.

Men yelled behind him.

A gun roared once...twice...three times.

The bullets sang over Mannion's head and to each side, screeching off rocks or plunking into trees.

He caught up with Ilsa, took her hand, and yelled, "Faster than you ever have, honey—*run!*"

Another gun roared behind them.

Ilsa screamed. Her hand slipped out of Mannion's hand, and she dropped.

CHAPTER 28

KING GROWLED, PULLING SAM OUT OF A LIGHT DOZE. The boy sat back against a cottonwood bole, arms crossed on his chest.

He opened his eyes.

King sat on the edge of the low bench they were on, staring out between a cedar tree and a wagon-sized boulder. The night was quiet and dark, only the rustle of a breeze in the brush below and to each side of Sam. Behind and above him was a steep ridge wall. Mannion had led him and the dog and both horses to a protected place, because he'd known he'd have to leave the boy alone to retrieve Sam's sister.

It was a job for Mannion alone.

Again, King growled very deep in his throat. Both ears were pricked.

"What is it, boy?" Sam asked.

He rose, picked up his Spencer repeating rifle, and walked over to drop to one knee beside the dog, staring through the same gap through which the dog was peering, obviously sensing something.

King glanced up at Sam, mewled softly, shifted his

weight from one foot to the other, then cast his gaze down to the dark, open bowl of ground below them, to the east, beyond where rocks and brush trailed down the side of the slope they were on.

Sam rested the Spencer's butt on his right thigh and ran his hand down the dog's head and back. "You see somethin' out there, boy?"

The dog continued staring into the night, working his nose.

Sam turned to where the three horses, Red, Lightning, and Honey, stood tied to a rope Mannion had strung between two cedars. Red and Lightning were staring down the slope in the same direction King was. Honey stood with her head forward, but she was giving her tail occasional, nervous switches.

"Hmm," Sam said, apprehension growing in him.

He remembered the tracks of the six men, bounty hunters, who were trailing Zeke Trainor and the other men who'd kidnapped Ilsa. It was a warm night, but a chill grew in him. He took the Spencer in both hands and squeezed it nervously. He swallowed, then touched the dog's head once more.

"You stay, boy. Stay, King. I'm gonna go down and take a look around."

He wanted to scout the slope silently. The dog would make noise and give him away. Besides, if the bounty hunters were down there, they'd have guns. King was protective of Sam and Ilsa, but he was no match for a gun.

The dog looked up at Sam and whined, shifting his weight from foot to foot again, sliding his bushy tail along the ground.

Sam rose, said quietly but commandingly, "Remember, you stay."

He slipped off through the gap before him and the dog, heading slowly off down the slope, wended his way slowly, quietly through the rocks and trees—mostly pines but with some desert oaks and cottonwoods, too.

As he walked, he held the Spencer straight out from his right hip. He paused to quietly work the trigger guard cocking mechanism, sliding a cartridge into the breech. Then he continued striding slowly down the slope, his gloved right index finger curled across the Spencer's heavy steel trigger.

His heart fluttered.

"Courage," he told himself. "Courage. You've come this far..."

Dark out here, though. Real dark...

Sam sucked back his fear and kept walking, wending his way down the slope. Brush made a dark, jagged line along a ravine cutting down the slope on his left. That brush could hide anyone. Hell, it could hide a whole bunch of people.

It could hide six bounty hunters out for the loot and wanting to scour their trail and their quarry's trail of possible competition. Even if that competition was Bloody Joe Mannion.

As he walked, Sam ran his tongue across his upper lip. It was pointless. His mouth was dry; he couldn't work up any spit.

He stopped suddenly, tightening his finger on the Spencer's trigger.

He'd heard something.

What?

It had sounded like a soft thump.

He drew a deep breath, trying to calm himself, and continued walking down the slope, angling toward the dark line of the brush on his left. It was from over there and down the slope a little farther that the sound had come.

A horse's soft whicker sounded in the starlit darkness.

Sam sucked a sharp, startled breath and stopped.

There was a horse out here.

Where? Down a little farther.

Resisting the urge to bolt and beat it back up to the relative safety of his camp and his dog—he felt so horribly exposed out here—he continued walking. A little fast now, hearing a soft ringing in his ears. The brush curved away as the ravine swung away to the left. Sam followed that curve, walking along the edge of the brush...and stopped suddenly with another startled gasp.

He found himself staring at the dark outline of a horse standing nearly straight ahead of him. The horse was saddled, and its reins dangled to the ground. It stared back at Sam, blue starlight glowing softly in its eyes.

Sam took two more steps and stopped.

He was close enough now that he could hear the horse—a rangy chestnut—breathing. It stomped a rear hoof then gave another louder whicker and shook its head so hard it nearly tossed off its bridle. Suddenly, the horse lifted its head toward the stars and loosed a shrill whinny.

Sam's heart banged like a cracked bell in his ears.

Then King started barking wildly back up the slope behind the boy. Sam couldn't take it anymore. His nerves were sizzling like the branches of a lightning-struck pine. He swung around and, holding the Spencer in both hands, ran back hard in the direction from which he'd come and where King was barking frantically, the barks growing louder as Sam closed the gap between himself and the dog.

Breaths raked in and out of Sam's lungs, his heart racing, bells of raw, wild fear tolling in his ears.

Cottonwoods and oaks swept past him. He swerved around or leaped over rocks, his boots thudding on the sandy ground.

Ahead and above, he could see King's outline as the dog, standing roughly ten feet down from the rocks forming their cold camp, peered into the brush on Sam's right now as he ran uphill toward the dog. King stood, tail arched, hackles raised, barking furiously at something in the brush-lined ravine.

Sam ran past the dog and slipped through the large rocks and onto the flat top of the slope at the base of the steep ridge, yelling, "Come on, King! Come on, boy!"

He turned back to where the dog ran through the rocks and into the camp, whining with fear and agitation.

Sam bent over, one hand around the Spencer, one hand on his knee, trying to catch his breath. Cold sweat dribbled down his cheeks.

Suddenly, King started barking again.

Sam turned to him. King gazed off behind Sam now. Sam just now realized the horses were prancing and whickering, pulling on their picket line.

Behind him, a man's harsh voice said, "Shut that damn dog up, kid, or I'll—"

The loud roar of a rifle cut off the man's sentence.

Sam looked down. He was holding the Spencer straight out in front of him now. Pale smoke curled from the barrel. He was facing the far side of the camp, to the right of the horses. He'd swung around and fired without realizing it but now he remembered the startled yell he'd given as he'd done so. He was staring at the silhouette of an improbably wide, thick man with a heavy red beard, hip-length deer hide coat, and a low-crowned black hat.

The man stood frozen, one foot forward, crouched slightly forward at the waist, half turned away from Sam, facing the startled horses.

Above the horses' whickering, Sam heard the man give a hoarse groan. He stumbled forward, sort of toward Sam but to Sam's left. He lowered his right hand. Starlight glinted off steel. The pistol barked, the orange flames stabbing toward the ground beside the man's right foot.

"Ah...*hell*!" the man said, and fell in a heap ten feet away from Sam.

Sam gave another shocked intake of air as another man's voice said behind him, "Why, you murderin' little bastard!"

Sam swung around yet again to see the silhouette of yet another man step through the rocks and into the camp. Another big man in a duster and high-crowned hat. He raised his right hand. Sam heard the dreadful click of a gun hammer being cocked.

Terror was a hot javelin hurled through Sam's heart.

Sam held the Spencer in both hands, but the rifle wasn't cocked.

The second man had him dead to rights.

Sam watched the gun come up and slide toward him, the man lowering his chin slightly to aim down the barrel. King growled and leaped—a dog-shaped shadow in the night. The gun flashed and roared, the bullet slicing through the air to Sam's left as King closed his jaws around the man's right wrist.

The man cursed and lurched back and to one side as King clung to his wrist, growling fiercely.

"Damn *dog*!" the man shouted, and hurled King off to one side.

King yelped as he hit the ground and rolled.

There was the ominous ratcheting click of the gun in the man's hand being cocked again.

But only after Sam had levered a fresh cartridge into his Spencer's breech.

"Die, you son of a bitch!" Sam yelled, aiming.

The Spencer roared, the rear butt plate slamming back hard against Sam's right shoulder, making the boy stagger back a step.

The man groaned and fired his revolver again wide as he flew back into the shadows between two large rocks. He struck the ground with a heavy thud and another groan. There was a great sigh of expelled breath followed by silence.

King looked at Sam, mewling softly.

Sam stared at the dead man before him then at the dead man behind him.

He'd killed both. The first man before he'd realized what he was doing. The second man to save his own life. His nerves sizzled just beneath the surface of his skin. His knees and hands were shaking.

Again, he'd killed.

It wasn't at all like the dime novels had described it.

It was a terrible, terrifying thing...even when it had to be done. He walked over to the man lying near the horses. He wasn't moving. He walked over to the man lying between rocks. He wasn't moving either.

Sam turned to King. The dog sat several feet away, looking incredulous.

Not sure what to think of the situation.

Sam didn't either.

He jerked with yet another start when distant gunfire crackled.

"Holy..." Sam said.

There'd been two quick blasts. A slight pause. Then

more rifles barked, echoing distantly, the echoes chasing each other toward the starlit sky.

Sam walked down the slope through the rocks and stopped, staring toward where the marshal had gone to fetch Ilsa. King came down to sit beside him, staring in the same direction. The dog whined softly, pricking his ears.

Sam stood there for a long time with his dog, staring toward the northwest, hearing the distant cacophony of more shooting, feeling sick to his stomach...

Wondering if he would ever see his sister and Marshal Mannion again.

Were he and King all alone in the world?

"That tears it!" he said, and turned to saddle Lightning.

CHAPTER 29

"ILSA!"

Mannion stopped, glanced down at the girl as she skidded to a stop and rolled onto her back, groaning.

Mannion swung around, saw the flash of two guns—one roughly fifty yards ahead and on his right, the other roughly seventy yards ahead and on his left. The pickets were running toward him, shooting and levering, shooting and levering, the bullets curling the air over and around Mannion and plunking into the ground before and behind him.

Mannion dropped to a knee and returned fire until he'd emptied the Yellowboy. The men behind him shouted and stopped firing, likely taking to ground to avoid Mannion's own lead, which was what Joe had wanted them to do.

Short of them taking his bullets, that was.

"Ilsa!" he said again, turning to where the girl was just then sitting up. He dropped to a knee beside her. "You hit?"

She raised her hand, brushed it across her face. "Just...

my cheek…" She held her hand against the left side of her face.

Mannion leaned close to scrutinize the bloody, three-inch line across the outside of her left cheek. Just a burn.

"Thank God," Mannion raked out, reaching down to take her hand, pulling her back to her feet. "We gotta keep running, darlin'. I'm gonna get you to cover then finish those jaspers. I hope you still got some wind left!"

"I do…I do…" she said, climbing to her feet.

"Come on!"

The ravine opened ahead of them, curving around from where Mannion had left it to access Trainor's camp. He climbed down into it and then reached up to help Ilsa down. She'd been tied and immobile so long, she appeared weak and uncertain on her feet.

God knew what else had happened to her.

No. Mannion knew. He could see it in her eyes.

He led her around a bend in the wash then stopped and eased her down behind a bulge in the eastern bank.

"You stay here, honey," he said, dropping to a knee beside her and sliding cartridges from his shell belt to thumb them through the Winchester's loading gate. "I'll be back in a few minutes."

She looked at him sharply, wrapped her hand around his forearm, squeezing. Starlight glinted in her eyes. "Sam?!"

"Safe." Joe thumbed two more rounds through the loading gate then jacked a live one into the action, off cocked the hammer and rested the barrel on his shoulder. "Stay here."

Again, she squeezed his arm, scowling incredulously. "How? How…?"

She wanted to know how they'd gotten out of the

mine. He smiled. "Long story. I'll tell you shortly. Both Sam and I will."

He squeezed her shoulder reassuringly then rose and walked back up the wash, heading back in the direction of Trainor's camp. Three were dead. Two more to go, including Trainor himself. Rage burned hot in Mannion, oozing up from deep in his belly to sear his heart, when he thought of what that jackal had done to young Ilsa. He would die hard for that.

He'd walked maybe a hundred yards when he stopped suddenly.

Hoof thuds sounded from the darkness ahead. Two riders were coming at fast trots. Joe could hear their enervated voices. They were mighty piss-burned—Trainor and the other picket.

Mannion dropped a knee in the shadow of the bank rising on his left. He held the Yellowboy low, caressing the hammer with his thumb, eager to finish Trainor and the other man.

As they came closer, Mannion could start to hear what they were saying:

"...Mannion...I know it was..."

The other man said something Joe couldn't make out, then: "...whole mountain down..."

"It was him, dammit!" Trainor's voice came, loud with anger and frustration.

The silhouettes of both horses and riders came on around a bend in the wash wall. They were a hundred feet away, still trotting, starlight glinting off their horses' bridle chains.

Mannion flared a nostril, shaped a grimly satisfied smile, and stepped out into the middle of the wash. The two riders didn't see him for several seconds. Then the one on the left said, "Whoa, whoa...hold up!"

Both men checked their mounts down.

The one on the left was tall. The other one, short. The one on the left was Trainor. He'd die first.

They froze in their saddles, drawing back sharply on their nervous mounts' reins.

They stared straight ahead at Mannion who held the Yellowboy on his right shoulder, no longer caring that starlight flashed off the receiver.

Trainor and the other man sat in stony silence. They each held a rifle across the pommels of their saddles.

"Should have killed you days ago, Trainor. The girl saved your life. You repaid her by... Well, you know what you did."

Mannion saw the whiteness of the man's teeth as Trainor stretched his lips back in a dog-like snarl. His eyes glinted angrily beneath his hat brim. "You go to hell, Mannion!" he shouted, jerking his rifle up.

Mannion was a full second faster.

Joe swung the Yellowboy around and shot the man out of his saddle before the rancher could get the Winchester settled. The shorter man was next, yelling and rolling ass over teakettle over his horse's tail as the horse whinnied and lurched forward, galloping off down the ravine behind Mannion. Neither man had gotten a shot off.

Both men lay groaning.

Mannion levered another round into the Yellowboy's action, stepped forward and stared down at the second man. He aimed the Yellowboy straight down and blew a .44-caliber hole through the center of the man's forehead, just above the bridge of his nose.

Mannion walked ahead and left to where Zeke Trainor writhed on the ground, trying to crawl away. He looked like a large crab in the darkness, clawing the pebbly floor of the wash, trying to shove himself ahead with his feet.

Mannion levered another round into the Winchester's breech.

Footsteps sounded behind him, and a girl's voice said, "No. Let me."

Mannion stopped, lowered the Yellowboy, and turned.

Ilsa walked up to him, gazed up into his face, her own eyes reflecting the glint of the starlight. "I've been thinking about this for a long time now."

She brushed past Mannion, walked up to Trainor, crouched over him, and slid the man's bowie knife from the sheath on his left hip. She glanced at Mannion and raked her thumb across the edge of the blade.

"Sharp."

Mannion smiled.

"No," Trainor said, still trying to crawl away. He brushed a hand across the holster on his right hip; his revolver was gone. He'd lost it in the tumble from his horse. "No," he said again. "Leave me." He looked up at Ilsa staring down at him, still holding her thumb against the bowie's blade. "Leave me...d-damn you! D-don't even think about it!"

"I'm not only thinking about it, Trainor," the girl said, softly, menacingly. "I'm going to do it, so you know what it feels like. The pain...the humiliation of being violated."

"Mannion, stop her!"

Mannion turned to Ilsa, placed a hand on her shoulder. "Do what you have to do, sweetheart. I'm gonna go into their camp and gather the loot."

He headed up the wash.

Behind him, Trainor said, "No...no...now, don't you—

ahhhh...oh, god...Mannion," the rancher bawled, "make her...make her...STAWWWPPPP!"

Mannion kept walking, grinning, as Trainor continued screaming and sobbing behind him. He didn't scream and sob for long. Soon, only funereal silence issued from the wash.

The gory deed had been completed. Revenge.

It might be a dish best served cold, but Mannion knew from experience it was as sweet as chocolate cake fresh out of the oven.

He walked into Trainor's camp and built up the fire so he could see to gather the loot. There was still another hour of dark left though the dawn was beginning to spread a gray smudge in the east. He fished the burlap bags of scrip and specie out of the outlaws' saddlebags, combining all the loot into one set of bags. He was glad none of the outlaws including Trainor had had time to spend any of it.

He took his time, wanting to get every coin and greenback.

When he was done, he rose and draped the saddle-bags over his left shoulder. Off in the darkness to his right, beyond where the two dead men lay, the horses were whickering and moving around uneasily. He thought it was himself and the smell of fresh blood that was making them nervous but then footsteps sounded in the trees around him.

Slow, crunching footsteps.

He peered into the darkness around the fire.

Four man-shaped shadows moved toward him.

Mannion looked at his Yellowboy. He'd leaned it against a tree ten feet away.

Too far away.

The four men—big, wool-and-canvas clad, and wearing weather-battered Stetsons—stepped up into the edge of the firelight, surrounding Joe. Milo Philpot stood directly across the fire at Mannion.

He was Mannion's size—broad-headed with tiny eyes set in deep sockets and a long, sandy beard with a thick mustache with upswept and waxed ends. The man's savagery radiated off him. You could almost smell it.

The other three looked similar. Well-armed men—several knives apiece as well as guns—more animal than men. They each held a rifle as they stood staring dully from the shadows, their hard, savage eyes glinting orange in the firelight.

"Been a long time, Mannion," Philpot said.

"Not long enough," Joe said with a sigh. He was all too aware that both his Russians were holstered, the keeper thongs in place across their hammers.

Philpot's men had him dead to rights.

The lead bounty hunter smiled inside his beard, showing two fanglike teeth the color of ancient ivory. "Thanks for combining the loot into one bag, Marshal." He smiled again, blinking. "We'll be taking it now."

He raised the Henry repeating rifle in his big, gloved hands, drawing the hammer back to full cock, pressing the butt plate against his right shoulder. He smiled as he aimed down the barrel at Joe's head.

He frowned suddenly when the frenetic tread of small, padded feet sounded in the woods behind him.

"What the hell?" said the man to his left.

They all had just started to turn toward the source of the noise—the quick footsteps and panting growing quickly louder...until the McDowells' shepherd-collie ran up out of the shadows. King gave a loud growl, launched himself off his back feet, arced up through the air, hackles raised, and closed his jaws around the back of Philpot's neck.

The bounty hunter screamed as he staggered forward, triggering his Henry wide of Mannion. The rocketing report was followed by a cacophony of gunfire issuing from the shadows around Mannion, who swung around to see the other three bounty hunters lurching this way and that, screaming and dropping their rifles, as bullets tore into them.

They danced around the edge of the firelight, savage faces bunched with agony, sidestepping and falling to lie in writhing piles around Mannion, who dropped the saddlebags, unsheathed his Russian from the holster on his right leg and drilled a round through Philpot's head just as the man, on his back with King on top of him, was unsheathing the big Smith & Wesson tied low on his own right thigh.

The man screamed, dropped the Smithy, and lay still, glaring up at Mannion, his eyes glassy in death.

Standing on the man's broad, lumpy chest, King looked up at Mannion and barked victoriously. Then he stepped off the dead man and lifted his leg on the man's head.

More footsteps sounded in the shadows. Ilsa stepped up out of the darkness to Mannion's left, a smoking Winchester in her hands. Likely Trainor's weapon. Sam stepped up out of the darkness on Mannion's right, his own smoking Spencer held high across his chest.

The sister and brother regarded the dead men around them then looked at Mannion. Blood shone on Ilsa's left cheek. Her hair hung wildly about her face. She looked like a Scottish princess warrior from medieval times.

Sam said, "There's two more where these came from up where you left me. I reckon they thought they were gonna scour both you and me off Trainor's trail while these four took down Trainor and got their greedy hands on the loot."

Mannion smiled. "Their mistake."

Ilsa said, "I heard them sneak into the camp after I'd finished Trainor."

"I heard shooting out this way," Sam said. "I galloped over on Lightning, left him off a ways, then ran into Ilsa in the wash." The boy turned to his sister and smiled.

Ilsa looked at Mannion. "Do you think this is the end of it?"

"Who knows?" Mannion said, looking around. "Who knows?" He turned to Ilsa and Sam. "But for now, I think it is."

He holstered his Russian and sat down heavily on a rock. He looked at the coffeepot hanging from a tripod over the fire. It gurgled quietly. "Coffee, anyone?"

It had been a long night. They still had a long ride to Del Norte ahead of them.

After the McDowells had spent a few days in Del Norte for rest, baths, and good meals at Jane's San Juan Hotel & Saloon, Mannion would see they got safely back to their humble home in the Stalwarts, back to Ilsa's pet raccoon and their cattle. Because he knew for these two wild children of the mountains—a little wilder now, stronger and wiser for all they'd been through in recent days—the Stalwarts were, indeed, home.

A fitting name for the home of these two. Three, rather, Mannion thought with a smile as he looked at the dog sitting at the boy's feet.

Sam sighed, shook his head. "Me? I could go for a

shot of whiskey. The unlabeled kind." He grinned at Mannion. "The kind you like, Bloody Joe."

"Sam!" Ilsa scolded.

They all laughed.

King barked.

Bestselling author "Mean Pete" Brandvold has been
spinning classic, action-filled western yarns for the past
25 years. In this Introductory Library, you'll find the
first book from each of 8 bestselling, fan favorite series,
offering you a mere taste of the smorgasbord served up
by the legend himself.

The Classic *Sheriff Ben Stillman Series* Begins...

Playing poker, smoking cigarettes, drinking whiskey—
retirement was treacherous business for ex-lawman Ben
Stillman. The best of life seemed to be past, but then the past
came looking for him... Can the worn-out old lawman live up to
the legendary lawman he once was?

Peter Brandvold has worked up the grittiest, bloodiest fast-action western in the *.45 Caliber Series*!

Cuno Massey's thirst for revenge runs deep. Deeper than his
skills. But when Rolf Anderson and Sammy Spoon killed his
stepmother and his father, nothing would stand in young Cuno's
way. He'd ride straight through hell for the bittersweet taste of
revenge...

Saddle up for the wildest, bloodiest Peter Brandvold series yet—*Yakima Henry*!

Half Indian and half white, Yakima Henry considers himself
lucky to have any job—even if it means just sweeping up the
local brothel. But when four hombres attempt to carve up one
of the house girls, Yakima gives them a taste of their own
medicine with his Arkansas Toothpick. Now, he's become the
girl's protector, and is on the run from a vicious bounty hunter.

A hot and heavy western noir... *The Saga of Colter Farrow...*

Colter Farrow may be young, but ever since his stepfather was savagely murdered, his blood has boiled with a rage as great as any man's. While trying to exact revenge, Colter ends up on the run from bounty hunters, outlaws, and a sadistic sheriff. Desperate and afraid, Colter is searching for freedom and a chance to return home to live a quiet, normal life.

This Prophet is riding to hell and back!

Lou Prophet's life as a bounty hunter has taught him one rule: You don't stop riding till the job is finished. Prophet is repeatedly caught in bloody crossfires and he is determined to show the outlaws that justice doesn't always wear a badge. Join the bounty hunter as he faces seemingly insurmountable odds at every turn...

The Revenger Series

Mike Sartain, The Revenger, grew up in the French Quarter of New Orleans where he was taught how to fight by some of the toughest, meanest SOBs in any port. He was taught how to love by some of the most beautiful women in the world...

Now, The Revenger rides for anyone who has an ax to grind...

Ride the rough, lawless trails of the western frontier with *The Rogue Lawman*!

Deputy U.S. Marshal Gideon Hawk was respected throughout the Territory as a lawman of principle—until Three Fingers Ned Meade threw him a curve. Meade killed Hawk's ten-year-old boy, and the grisly act drove Hawk's grief-stricken wife to hang herself. Now, robbed of kin, Hawk sets out on a brutal quest to find the man responsible—at any cost.

Get ready for a dose of action and adventure and a heaping helping of western justice with *Bloody Joe Mannion*!

"Bloody" Joe Mannion is a town tamer of great renown. His temper is just as famous. Known as the most uncompromising lawman on the Western frontier, he's been the town marshal of Del Norte in the Colorado Territory for the past five years. Now, Bloody Joe will risk everything, including his life, the town, and a hail of hot lead!

The Peter Brandvold Introductory Library includes the following titles:

Once a Marshal (Ben Stillman 1)

.45 Caliber Revenge (.45 Caliber 1)

The Lonely Breed (Yakima Henry 1)

The Guns of Sapinero (Colter Farrow 1)

The Devil and Lou Prophet (Lou Prophet 1)

A Bullet for Sartain (The Revenger 1)

Rogue Lawman (Rogue Lawman 1)

Bloody Joe (Bloody Joe Mannion 1)

AVAILABLE NOW

ABOUT THE AUTHOR

Peter Brandvold grew up in the great state of North Dakota in the 1960's and '70s, when television westerns were as popular as shows about hoarders and shark tanks are now, and western paperbacks were as popular as *Game of Thrones*.

Brandvold watched every western series on television at the time. He grew up riding horses and herding cows on the farms of his grandfather and many friends who owned livestock.

Brandvold's imagination has always lived and will always live in the West. He is the author of over a hundred lightning-fast action westerns under his own name and his pen name, Frank Leslie.

Made in the USA
Las Vegas, NV
26 January 2025